*You're a
Privileged
Woman.*

INTRODUCING
PAGES & PRIVILEGES™.
It's our way of thanking you for buying
our books at your favorite retail store.

*G*ET ALL THIS *F*REE
WITH JUST ONE PROOF OF PURCHASE:

◆ **Hotel Discounts** up
to 60% at home and
abroad ◆ **Travel Service**
- Guaranteed lowest
published airfares
plus 5% cash back

**$50
VALUE**

on tickets ◆ **$25 Travel Voucher**
◆ **Sensuous Petite Parfumerie** collection

◆ **Insider Tips Letter**
with sneak previews
of upcoming books

*You'll get a FREE personal card, too.
It's your passport to all these benefits– and to
even more great gifts & benefits to come!*
There's no club to join. No purchase commitment. No obligation.

Enrollment Form

☐ *Yes!* I WANT TO BE A *PRIVILEGED WOMAN.*

Enclosed is one *PAGES & PRIVILEGES*™ Proof of Purchase from any Harlequin or Silhouette book currently for sale in stores (Proofs of Purchase are found on the back pages of books) and the store cash register receipt. Please enroll me in *PAGES & PRIVILEGES*™. Send my Welcome Kit and FREE Gifts -- and activate my FREE benefits -- immediately.

More great gifts and benefits to come like these luxurious Truly Lace and L'Effleur gift baskets.

NAME (please print)

ADDRESS   APT. NO

CITY   STATE   ZIP/POSTAL CODE

📖 **PROOF OF PURCHASE** *SAMPLE ONLY*

Please allow 6-8 weeks for delivery. Quantities are limited. We reserve the right to substitute items. Enroll before October 31, 1995 and receive one full year of benefits.

**NO CLUB!
NO COMMITMENT!**
Just one purchase brings you great **Free Gifts
and Benefits!**
(More details in back of this book.)

Name of store where this book was purchased_____

Date of purchase_____

Type of store:

☐ Bookstore ☐ Supermarket ☐ Drugstore

☐ Dept. or discount store (e.g. K-Mart or Walmart)

☐ Other (specify)_____

Which Harlequin or Silhouette series do you usually read?

📖 **Pages & Privileges**™

Complete and mail with one Proof of Purchase and store receipt to:

U.S.: *PAGES & PRIVILEGES*™, P.O. Box 1960, Danbury, CT 06813-1960

Canada: *PAGES & PRIVILEGES*™, 49-6A The Donway West, P.O. 813, North York, ON M3C 2E8   **PRINTED IN U.S.A**

His breath hissed out.
"So that's your game."

" 'Tis no game, Ian."

"Listen to me, Madeline, and listen well. If it costs me all the fiefs I hold of Henry, you and the man you took as lover will not win at this."

Flushing, she pushed herself to her feet. "He's not my lover!"

"Then why do you want the freedom to wed where you will, if not with Guy Blackhair? What other poor fool have you smiled upon and teased and offered your body to, as you did to me?"

"There is no other man," she spit, flicked to the raw. "None! But when I choose the man I will wed, 'twill be one I may smile upon without being called to task for it. One I may tease and laugh with and…and lust for with all my woman's passion, without being thought a whore!"

Dear Reader,

With a writing workday that often begins at 5:00 a.m. and can run until 10:00 p.m., it's no wonder that Merline Lovelace has already made a name for herself in both the historical and contemporary romance fields, even though her first book was only published in 1992! This month we are delighted to bring you Merline's new medieval tale, *His Lady's Ransom*, the sweeping story of a nobleman who sets out to discourage his brother's infatuation with a notorious woman, only to find himself under her captivating spell. And don't miss Merline Lovelace in our August short-story collection, RENEGADES, featuring *New York Times* bestselling author, Heather Graham Pozzessere, and our own Theresa Michaels.

And be sure to keep an eye out for *Once a Maverick*, the first in a Western trilogy featuring the infamous Kincaids, by award-winning author Theresa Michaels, whom *Romantic Times* has described as a woman who "has a rare and welcome ability to move the heart and touch the soul..."

Also this month are a new title from Nina Beaumont— the author of *Across Time*—*Tapestry of Dreams*, a passionate tale of danger and desire, and a new Western from author DeLoras Scott, *Addie's Lament*, the heart-warming love story of a young woman determined to make a better life for herself and the man who seems to always want to get in her way.

Whatever your taste in historical reading, we hope you'll keep an eye out for all four Harlequin Historical titles, wherever Harlequin books are sold.

Sincerely,

Tracy Farrell

Please address questions and book requests to:
Harlequin Reader Service
U.S.: 3010 Walden Ave., P.O. Box 1325, Buffalo, NY 14269
Canadian: P.O. Box 609, Fort Erie, Ont. L2A 5X3

HIS LADY'S RANSOM

MERLINE LOVELACE

Harlequin Books

TORONTO • NEW YORK • LONDON
AMSTERDAM • PARIS • SYDNEY • HAMBURG
STOCKHOLM • ATHENS • TOKYO • MILAN
MADRID • WARSAW • BUDAPEST • AUCKLAND

ISBN 0-373-28875-9

HIS LADY'S RANSOM

Printed in U.S.A.

Books by Merline Lovelace

Harlequin Historicals

Alena #220
Sweet Song of Love #230
Siren's Call #236
His Lady's Ransom #275

*Destiny's Women Series

MERLINE LOVELACE

As a career Air Force officer, Merline Lovelace
served tours of duty in Vietnam, at the Pentagon and
at bases all over the world. She met and married her
own handsome warrior hero twenty-four years ago,
with whom she's shared a lifetime of adventure and
romance.

Merline loves to read and write stories set against
dramatic historical backdrops. Look for her next
book, *Lady of the Upper Kingdom,* coming soon
from Harlequin Historicals. In this tale of ancient
Egypt, a captain in Alexander the Great's invading
army tangles with an acolyte of the temple of Bastet,
the great cat god of the Pharaohs.

To Maggie Price and Nancy Berland, two superb
authors, wonderful critique partners and the kind of
friends who make this business of writing such a
joy—it wouldn't be half so much fun without our
Wednesday-night sessions!

Chapter One

Wyndham Castle
Cumbria, Northern England
The Year of Our Lord 1188

"I tell you, Ian, the lad's besotted with that—that slut. You must do something!"

Ian de Burgh, earl of Margill, baron St. Briac, lord of Wyndham, Glenwaite and other holdings in northern England and Normandy, paused in the act of donning his shirt and glanced at the woman who paced in front of the huge hearth.

"You look much like a peahen who's been chased around the bailey by a playful cat, Lady Mother." Affectionate irreverence laced his low north-country drawl. "Your feathers are all aruffle."

Instinctively Lady Elizabeth lifted a hand to smooth her silvered hair under its gossamer silk veil. Her huge brown eyes took on the look of a wounded doe's, and the frown marring her delicate features lightened to a winsome expression, one Ian knew full well. It had often reduced his father, a warrior feared throughout England and Normandy, to helpless resignation. In Ian's youth, that same expression had sent him scurrying on many an errand for his beautiful, gentle stepmother.

His grin softened to a smile of genuine warmth as he took in her woe-filled countenance. He jerked his chin at his squire, and the brawny youth went to shoo away the clutch of servants who had attended their lord while he soaked away the dirt of travel. As the squire cleared the room, Ian went forward to take his mother's hand.

"Come, Lady Mother, surely 'tis not so serious as you seem to think."

"It is," she insisted, clutching at his fingers. "You cannot know, Ian. You've been gone for nigh on a year. First to Ireland, then to France, in this damnable war."

She stopped as her eyes caught sight of a wound exposed by the open ties of his linen shirt. Tugging at Ian's arm to bring him down to her eye level, she examined the red, raw cut that traced his collarbone.

"Who stitched this?"

"The churgeon, after the battle at Châteauroux."

Ian suppressed a wince as she probed the tender flesh with one finger, clucking under her breath. A glancing blow from a sword had slipped under his mailed coif and sliced through the padded leather gambeson he wore beneath. The wound was not deep, but long and ragged.

"Well, 'twill leave an ugly scar, but 'tis healing cleanly, so I won't resew it."

She sighed, and Ian saw again the concern that had bracketed her forehead ever since she'd come to his chamber to give him the blue wool surcoat lined with vair that she'd lovingly fashioned for him in his absence.

"Don't fash yourself, Lady Mother," he said. "Will's but seventeen, after all, and won his spurs only six months ago. He's just feeling his manhood, paying court to his first ladylove."

Lady Elizabeth shook her head. "You've not seen him since his knighting. I tell you, Ian, Will's smitten with that bitch."

Ian's brows rose at the uncharacteristic harshness of his stepmother's words. Known as much for her gentleness as for her charity to the poor, Lady Elizabeth rarely spoke ill of anyone, much less a woman she'd never met.

"So Will's smitten," Ian replied with a slight shrug. "It won't harm him to gain a little experience with such women before he takes his wife."

The hurt flooding Lady Elizabeth's brown eyes made Ian realize his mistake at once.

"William's not like you, my son," she said, with only the faintest hint of reproach. "He has not the sophistication for the games played by the women of the king's court. Nor the endurance to enter into them so enthusiastically."

Ian bit back a smile. When he attended his younger brother's investiture some six months before, he'd discovered that the handsome, irrepressible young knight had already gained a formidable reputation for endurance among the ladies. But Ian knew better than to share that information with Will's doting mother.

"You worry needlessly, my lady. Will is young enough yet to enjoy his new status as knight, and man enough to know his responsibilities to his betrothed. He but dallies with this woman."

Elizabeth sighed. "At first I, too, thought 'twas naught but a boy's infatuation. But of late William's every letter speaks only of his Madeline de Courcey. She's bewitched him, I tell you."

The genuine distress on her face told Ian that she was more worried than he'd first thought.

"Sit down by the fire while I finish robing," he told her with a smile. "Then we'll thrash this out."

When he joined his mother beside the fire a few moments later, Ian stretched his long legs out and heaved a sigh of contentment. Sweet Jesu, it felt good to be home again.

"Will you have wine?" Lady Elizabeth asked.

At his assent, she nodded to the maidservant who crouched beside the fire. The girl wrapped a thick pad around the poker buried in the coals. Plunging the hot iron into a pitcher of wine, she let the liquid sizzle for a moment. The scent of precious cinnamon and nutmeg filled the air.

She poured the mulled wine into a silver cup and handed it to Lady Elizabeth, her eyes respectfully downcast. She handed another cup to Ian, but there was more invitation than respect in the look that accompanied the wine. Her gaze traveled the length of Ian's outstretched frame, then back up again, and a smile tilted her lips.

The girl's bold assessment earned a scowl from Lady Elizabeth and an answering smile from Ian, who ran an equally appreciative eye over her pale hair and well-padded figure. He watched the saucy maid's hips twitch as she left the room. On the instant, the lethargy wrought by his bath and this quiet moment by the fire receded, and Ian revised his plans for later that evening.

"Do you know this Madeline de Courcey?" His mother's voice pulled his eyes and thoughts from the enticing rear.

"I met her once, years ago," he responded. "She was just a maid then, a plain little thing with big eyes and skinny arms. She didn't strike me as having any special witching powers."

"Since then she's buried two husbands," Elizabeth retorted. "Both died within a twelvemonth of marriage to the woman," she added darkly.

"Her first lord had some sixty years under his belt when he took his child bride, as I recall. 'Tis no wonder he expired."

"And her second? He was young, and most robust."

"The second met his fate on the battlefield, leading an insane charge against a vastly superior force. The fool didn't wait for reinforcements."

"And why would any knight attack against such overwhelming odds?"

"Maybe because he had more courage than brains," Ian replied with a shrug, having once served with the well-muscled but incredibly thick-skulled young knight.

"Or mayhap because the king's son arranged the order of battle when the man objected to his interest in his wife," Lady Elizabeth suggested. "'Tis common knowledge that this Madeline de Courcey has Lord John under her spell."

Ian knew that the king's youngest son, for all his show of knightly presence in the recent wars, had little say in the order of battle. King Henry, the second of that name, directed his forces with the same demonic energy and efficiency he brought to the governance of his vast dominions in England and on the Continent. Ian knew, as well, however, that the Lady Elizabeth would not be deflected by logic when the interests of one of her brood were at issue. Not wanting to offer her the discourtesy of an argument, he took a sip of his wine and smiled lazily.

"When I saw William last, he spoke only of the battles he'd been in, and his knighting. He said nothing of this Lady Madeline, nor of any lady in particular."

"William met her shortly after, when she once again became the king's ward, upon her second husband's death."

"What, does she reside in the king's household, and not at one of her dower estates?"

Lady Elizabeth nodded. "'Tis said John himself begged the king to bring her back. Will has written of nothing but the accursed woman since. He raves about her wit, and her charm, even her seat on a horse!''

Ian smiled inwardly at the pique in his mother's voice and made a mental note to speak to his brother about the detail he included in his letters in the future.

''You think I exaggerate?'' Lady Elizabeth sighed. ''Here, read for yourself.''

She pulled a much-worn parchment from the folds of her robe and passed it to him. Leaning toward the flickering fire, Ian scanned his brother's all-but-illegible script. Despite his best efforts, he couldn't hold back a grin at the flowery, poetic words Will used to describe his ladylove. This atrocious poetry would cause his brother to writhe in embarrassment when he had a few more years and a few more women to his credit.

Ian's grin slipped, however, when he read the last paragraph. In it, Will compared Lady Madeline to his betrothed, and found the young girl he'd been promised to since early childhood sadly lacking.

''Just so,'' his mother commented, seeing his expression. ''Surely William cannot want to break his betrothal! His father arranged it before he died and pledged his most solemn oath.''

''Nay,'' Ian responded, his tone thoughtful. ''Will doesn't take his honor so slightly that he would disavow a sacred pledge made in his name.''

''But he's never expressed the least dissatisfaction with his betrothed before. She's a gentle, well-mannered girl, and will make him a comfortable wife.

As many times as we brought them together as children to make sure they would suit, they've come to know each other well.''

Ian saw the worry clouding Lady Elizabeth's eyes and put aside his own disturbing thoughts. Taking her hands in a warm hold, he slipped into the familiar role of protector and head of a vast network of responsibilities. It was a role he'd worn for some ten years and more, one that sat easily on his shoulders.

''Don't fret, Lady Mother. Will's but sampling his first taste of courtly love. If it eases your mind, I'll speak to him when I go south about fixing the date of his marriage. The prospect of assuming full management of his own lands and those of his wife should distract him from this Lady Madeline.''

Lady Elizabeth turned her face up to Ian's, her lips lifted in the glowing smile that had won his father's heart so many years ago and was yet undimmed by time. ''Thank you, my son. I knew I could depend on you to take his mind from that . . . that female.''

Ian drew her up and kissed her cheek. ''Aye, you can depend on me.''

He led her from the lord's chamber and down the flight of stone steps to the great hall, his eyes thoughtful. For all his easy assurances to Lady Elizabeth, Ian wasn't as confident in the matter as he'd let on. The tone of Will's letter disturbed him. It held less of the gushing moonling and more of a man caught in the throes of passion than Ian wanted to admit, even to himself.

Moreover, he much disliked the idea of Will being enthralled by a woman rumored to be mistress to the king's son. The Angevins loved and hated with equal passion, and John was as much a spawn of King Henry and Queen Eleanor of Aquitaine as any of their hot-blooded brood. The youngest of their eight children, John was also the king's most beloved son—the only one, Ian thought wryly, who had not yet rebelled against his father's heavy hand. 'Twould not do for Will to earn John's enmity, and mayhap the king's, by toying with the young lord's mistress.

As Ian escorted Lady Elizabeth across the great hall, he returned the greetings offered by passing servants and the vassals assembled to welcome him home and hear the news. Surrounded by the familiar noise and clatter of the feast ordered in honor of his homecoming, Ian gradually relaxed. The habit of caring for his large, boisterous family was so ingrained that he had no doubt of his ability to extricate William from this Lady Madeline's coils, if he found it necessary to do so.

"Ian!"

He loosed his hold on Lady Elizabeth just in time to catch a flying bundle of robes and long honey-colored braids.

"Oof!" He made a show of stumbling back with his laughing, squealing younger sister in his arms. "You've gained at least a stone since last I was home, Cat. And at least two score new freckles."

Lady Elizabeth watched with an indulgent smile as Ian teased her youngest chick, a budding, blushing maid of some ten summers, then turned to take an equally lively greeting from her next youngest.

"Ian," the boy exclaimed, "you must tell me every detail of the battle at Châteauroux! The other pages have promised to share their sweets with me for a month if I relay the exact order of the siege."

Ian ruffled Dickon's thick golden hair and answered his eager questions while Catherine hung on his other arm. Watching them, Lady Elizabeth felt her heart contract with love. Their tawny heads shone in the light of the torches placed around the hall. The three were so alike in color most people forgot they were but half brother and sister.

Ian looked older than his eight-and-twenty years, Elizabeth thought, ascribing it to the months of war from which he'd just returned. With rest, nourishment and her watchful care, he'd soon lose the lines of strain etching deep groves beside his dark blue eyes and the gauntness from his chiseled cheekbones. He'd have to be fattened up a bit, too, she decided. Although his thighs and muscles were roped with hard muscles, his long frame was far too thin, in her opinion.

She breathed a small sigh, wishing once again that Ian would seek another wife. One who would take him in hand, fuss over him and give him the love he deserved. One who would breed him fine sons and daughters. The maid he wed as a youth had been far too timid and delicate to curb his independent ways. And since the girl's death from ague after a scant year of marriage, Ian had become much too comfortable with his stable of willing bedmates to seek out another bride. He had his mother and a throng of loving sisters to see to his household needs, or so he protested whenever Elizabeth brought up the subject. Why should he take a wife?

Elizabeth stood a moment longer, observing the play of light on the golden heads still bent in cheerful discourse. She'd been blessed with a fine brood, six babes of her own who lived past infancy and a tall, handsome son of her heart. They were her life, and she would give her life to keep any one of them from harm.

The thought brought her brows together, and her hand sought the folded parchment in her pocket. Praise God Ian was home. Ian would speak to Will. He'd end the boy's infatuation with a woman whose unsavory reputation had penetrated even these remote northern reaches. Knowing that the matter was all but done, Elizabeth moved forward to join her lively family.

Bad weather and the myriad demands on a lord who had been absent for many months delayed Ian's departure for the south. He spent a week at Wyndham, his principal holding, settling disputes among his tenants and overseeing the refurbishment of the armory after the depredations of the recent campaign.

Wet snow blanketed the hills the following week, making travel to his outlying manors an unpleasant chore and slowing progress between each of his demesne properties. Consequently, when he headed

south the second week in February to attend the king's
wearing of the crown, he found the roads turned to
mud. His troop was slowed by great processions of
mounted knights moving their households from
properties denuded of winter provisions to other
holdings, as well as throngs of pilgrims, road merchants and jugglers. Where their ways converged, Ian
offered travelers the protection of his troop against the
bandits that ravaged the countryside.

After a week of slow progress, Ian neared the red
sandstone walls of Kenilworth Castle. Appropriated
as a royal residence a decade before, Kenilworth stood
as a massive symbol of safety and comfort. Ian rode
through its thick barbican with weary relief.

Within an hour, he'd found his assigned rooms,
given his mail and weapons into his squire's care and
prepared to go in search of his younger brother. As it
happened, Will came charging down the drafty corridor just as Ian opened the chamber door.

"Ian!"

Will's enthusiastic greeting propelled them both
back across the threshold. He buffeted Ian on the
shoulder with all the enthusiasm of a youth of seventeen summers and the unrestrained strength of a year-
ling bull. He already matched Ian's not inconsiderable
height and promised fair to overtake him in weight
before long.

"Jesu, lad," Ian protested, laughing. "Is this the
training a knight of the royal household receives? To
all but knock his lord and guardian to the floor in
rough greeting?"

"Ha! The day I knock you to the floor I will know myself truly a knight."

The two brothers grinned at each other, remembering the many wrestling matches and mock combat they'd engaged in. Ian had never coddled his younger brothers, knowing they would need all their strength of arm to survive. The boys had taken many a toss from their horses in their youth and thumped the floor regularly in their efforts to best their older brother.

Throwing an arm across the young knight's shoulders, Ian led Will back into his chambers. A roaring fire snapped in the great stone hearth in a vain attempt to ward off the icy February drafts that whistled through the tall mullioned glass windows.

The flickering flames illuminated the full glory of Will's attire. Brows raised, Ian ran admiring eyes down the brilliant turquoise surcoat that sat easily on the young man's broad shoulders. The wool gown sported rich embroidery along its neck and hem in an intricate pattern of mythical beasts and twisting vines. Lady Elizabeth must have spent months setting the stitches in precious gold and silver thread.

"Well, if you haven't learned any manners in your time at court, at least you've acquired an elegant air. You shine from head to toe," Ian intoned in awe. "Our lady mother will be pleased to know her efforts to display your curls to best advantage are finally appreciated."

A dull red crept up William's throat, but he laughed and raked a hand through his thick golden mane. Brighter by several shades than Ian's own tawny hair,

Will's shining curls were the bane of his existence and the object of his sisters' undying envy.

"I but dress to keep up with the courtiers," he protested. "I swear, Ian, with every shipment of goods that comes from Jerusalem, the knights at court bedeck themselves ever more gaudily. 'Tis like attending a damned May fair to walk amongst them."

"And you the beribboned Maypole, towering above them all," Ian teased good-naturedly.

"You could use some peacocking yourself," Will retorted, giving his brother's ringless hands and dark blue surcoat a candid once-over. "If you would not shame me, at least wear something other than those boots when you go to take the evening meal."

"Nay, I'd look the fool in shoes such as yours, falling flat on my face every time I tried to take a step."

Will lifted a huge foot clad in felt slippers with toes so long and pointed they had to be curled back and caught with garters below his knees.

"'Tis a ridiculous fashion," Will agreed with a laugh. "But a fellow must wear them, or look the country bumpkin to all the ladies."

"You've much yet to learn of women, if you think 'tis your shoes that interests them."

To Ian's surprise, Will failed to respond to his wry comment. The laughter faded from the boy's face, to be replaced by an expression containing an equal mixture of earnestness and defiance.

"I know I have much yet to learn of women, Ian, but I'm not quite the fool our mother thinks me. I'm neither besotted nor bewitched. Nor do I need you to turn me from my 'silly' infatuation.''

Ian stifled an oath as he surveyed his brother's stiff countenance. Evidently the Lady Elizabeth had written to advise Will of her misgivings and of her request for Ian's intervention in his brother's affairs. Shrugging off a momentary irritation at his mother's interference, he led the way to two armchairs set before the fire. He poured two goblets of wine, passed one to Will, then stretched his long legs out to the fire.

"I'll admit I've had some difficulty visualizing myself in the role of protector of your virtue," he said lazily. "Especially since I was the one who sent two eager kitchen wenches to the barn to help you lose it some years ago."

Will sputtered into his goblet, and an ebullient smile once more brightened his face.

"I didn't think you'd dare come down heavy on me, Ian. You, of all people! You've not been exactly continent since your lady wife died these many years ago. Still, my mother's latest missive all but shriveled my manhood with dire threats of what you'd do if I did not cease my...my preoccupation with the Lady Madeline."

Ian's lips twitched. "Mothers do tend to see these things differently."

"Yes, well, this...this *is* somewhat different, Ian." Will's broad smile took on a tentative edge once more, and he leaned forward in his seat. "The Lady Madeline is different. I've never met anyone like her."

"That's what you said about the chandler's daughter, the one with the astonishing repertoire of tricks with candles," Ian commented dryly.

"She's not like that!"

"Nay? Nor like the two sisters of the count de Marbeau, the ones who—?"

"I would not have you speak of the Lady Madeline in the same breath as those two."

The cool command in Will's voice made Ian's brow arch in surprise. He set aside his wine and studied his brother. The boy's—no, the young man's—face wore a mask of wounded dignity. Ian had enough years of experience dealing with youthful squires and pages, guiding their transition from boy to knight, to know when to prick their pretensions and when to listen.

"Very well, I will not speak of her thus," he told Will easily. "You speak, instead. Tell me of this paragon who has you arrayed in your finest velvet robes and gold rings."

"She's . . . she's special, Ian. Charming and gracious, with a laugh like silver bells carrying on the summer breeze."

Ian's brow inched up another notch, and Will leaned forward, his blue eyes shining with sincerity.

"She's not beautiful, exactly, but makes all other women pale in her company. And kind—she's kind to a fault."

"She'd have to be, to pay any attention to a clumsy-footed clunch such as you," Ian agreed.

Will nodded, in perfect accord with this description of one whose inheritance rivaled those of the wealthiest knights in England and whose form was fast fulfilling its promise of raw strength and masculine beauty.

"She tells me I'm but a callow cub, as well," he admitted, sheep-faced. "But she's given me her hand twice in the dance, and I have hopes of wearing her token in the tourney."

As he proceeded to describe the Lady Madeline, Will's stock of poetic phrases ran out long before his enthusiasm for his subject. By the time Ian had suffered hearing how her hair gleamed like the glossy bark of a towering chestnut tree for the third time, and how her eyes sparkled like the veriest stars several times over, he'd heard enough to make him distinctly uneasy.

To his experienced ears, it sounded as if the lady but played with Will. She enticed him with smiles, yet kept him at arm's length with a show of maidenly reserve. Such false modesty from one who had buried two husbands and was rumored to bed with the king's son grated on Ian. Hand upraised, he called a halt to Will's paean to the lady.

"Enough, man, enough! You make my head ache with all your mangled poetry. Let's go down and seek out this exemplar of womanly virtues. I would see if she lives up to half of your honeyed words."

Will clambered to his feet with boyish eagerness. "Aye, let's go. I'm anxious for you to meet her."

"No more than I am," Ian responded easily, but his eyes were hard as he followed Will from the chamber.

They made slow progress across Kenilworth's vast hall, as many acquaintances called greetings to Ian. All the great barons owing homage to King Henry were summoned thrice yearly for these state occasions, held in conjunction with church feast days. It was an opportunity for the king to consult with his barons, and for the lords themselves to share news and gossip. Those who had not provided knight's service in the latest war were anxious to hear Ian's account of the action. Will lingered by Ian's side for a while, then spotted a small knot of courtiers at the far side of the hall. He nudged his brother in the side with an elbow.

"'Tis her, Ian. The Lady Madeline. I would go and speak with her. Join me when you can."

From a corner of his eye, Ian watched his brother's passage across the hall. His lips tightened at the fatuous expression that settled on Will's face as he bent over the hand of a slight figure in a flowing crimson gown.

Seeing her from across the hall, Ian's first impression of the Lady Madeline was that she hadn't changed much from the mousy young maid he half remembered. Surrounded by a ring of richly dressed men and elegant women, her slight figure was barely visible. He could just make out her profile, with a nose more short and pert than aquiline, and a chin more distinguished by its firmness than by soft, rounded feminine beauty. From the little Ian could see of her braided hair, caught up in two gold cauls over her ears and covered with a silken veil, it appeared more brown than the bright chestnut Will had rhapsodized over.

Some of the tension in Ian's body eased. Whatever the rumors about the Lady Madeline's charms, she did not appear to be the sultry beauty Ian had feared. It shouldn't be all that difficult to detach Will from her circle.

At that moment the lady looked over her shoulder in response to a remark made by the elderly knight at her side. Flaring torches set in iron holders high above illuminated her face as she made some teasing reply.

A slow, provocative smile transformed her nondescript features. Green eyes, so bright and luminescent a man could lose himself in them, glowed with mischievous, tantalizing, stunningly sensual laughter.

Ian drew in a sharp breath, feeling the impact of those incredible eyes like a mailed fist to his stomach.

Chapter Two

Madeline's low, merry laugh rippled through the crowd of courtiers surrounding her.

"Nay, Sir Percy," she told the grizzled knight who hovered at her shoulder, "you may not have my garter. Imagine what people would think if you were to wear such an intimate item in the tourney."

"They would think what is my fondest desire, lady."

"Oh, so?" she said teasingly. "And just moments ago I heard you say you desired above all else to win a certain war-horse, if you could but unseat its owner. 'Tis the trouble with you fearsome knights. You know not whether you want first your horse or your lady."

The courtiers around her burst into laughter as the older knight began a gallant repartee, trying to convince her that she owned his heart. Madeline turned aside his flowery phrases with practiced ease, enjoying the lively give-and-take. Her eyes sparkled as Sir Percy effusively professed his devotion. When the older knight paused at last, William edged him aside with more boyish eagerness than polished address.

"Lady, may I take you in to supper?"

"Nay, Sir William, I am promised." Madeline hid a smile at his crestfallen face. "But I'll save a dance for you later. The rondeau, perhaps? 'Twill do my image no end of good to be partnered by the handsomest young knight at the king's court."

Will nodded eagerly and bent over her hand, his bright curls shining against the crimson of her sleeve. Madeline's gaze softened at his reverent salute. In truth, he was a comely lad, with a friendly, open disposition to match his well-proportioned frame. That he'd already made a name for himself on the tourney field and in several battles didn't detract from the air of youthful exuberance that she found so refreshing.

"Will you at least allow me to bring my brother to meet you before the boards are laid?" he asked, retaining her hand until she slipped it from his grasp.

"What, has he arrived at last? The earl of Margill? The same glorious knight and fearless warrior I've heard so much about these last weeks?"

"Don't tell him I described him thus," Will begged, grinning down at her. "In his presence, I refer to him as the biggest churl in Christendom! Give me leave, and I'll deliver him to your side this instant."

Madeline nodded her assent, curious to meet the man whose sayings and accomplishments peppered William's conversation with unconscious frequency. In the weeks since the youth had drifted into her circle—nay, blundered into her circle, for with those huge feet, the lad would never drift—she'd heard much of this esteemed older brother. She had a vague memory of meeting him once, long ago, when she'd wed her first lord. She'd been too young and too nervous to remember much of the crowd of knights and ladies who attended the festivities. But if she could not recall Ian de Burgh in any detail, there were many women here at Kenilworth who could. Since her return to court, Madeline had heard more than one lady sighing over the earl's beguiling blue eyes and lazy smile. From their tittering, giggling comments about his person, Madeline had formed a mental image of a peacock on the strut.

At length Will elbowed his way back into the circle surrounding her. Madeline looked up, and her gaze locked with a pair of midnight blue eyes, startling in a face so tanned by sun and wind. A shock of sheer awareness darted down her spine.

This was no puffed-up courtier, impressed by the power and authority of his huge estates.

This was a man in his prime, a knight honed to a muscled leanness by vigorous activity, and tougher by far than his tawny-haired, chiseled handsomeness would suggest.

Madeline swallowed. Having twice been wed, she was yet a stranger to the feeling that suddenly coursed through her at the sight of this tall, broad-shouldered man.

"I would present my brother, Lord Ian," Will said eagerly. "He's professed himself most anxious to meet you."

"Indeed, my lady, after hearing Will's flowing verses, I could scarce wait to meet the object of his poetry."

Recovering her poise, Madeline threw the youth a look of mock dismay. "Oh, no, Sir William! You've not subjected your brother to those verses!"

"Indeed he has," de Burgh drawled. "All of them. Several times over."

To her surprise, Madeline felt a flush rising above the square cut bodice of her gown. By the holy Virgin, she hadn't blushed in years. But for some reason the thought of the earl reading those outrageous descriptions of her face and form disconcerted her.

Undaunted by their disparagement of his compositions, Will gave a cheerful grin. "My verses will improve with practice."

"I hope so," his brother interjected smoothly, "else the lady will not allow you to continue to pay homage at her skirts."

Madeline's eyes flashed up to meet the earl's. Was she the only one who heard the soft warning in his words? Or sensed intimidation in the way his hand closed over her upper arm, to ease her away from the rest of the group?

Apparently so. When he suggested casually that he wished to further her acquaintance where there was less noise, Will nodded in acquiescence, and the rest of her circle stood aside. The conversation behind her picked up with barely a pause as Madeline found herself heading toward a nearby alcove.

She fought a ripple of annoyance at the way the man detached her from her friends with such effortless skill. She wasn't used to being led away without being consulted as to her own wishes in the matter. She wasn't used to being led at all. Tugging her arm from his firm hold, she turned to face Ian. Madeline allowed no trace of her irritation at his high-handed manners to show in her voice, or in the half smile she sent him.

"I gather you wish to speak with me privately because you're concerned about your brother's choice of an *objet d'amour.*"

His sun-bleached brows rose. She'd taken him aback, Madeline saw with some satisfaction. She suspected it wasn't often that anyone did so.

"You believe in plain speaking, I see," he commented after a moment.

"Yes, I do. It saves much time and misunderstanding. And spares me unsubtle warnings such as you issued just now."

After a brief hesitation, he made a slight bow. "My pardon, Lady Madeline. I hadn't realized I was being so clumsy in my address."

He leaned back against the stone wall, his arms folded, and ran his eyes slowly over her face. At his appraising look, Madeline fought the flush that threatened to stain her bosom once again.

"'Tis one of the things I like most in your brother," she said with faint challenge. "He is refreshingly open and honest."

"Aye, he is that. And as yet untainted by the ways of the court."

"You fear I will be the one to taint him?"

"This is plain speaking indeed," the earl murmured, straightening.

"I'm neither stupid nor a timid maiden, my lord. I know well what is said of me. And I know, as well, that Will's family is concerned for him. Or so I've been advised by half a dozen of the older tabbies at court," she finished dryly.

To Madeline's surprise, his blue eyes lightened with rueful laughter. For the first time, she witnessed the beguiling charm the other ladies of the courts had tittered about whenever Ian de Burgh's name was mentioned.

"'Twould appear my lady mother is most industrious in her correspondence."

Madeline's own lips curved in instinctive response to the smile creasing his lean cheeks. "And you, my lord? Do you share your mother's concerns?"

"I? I begin to share my brother's interest."

His soft, slow drawl raised ripples of pleasure all along Madeline's nerves. When the man chose to be charming, he did so with a vengeance, she thought somewhat breathlessly. That particular combination of gleaming eyes and crooked grin was enough to make any woman's breath catch in her throat. She ran her tongue across suddenly dry lips and sought for something to say.

"Your pardon, my lord, my lady."

She turned to see one of the household pages standing just beyond the alcove. The golden lion, symbol of the house of Plantagenet, shone on the boy's red tunic.

"They're laying the boards and will soon begin to serve. Lord John sent me to escort you to your seat, my lady."

"Aye, I'll be with you shortly."

Madeline turned back to finish her conversation with the earl. She had yet to assure him that he need not worry about Will. The boy's adoration amused her, but she'd been in the world enough to know how to let down a young knight without shattering either his pride or his illusions.

The earl's closed expression stopped the words in her mouth. No trace of either laughter or friendliness lingered in his eyes. Confused, Madeline stared up at his tanned face.

He bent at the waist in a bow so shallow it was more insult than salute. "Don't let me keep you from a royal summons, madame."

His cold tone sent a spear of regret through her so swift and sharp she had to bite back a small gasp. So he, like all the others, disparaged her friendship with John. This knight, whose reputation with women was common knowledge, dared scorn her.

Madeline knew well the rumors that flitted through the court about her, skittering here and there through the castle halls like old rushes stirred by the drafts that swept the winding corridors. 'Twas widely believed that the king's son took her to mistress. If John led her in the dance, heads would bow and whispers pass from mouth to mouth. If she danced with another knight, knowing eyes would flash the message that she sought another husband to wear the cuckold's horns while she dallied with the king's son. After all, she'd held the man enthralled since childhood and through two marriages.

Normally Madeline dismissed the whispers with the ease of long practice. The look in de Burgh's eyes, however, pricked at her pride.

Lifting her chin, she nodded coolly. "Aye, I must not keep the prince waiting."

Allowing none of her inner turmoil to show in her face, Madeline followed the page through the throng filling Kenilworth's vast hall and took her seat at the high table beside the man who was youngest son to King Henry and Queen Eleanor.

Her usual place was lower, well below the salt, with the other maidens and widows in warship to the crown. But with the king not yet arrived and Richard Lionheart otherwise disposed, John had ordered the seating this night to suit his own preferences. Madeline bit back a sigh as she caught the sly glances thrown her way from those seated at the lower tables. By elevating her well above her station, John had once again fueled the rumors about them. 'Twould do no good to protest, however. It never did. Spoiled, darkly handsome, and indulged by his father from earliest infancy, the young lord was rarely denied his wishes.

"Why don't you eat?" he asked when she took a meager helping from the dish of eels stewed in honey and wild onions that a perspiring page presented. "You'll never attract another husband if you don't fatten up and fill out your gowns more. You were ever flat as a sword blade, Maddy."

Her gaze flew up to meet his dancing black eyes. "Aye, and you were ever ready to tell me so, my lord. You'll never know how much I feared my first wedding and bedding because of your slighting comments about my shape when we were children."

"Ha! That doting old fool who wed you cared not about your shape. He was as beguiled as they all are by your green eyes and ripe lips."

The lips under discussion lost their ripeness. Slowly Madeline set down her two-tined fork—a recent introduction to the court—and turned to give the man beside her a level look.

"I've valued your friendship since I first came to your mother's household these many years ago. But I'll not allow you to speak so of the man who wed me. He was good, and kind, and treated me most gently."

"He was also so old his knees rattled when he walked." John held up a hand. "Nay, nay, do not glower at me. He was good and kind, if so you say."

He waited until she had given a stiff nod and picked up her fork once more, then grinned wickedly.

"But I'll warrant you enjoyed your second wedding and bedding far more."

"Jack-a-napes," Madeline sputtered, using the nickname she'd called him by privately since they were four years old. "Do not start on that again!"

He leaned forward, his shoulder brushing hers. "Come, Maddy. Your second lord may have had wool for brains, but he was rumored to have the accoutrements of an ox. Were the pleasures of the marriage bed all that they're rumored to be?"

"You'll find out when you consummate your marriage to the Lady Isabel," Madeline replied lightly. "As if you didn't already know!"

At the mention of his betrothed, John's eyes lost their dark light. He drew back and lifted his wine goblet to his lips.

Madeline stabbed at a slithery eel and cursed herself under her breath for her slip. As the youngest of the king's eight children, John had no hereditary duchies to claim as his own, and much resented his landless state. To rectify this situation, King Henry had debated endlessly whether to strip his other sons of some of their lands to give John a heritage. He'd also betrothed him as a young boy to Isabel of Gloucester, Strongbow's great heiress, a cold, supercilious girl. Despite the fact that Isabel's holdings constituted as yet his only estates, or mayhap because of it, John secretly despised the dark-haired heiress. He was careful not to show his dislike, but Madeline knew of his disdain for his betrothed, as she knew most of his innermost thoughts.

Almost since the day she'd come into the king's wardship, a lonely little four-year-old, John had been her friend and companion. Madeline could recall as if it were yesterday the rainy April morning he'd released her, white-faced and stiff with fright, from the dark privy a mischievous playmate had locked her in hours before. On that day, he'd become her instant hero.

Madeline often wondered at the unlikely friendship that had sprung from that inauspicious meeting. Although the son of the most powerful king in Christendom, John had always alternated between flashing smiles and dark melancholy. Madeline, by contrast, was the orphan of a minor baron and found easy release for her ready laughter. Yet, whenever the young lord could steal away from his tutors and Madeline from her duties to Queen Eleanor, the two children would explore the gardens or the stables, tearing hose and skirts in their adventures. Over the years, the friendship between the prince and maid had grown haphazardly, in fits and starts, but grown it had.

Not even Madeline's two marriages, as brief and as fruitless as they'd been, had lessened the bond. Her first lord, a kind, chivalrous old knight who professed himself delighted with his child bride, had taken her into his household when she was twelve. Spoiled and petted and shamelessly indulged, Madeline had gone willingly to his bed to consummate their marriage two years later. When he died within a twelvemonth, the king had taken the young widow into wardship once again.

King Henry himself had chosen Madeline's second husband, a brawny but slow-witted young knight who'd all but fallen over his feet in his desire for the lady. The knight had gladly paid the exorbitant bride price into the royal coffers, reverently and most satisfactorily bedded his wife—at least in his mind—then promptly lost his life in a mad charge across a battlefield.

Now she was once more the king's ward. At John's request, she'd been brought back to reside within the royal household, while castellans managed her estates and rendered their revenues to the crown. Madeline didn't mind. 'Twas the only home she'd ever known, after all, and John the only constant in the shifting world in which she'd come to womanhood. This time, her friend had promised her, she would not have to leave until she so chose. This time he'd used his influence with his father, who'd agreed Madeline would have a say in the choice of her next lord.

Her next husband would not be quite as old as her first, Madeline had already decided, nor as foolhardy as her second. She wanted a man strong enough to hold her lands and mature enough to manage them wisely, yet young enough to laugh with. Someone to stoke the fires of passion that flickered within her but had, as yet, not been fanned to flames.

Unbidden, Madeline's gaze drifted down the boards and met that of Ian de Burgh. At the look in his blue eyes, she stiffened. Suddenly the sweetmeat she had just bitten into tasted like ashes in her mouth.

She'd hoped, nay dreamed, for a husband such as Lord Ian. One whose body made her breath catch and whose eyes bespoke intelligence and wit. But the scorn

that now curled his mouth made a mockery of her
dreams. Better by far to take one of those who dangled after her, Madeline decided with a sigh, than to
waste her wishes on a man who clearly believed the
court's gossip. Swearing a silent vow to avoid the earl
in the future, Madeline gave her attention to the
prince.

As the days passed, Ian felt both his ire and his unwilling fascination with Lady Madeline grow in equal
measures. The lady was like a moth, he decided, light
and frivolous, fluttering from one man to the next.
With the king's arrival, Kenilworth Castle was filled
to overflowing, yet Ian had only to walk past a
crowded salon to hear her merry laughter. He couldn't
stroll into the great hall of an evening without seeing
a knot of courtiers clustered about a slender form and
knowing she was holding court.

She was discreet enough not to flaunt her relationship with the king's son in his father's presence, but
she flirted with every other male in the castle, it
seemed.

Every male except him.

Ian shrugged, telling himself that he cared naught
about the lady's cold stare when he'd chanced upon
her in the corridor yestereve, but in truth he was no
more used to being snubbed than he was to having his
brother ignore his subtle tugs on the reins.

Despite his efforts to detach Will from the lady's
circle, the lad was well and truly smitten. He'd join Ian
in the hunt with great good humor, and participate

vigorously in the games leading up to the great tourney that was to begin in a few days. But, like an iron
filing drawn to a lodestone, Will would find his way to
the lady's side as soon as he could.

As he had tonight.

Thoroughly disgusted, Ian watched his brother lead
the lady through a stately dance, his bright head
clearly visible above the rest of the crowd. Clad in a
richly embroidered robe of shimmering blue silk, Lady
Madeline looked slender and graceful next to Will's
towering bulk.

Forcing himself to remain casual, Ian intercepted
Will after the dance ended and steered his brother to
a quiet corner. A passing page provided them both
with wine, which Will downed in long, thirsty gulps.

"I tell you, Ian, this dancing is a warm business,"
he confided, wiping the sweat from his brow with one
arm.

"More like 'tis all the layers of finery you've
adorned yourself with," Ian responded with a grin.

The brothers exchanged good-natured insults for a
few moments, before Ian led the conversation to the
issue that concerned him. "You should not be quite so
particular in your attentions to the Lady Madeline,"
he suggested casually.

Will's smile slipped a bit, and a hesitant expression
crept into his eyes. "Why not?"

"'Twill give her the idea that you wish more than
just a pleasant dalliance."

The lad's face took on a closed expression, as though he weighed matters in his mind that he could not, or would not, share.

Ian felt a stab of hurt. Never before had Will been the least reluctant to discuss his amatory adventures or seek his older brother's counsel on such matters. Swallowing his anger at the woman who had caused this sudden caution in his open, trusting brother, Ian shrugged. "She's a widow, after all, on the look for a new husband. You shouldn't monopolize her time, nor distract her from her task."

"Is it so improbable that Lady Madeline might want me as a husband?" Will asked slowly.

Ian threw him a sharp glance. "You are betrothed."

"Aye." Will gnawed on his lower lip for a long, hesitant moment. "But the last time I was in the north, Alicia seemed to find little joy in the prospect of marriage with me. Mayhap she would be better matched with someone else."

Ian's brows soared in surprise. "Are you saying she wants release from the betrothal? Our lady mother mentioned nothing of this when I was home."

Will shook his head, clearly miserable. "Nay, Ian. Alicia would not ask for release. She's such a mouse, she would not have the courage. But... but neither does she invite my kisses."

Ian wavered between exasperation and amusement. Will's next words, however, erased all inclination to laugh.

"Lady Madeline doesn't shrink away and call me a heavy-handed brute when I take her arm."

"Nay, I'll wager she does not," Ian drawled. "She's more used to men by a goodly measure than is Alicia."

A frown settled between Will's brows at this description of his ladylove. Satisfied that he'd planted at least a seed of doubt, Ian turned the subject. He'd heard enough to know that Will would not disgrace himself by forswearing his vows, though the lad longed for this Madeline de Courcey with all the urgency of a young man in the throes of his first love.

There was only one solution, Ian concluded, and that was to convince the woman herself to call a halt before the boy's heart took a serious blow. Or before he earned the enmity of the king's son with his pursuit of the lady. Sending Will off with the suggestion that he find himself a flagon of ale or a willing wench, or both, Ian decided that 'twas time he and the Lady Madeline finished their discussion of some days before.

With the skill of the hunter cutting his prey from the herd, Ian separated the lady from the women she walked with in the castle gardens the next afternoon. Holding her hand longer than was either polite or necessary, he gave the other ladies a slow grin and the unmistakable hint that he desired private speech with Lady Madeline. Despite Madeline's raised brows and stiff rejoinder that 'twas too cold and damp for conversation, the other women fluttered off, casting more

than one arch glance over a cloaked shoulder. As soon
as they had disappeared around a bend of the intricate evergreen hedges that made Kenilworth's gardens famous, Madeline snatched back her hand.

"I much mislike this tendency you have to separate
me from my companions, my lord. Do not do so
again."

Ian stared down at her flushed face. Whether it was
the cold February wind that had put the pink in her
cheeks or his own determined tactics, he neither knew
nor cared. But the sight of her creamy, rose-tinted skin
and huge, flashing eyes framed by a blue wool hood
lined with sable made Ian suck in a quick breath. Irritated that she would cause such a reaction in him, he
folded his arms across his chest.

"And I much mislike seeing my brother make a fool
of himself over one such as you, my lady. You will
cease your attentions to him."

Her breath puffed out in a little cloud of white va-
por. "One such as I?"

"Come, you told me yourself that you preferred
plain speaking."

To his surprise, a gleam of wry laughter appeared in
her expressive eyes. "'Tis one thing for me to speak
plainly about myself, my lord. 'Tis another thing altogether for you to do so."

Despite himself, Ian felt an answering grin tug at his
lips. "I see. 'Tis well I know the rules before I play the
game."

"The game?"

"Aye. 'Tis what you do, is it not? You draw men in with your laughter and your merry eyes, and play with them. You're most skilled at it."

She drew back and surveyed him thoughtfully. "I'd thank you for the compliment sir, if I thought it one."

"Oh, it is, most assuredly."

Ian brushed a knuckle down the alabaster coldness of her cheek. She jerked her head back, startled and a little breathless. Her fingers curled under her chin.

"I would be drawn by those eyes myself," he murmured, "were I not reluctant to poach in my brother's preserves."

Madeline stared up at him, confused by the conflicting emotions he generated within her breast. With every double-edged word he spoke, he seemed to be offering her insult. But the lambent gleam in his dark blue eyes, and the way his hand now cupped her chin in a warm, hard hold, fanned a tiny flame within her. When it came to playing the game, Madeline decided, this man was more skilled by far than she.

"My lord . . ." she began, embarrassed at the breathless quality of her voice.

"Aye?"

His murmured response sent a tingle of awareness shimmering down her spine. Or mayhap it was the feel of his callused fingers on her skin. Or the scent that drifted to her on the cold, crisp air of leather and dry wood and male.

"You need not worry about William."

"Need I not?"

Madeline's hood slid off her hair as she tilted her head back to look up into the face above her. The winter sun painted his high cheeks and square, blunt jaw. It was a strong face, Madeline decided, echoing the character of its owner.

"Nay, you need not," she replied lightly. "I will ensure he takes no hurt. As you said, I'm much skilled at this game."

The hold on her chin tightened suddenly. Madeline blinked in surprise as his eyes took on the silvery sheen of old slate.

"You mistake Will's character, lady. Unlike your husbands, my brother is neither old nor thick-skulled."

"What are you speaking of?" she gasped.

"I won't allow Will to break his betrothal and marry you," he replied with knife-edged bluntness. "However well you play this game of yours, you'll not put cuckold's horns on my brother while you dally with the king's son."

Madeline jerked her chin out of his hold, stunned by his attack. "How—how dare you speak to me so!"

"I dare because Will is my responsibility."

"You take your responsibilities too heavily," she said, gathering her skirts. "William is a man, fully grown and knighted. 'Tis time you let him think for himself."

She whirled, intending to stalk out of the garden, but a hard hand grasped her arm and whipped her around.

"I tell you now, he'll not break his betrothal. Will has more honor than you appear to credit him with. He's...infatuated with you, 'tis all."

"If infatuation is all it is, you need not worry," Madeline snapped, tugging furiously at his hold.

"Cut the strings you keep him dangling by, or I'll cut them myself, in a manner you'll like not."

Incensed, Madeline swung back to face him. "You may take your threats and your insults straight to the reddest, hottest flames of hell, my lord, and yourself with them."

His jaw clenching, he caught both of her arms in an iron, unbreakable hold. "Let the lad be, lady."

"Why should I do so?" she retorted, stung by the flat coldness in a voice that had sent a shiver of delight through her only moments before. She wanted to hurt this man, as he'd hurt her. Humble him. Cause him to sweat under his fur-lined surcoat. If this...this dolt wanted to think she sought to ensnare his precious brother, then she'd not disabuse him of his folly.

Without giving him time to reply, she rushed on. "The boy's besotted, any fool can see that. And he has lands and incomes greater by far than my previous lords," she ended on a sneer.

He tightened his grip, drawing her up, until her toes just touched the stone walk and her head tilted back. A muscle twitched at one side of his jaw.

Madeline watched it, fascinated and a little frightened. She swallowed, thinking that mayhap she'd been a little too precipitate. Wetting her lips, she drew in a deep breath.

"My lord..." she began.

"Will's estates and income are under my control." He ground out the words. "If 'tis moneys you want, you play with the wrong brother." He drew her against him, banding her body to his with an arm around her waist.

"My lord!"

"Why not try your games with me, Lady Madeline?" he taunted softly. "Let's see how skilled you really are."

She splayed her hands against his chest, pushing against the hold that held her locked to him in such intimate embrace. "I thought you did not hunt in your brother's preserves!"

"That was when I believed Will the hunter. I see now he's the quarry, instead."

Madeline arched backward, and realized immediately her mistake. Her hips pressed hard into his. Through the thick layers separating them, she could feel the unyielding strength of his thighs, the flat planes of his belly. And something else. Something that grew harder with every effort she made to twist free.

She was the king's ward, Madeline thought incredulously. She could claim royal protection. Yet this arrogant knight appeared to care naught. He would take her here, on the bare, windswept ground, did she let him!

"You'd best beware," she warned, breathing hard. "'Tis also royal ground you poach upon."

She'd meant to remind him that she was under the king's protection, but she saw at once he'd mistaken her meaning. Disgust flared in his eyes, the same disgust she'd seen when he looked upon her at the high table, seated beside John. Before she could make clear her meaning, or even decide if she wanted to, he tangled a fist in the silk anchored over her braided hair and angled her face up to his.

"Well, at least we know the game is plentiful," he told her grimly, then bent and took her lips with his.

It was a kiss intended to convey more insult than passion, and it did. His lips were hard and unyielding, taking rather than giving. They branded her. Seared her. Humiliated her as no spoken insult could have. Never in her brief years of marriage had Madeline felt so used or so dominated by a man.

He shifted, widening his stance. Madeline gave a muffled squeak of dismay as she felt herself bent backward over his arm.

Her distress penetrated the fury ringing in Ian's ears. Christ's bones, he hadn't meant to savage the woman, only to show her whom it was she had pitted herself against.

Not unskilled himself in the games played between men and women, Ian brought her up against him and savored the unexpected pleasure that shot through him at the feel of her body arching into his. He gentled his kiss, and his lips molded hers, tasting instead of torturing, teasing instead of taking.

She gave a soft, breathless moan, and her fingers loosed their clawing hold on his arms.

Ian lifted his head, his nostrils flaring in fierce male satisfaction at the sound of her surrender. His conscience screamed 'twas Will's love he held in his arms, but when she stared up at him, her huge eyes dazed, he could not have loosed her had his life depended on it.

Madeline drew in a shaky breath, trying to gather her disordered senses. Anger coursed through her, so fast and hot she shivered with the force of it. And stunned astonishment that the earl would use her like some kitchen wench. And desire. Hot, shameful desire.

Her lips throbbed from the force of his, and when he lowered his head to kiss her once again, Madeline knew she had to win free of him.

Abandoning all pretensions to courtly sophistication or dignity, she did what she'd done once before, when she and John were but six and he wrestled her to the ground in an argument over a frog they'd found.

She bit her tormentor. Hard.

The earl jerked back with a startled oath.

Madeline twisted out of his arms. Had it been a sword, the glare she gave him would have sliced off his manhood. Picking up her skirts, she stalked out of the garden.

Chapter Three

Madeline spent a restless night, tossing and turning on the thick fur-covered pallet on the floor. Not for anything would she have shared the curtained bed with the other women assigned to the tower chamber. Her long, frightened hours in the dark privy as a child had given her a dislike of confined spaces that she'd never lost. She far preferred a scratchy mattress of straw to the closeness of the wood-framed bed.

The other ladies considered her strange, she knew, to forfeit warm comfort for a mat on the hard floor. Or, worse, they thought her sly beyond words, placing her pallet near the door so that she could slip away unnoticed to go to her lover's bed. Madeline could have told them of her childhood fright, but her pride refused to admit such silly weakness to any but John. Besides, she'd long since learned not to care what others thought.

So why did the scorn of one particular earl raise her ire so? she wondered irritably, curling her body into a tight ball under the furs. Why did she clench her teeth in the predawn darkness at just the memory of his punishing kiss? Why should she care if he, like all the others, believed her mistress to the king's son?

'Twas no disgrace to take a lover, after all. Queen Eleanor herself had postulated the rules for courtly love years ago. Following well-established procedures, a knight pursued his *objet d'amour* with poetry and song and feats of arms, using all his skills to win his lady's favor. Once she accepted him as her lover, a lady was bound to her knight even more than to her husband—at least in the songs of the troubadours.

All too often, Madeline acknowledged sardonically, courtly ideals and reality clashed, sometimes with brutal results. More than one lady discovered in the arms of her chivalrous love had been beaten or even killed by her lord. Only last year, one enraged husband had served his wife her lover's heart on a golden plate, forcing the horrified woman to partake of it before he threw her from a tower window. The queen's courtiers still argued the lovers' rights in that sad affair, much good it did the unfortunate pair! The bald fact was that church and canon law gave a husband absolute mastery over his wife, whatever the troubadours might sing.

Which was why Madeline intended to use all her influence with John to ensure that she had a say in the choice of her next husband. Whichever lord she chose, he would *not,* she decided, bear the remotest resemblance in face, figure or temperament to Ian de Burgh.

She snuggled deeper in the furs, pitying the poor woman given to the man as wife. She knew he was a widower of some years' standing. Although she didn't believe the earl quite so barbaric as to cut out a rival's heart, he would no doubt make a most exacting husband. That lazy smile hid a ruthlessness Madeline had herself tasted of just yesterday. She slid a hand from under the coverings to touch her lips, still swollen and tender from his kiss. How dare he use her so, as though she were some kitchen wench, his for the taking! She hoped with all her being that Lord Ian's lip throbbed far more painfully than did hers this morn.

"The devil take the man!" Madeline muttered, shoving aside her furs.

The rushes covering the stone floor rustled as the slumbering form on the pallet beside hers stirred. "Be ye awake, mistress?" a sleepy voice asked. "So early?"

"Aye, Gerda. Come, get you up and help me dress. I would attend early mass this morn, that I might break my fast before I ride out to watch the tourney."

The maid rolled over on one broad hip, yawning prodigiously and scratching her hair under the nightcap she wore as protection against the chill night air. At her movement, the other maids began to stir, as well. Soon the chamber was filled with the rustle of straw pallets being rolled up and the clatter of wooden shutters thrown open to allow in the faint glow of dawn. One by one the other ladies burrowed out from the curtained nest and began their morning toilets.

"Will ye wear your red?" Gerda asked, rummaging through the tall parquet-fronted chest that held the ladies' robes.

"Aye, and be careful with that veil!"

Madeline's warning came too late. The gossamer silk head covering Gerda reached for snagged on a wooden peg and tore. The maid's brown eyes flooded with remorse as she held up the ruined strip of crimson silk.

Shaking her head, Madeline poked two fingers through the ice encrusting the washbowl, then bent to splash her face with the frigid water. 'Twould do no good to remonstrate with the maid. She had the clumsiest hands in all of England. A sturdy lass whose mother had attended Madeline as a child bride, Gerda had neither her dam's light touch with delicate linens nor her skill with the needle. In truth, she was more apt to step upon the hem of her mistress's robe and rend it than not. But, though she tried Madeline's patience, she was fiercely loyal and devoted to her mistress. In Madeline's mind, such loyalty more than compensated for the girl's heavy hands. Still, there were times . . .

"Here, let me."

Shivering in her thin wool shift, Madeline took the scarlet bliaut from the maid's fumbling fingers. She pulled the robe over her head and thrust her arms through its wide fur-trimmed sleeves, then twisted sideways to reach the laces. A rich Burgundian red wool edged with sable, the bliaut fitted tightly over her bust and waist, then flared in thick folds over her hips.

Sitting on a low stool, Madeline pulled on brightly embroidered stockings and broad-toed boots. She winced as Gerda fumbled a comb through the heavy mass of her hair, then rebraided it with rough, if competent, hands. Bending to retrieve the wooden pins the maid had dropped for the second time, Madeline herself stabbed at her scalp to anchor the braids to either side of her head. At this rate, she'd miss not only early mass, but the escort to the tourney field, as well.

At the thought of being confined to the castle all day, Madeline threw her fur-lined mantle over her shoulders and hurried out of the tower room. Lifting her skirts to avoid the occasional droppings deposited by the hounds during the night, she sped through the drafty halls. In the distance she heard the faint echo of the priest's voice lifted in holy song. Breathless, she rounded the corner that led to the chapel—and careered headlong into a solid, wool-clad chest.

The man she collided with wrapped an instinctive arm around her waist. Madeline found herself held firmly against a hard, muscled plane. A chuckle rumbled in his broad chest under her ear.

"'Ware, sweetings. Such impetuous haste is ever the downfall of man and maid."

Biting back a groan, Madeline fought the urge to bury her face in the smoky wool. She had no difficulty recognizing the rolling north-country burr of the man who held her, or the huge feet of the one who stood beside him. Drawing in a deep breath, she drew back slowly and raised her eyes to Ian de Burgh's.

The laughter faded from his eyes when he saw who it was he held. His arm dropped to his side, freeing her.

Madeline stepped back. "Your pardon, my lord." She forced the words out through stiff lips.

"Lady Madeline!" William's exclamation drew her attention. "I hope you took no hurt."

She managed a small laugh. "Nay, none, except to my dignity."

Will stepped forward and made as if to take her arm.

"Truly," Madeline snapped with something less than her usual mellifluous charm, wanting only to be away from both of them, "I'm fine. 'Tis your brother who took the brunt of my charge. Look instead to him."

Undaunted by her sharpness, Will gave a good-natured laugh. "In truth, he does need someone to protect him from the women of this castle. Yestereve he was marked by a jealous wench, and today he's all but brought to his knees by a lady half his size."

At the lighthearted words, Madeline's gaze flew to the discolored swelling on the earl's lower lip. Her own mouth curled in a faint sneer. "A jealous wench?"

Will's grin widened. "Well, that's how I describe her. My brother's description is not fit for the ears of a lady."

One sable brow arched. "Oh, is it not?"

"'Tis not fit for polite company, at any rate," Ian drawled.

Madeline bit back a gasp at the implied insult behind his words. 'Twas plain to her from his careless tone that he chose not to number her among the "polite." At that moment, with the icy drafts swirling about the hem of her skirts and the distant chanting from the chancel sounding faint in her ears, Madeline swore she would bring this man low. She didn't know how, nor when, but she would see him humbled if 'twas the last thing she did on this earth.

One sure way, she fumed, would be to tell Will just how his esteemed brother had earned that bruise on his lips. She could imagine the young knight's reaction to the knowledge that his hero had molested the lady he himself revered. She debated within herself, torn between the desire to hurt the earl and a reluctance to do the same to Will.

De Burgh must have read her intentions in the angry glitter that sparked her eyes. His own narrowed, and he took a half step toward her. His brother's voice forestalled whatever it was he would have said to her.

"My lady..."

With a start, Madeline saw that Will had stepped to her side. She glanced up and saw shy devotion writ plain on his handsome face. Sighing, she realized that she could not willfully cause the boy pain to satisfy her own need to prick the earl.

"If it please you, I would beg a favor to wear in the tourney."

When she saw the sudden scowl on the earl's face, Madeline knew she had the instrument of her revenge at hand. She had no intention of letting Will's infat-

uation ripen into something deeper, but de Burgh
didn't believe that. So be it! If he wished to worry and
stew, she'd give him something to worry about. She
was a master at this game he'd accused her of playing. She'd learned it from Queen Eleanor herself, a
woman who'd enthralled two kings. Madeline would
see that Will took no real hurt of her, but, by the Virgin, she'd make his brother squirm in the process.

Slipping easily into a role that was second nature to
her, she gave a tremulous sigh of regret. "Alas, Sir
William, I can't bestow that which is already given.
Another knight has claimed a token of me."

"Then I'll wrest it from him by force of arms," Will
bragged with the utter confidence of youth. "Only tell
me who carries it, and I'll see that we ride on oppos-
ing sides."

"La, sir, you know I cannot reveal my champion's
name."

The merry little laugh, the sidelong glance from beneath lowered lashes, the slight pout—all were instinctive to a woman schooled in such sophisticated
badinage. Madeline performed them with a skill that
brought a flush of desire to Will's open face and a
flash of disgust to the earl's eyes. Telling herself that
she was well pleased with both reactions, Madeline
ignored the man and smiled prettily at the youth.

"Come, sir, let me pass, else you will miss the call
to arms."

"My lady—"

"Enough, halfling." De Burgh's voice held no hint
of the anger Madeline saw in the cold blue of his eyes.

"Do you not see the lady has made her choice, and 'tis not you."

"Not this day," Will conceded cheerfully. He reached for Madeline's hand. "But mayhap another."

When he lifted her fingers to his lips, Madeline couldn't help but be touched by the reverent salute. Her gaze softened as it rested on the golden head bent over her hand. Any tender feelings stirring in her breast died aborning, however, when she looked up and met the earl's icy glare. Throwing him one last, mocking glance, she tugged her hand free.

"Aye, mayhap another, day," she told Will sweetly. Lifting her skirts, she glided by the two men.

With every ounce of willpower he possessed, Ian fought the urge to reach out and grasp the woman as she swept past. He wanted to shake her, as much for keeping Will dangling on her silken strings as for the taunting look she'd given him. Her mocking glance told him more clearly than words that she had thrown down the gauntlet. The battle between them was now a full-scale, if undeclared, war. One she would not win, Ian vowed, watching the sway of her hips as she walked away.

Will's bemused voice cut into his preoccupation.

"Do you think 'tis the king's son who claims her token?"

Ian drew in a quick breath and faced his brother. He'd never coddled Will, nor spoken less than the truth to him. "If half the rumors whispered about him and the Lady Madeline are true, he claims more than a token."

"Nay, he does not."

The flat assertion brought Ian's head around slowly. "You have some knowledge of the matter that others lack?"

Will shrugged. "I know you think me besotted, Ian, and well I may be. But I'm not a fool. I...I've watched my lady from afar these many weeks, and seen her in every mood. Laughing. Playful. Sometimes scolding, often mischievous. But never, never, have I seen wanton."

Ian clenched his jaw as he conjured up an image of Lady Madeline bent over his arm in a winter-swept garden, her small bosom heaving and her huge eyes alight with emerald flames.

"She...she has a flirtatious nature," Will admitted hesitantly, then flushed, as if it ill became a knight to acknowledge his lady's faults, "but not a licentious one."

At the simple declaration, Ian felt his temper push hard against its careful bounds. "Will, listen to me. This lady is not for you. Whether she beds with them or not, she plays with princes."

A troubled frown creased Will's forehead. "I know. And I fear for her, Ian. Although I don't believe the rumors about my lady, there are those who do. Lady Isabel de Clare, for one. She looked ready to claw Lady Madeline's eyes the last time she was at court."

Ian drew in a slow breath. The jealousy of John's betrothed was no light matter. A great heiress, Isabel was known for her temper, and was not above arranging a rival's death. It wouldn't be the first time a mistress was so disposed of. Queen Eleanor herself was rumored to have poisoned her husband's leman, Rosamund the Fair, and thus earned the unceasing enmity of the king who had once loved her.

To his disgust, Ian felt a new worry curl deep in his belly. His concern was Will, he told himself, only Will. But the thought of Madeline's gleaming eyes dulled with pain and her red, ripe lips blue with the cold of death made his hands close into tight fists. Damn the woman, he thought, even as his agile mind worked at the knots that now seemed to ensnare them all.

Will's unaccustomed solemnity vanished. He grinned at his frowning brother with all the bravado of a newly knighted youth. "The only recourse is for me to challenge the prince in the tourney today. I'll dump him on his arse and claim my lady's favor, as well as a fat ransom from the king for his precious son!"

"And you think yourself not a fool," Ian replied dryly.

Will laughed and clamped an arm around his brother's shoulders. "Come, we'd best find our squires and arm, lest we miss the tourney altogether. If the bishops have their way, we may not have many more to ride to."

As he strolled through the vaulted corridors with Will, Ian almost wished that the bishops had indeed prevailed in their futile attempt to gain the king's sanction against the tourneys held in conjunction with feast days. The church, it seemed, objected to the carnage that often resulted, claiming it profaned the holiness of the occasion.

Having participated in many tourneys, Ian knew well that death was not an infrequent occurrence in the great, brawling free-for-alls, in which squadrons of mounted knights charged across a broad plain at opponents coming from the opposite direction. Although the object was to take prizes for ransom and not to kill or maim, combatants fought with the same sharpened lances and swords they used in battle. More than one knight, stunned from repeated blows to the helm, fell from his saddle and was trampled to death. Others died from wounds inadvertently given in the heat of battle. The king's fourth son, Duke Geoffrey, traitor that he was, had died just last year during a tournament given in his honor by King Philip of France.

His mouth grim, Ian swore a silent vow that the king's youngest and favorite son would not meet a similar fate at Will's hands this day. Nor would he allow his brother to earn the prince's rancor by battling with him to win Lady Madeline's favor.

Ian had time yet for a word with the marshal who arranged the order of the tourney. He'd make sure Will rode with, and not against, the prince. And then, he swore savagely, he'd put an end to the Lady Madeline's game once and for all.

Cursing the female who had brought them all to this dangerous pass, Ian strode into his chamber and bellowed for his squire.

* * *

"Look, Lady Madeline, is that not the cub who would claim your favor? The one with the *bordure d'or* around his chequy shield? There, leading the charge?"

Madeline's breath frosted in the cold March air as she brushed her veil out of her eyes and followed the direction of Lady Nichola's outstretched arm. Muted thunder from a hundred or more pounding hooves rolled up from the valley below. Squinting at the galloping, unformed mass of men that charged across the flat valley floor, Madeline tried to find the checkered blue-and-white shield bordered in gold that Lady Nichola alluded to.

"Nay, I cannot tell. They're too far afield."

"I wish we could descend this hill and go closer to the fray," one of the other women complained. "I can see naught from here."

"'Tis not safe," the squire charged with escorting them repeated. "The battle rages where it will."

Lady Nichola straightened in her saddle. "Look, Madeline! There he is! Isn't that your young swain, riding against the prince?"

Madeline put up a hand to shield her eyes and peered through the morning haze.

"Sweet Jesu, there's a man," her companion murmured breathlessly. Then she gasped. "But 'tis not your cub after all. 'Tis his brother. See, there's the golden hawk of St. Briac quartered in the corner of the shield."

'Twas indeed Ian de Burgh, earl of Margill, baron St. Briac, who led the charge, Madeline saw at last. As she watched, biting her lower lip, he bore down on an armored knight mounted on a magnificent black destrier that bore the prince's trappings. Above the thunder of hooves striking hard earth, the sound of steel ringing against steel rose in cold air.

"Take him," Madeline whispered fiercely, wanting John to triumph as much as she wanted the earl to take a blow. "Knock him senseless."

"Oh, he did!" her companion trilled in delight. "He did."

To her profound disappointment, Madeline saw that the wrong man had carried the day. 'Twas John who wavered in his saddle, clearly dazed from a blow that had slipped under his guard and dented his golden helm. Fear knotted suddenly in her chest as she watched him tip slowly sideways.

Holy Mary, Mother of God, don't let him fall, she prayed desperately, her hands pressed to her mouth. With a sob of thanksgiving, she saw de Burgh spur his mount next to the black and catch the stunned man before he could slip out of the saddle. When John regained his seat, de Burgh leaned forward to catch the black's reins, then threaded through the surging mass to the woven wicker pen where squires waited with fresh arms and saw to the needs of captured knights.

The lists, as the safe haven was termed, lay directly below the hill where the women watched. In some disgust, Madeline saw de Burgh remove his great bucket-shaped helm and run a hand through sweat-flattened, sun-streaked hair. The prince did the same. Even from her high perch, Madeline could see John's rueful laugh as his gloved fingers measured the dent in the gilded metal. The two warriors, only moments before fierce enemies, now stood side by side in companionable accord.

The battle was done soon after that. A few knights fought on, their frenzied fight carrying them far across the broad valley and through a small village that lay in their path. Frightened serfs peered out of mud-and-wattle huts as the war-horses churned their fresh-turned plots into a muddy morass. But one by one the victors claimed their prizes, and the clash of sword on shield slowly died away. The weary knights retired, captives in tow, to the lists.

The sound of horns cut through the cold air as the king himself rode out to acknowledge the victors of this engagement. Although now well past his fiftieth summer, King Henry was still a formidable figure in the saddle. He sat tall and straight, the golden lion emblazoned on his tunic catching the sun's gleam. Pausing before his son, he said something to John, who shrugged. The king rested his forearms across the cantle and leaned down to hold discourse with Lord Ian.

They were settling the terms of the ransom, Madeline knew. De Burgh would claim John's destrier, of course. The costly war-horse, worth more than a small manse, always went to the victor. Most like, Ian would also come away richer by a fortified castle or two—as if a person of his wealth needed them, Madeline sniffed. Of a sudden, her enthusiasm for the tourney faded.

"'Tis colder than a sow's belly out here," she said to Lady Nichola. "What say you we return to the castle?"

The other woman laughed and tossed her veil over her shoulder with a coquette's practiced ease. "As you will. I'll admit my toes are like to fall off, they're so frozen. I just hope I get the use of them back before the banquet and dancing tonight."

As they galloped across the winter-browned earth, their escort at their heels, Madeline decided to use the hours this afternoon to prepare for the great feast that would celebrate the tourney. Will would follow at her heels most of the night, if she let him, which would displease his brother mightily. If she had to deflect de Burgh's cold glances all night long, she needed the armor of her best looks. Ignoring a twinge of guilt at using the boy as a pawn in what had become a silent war between her and his brother, Madeline plotted her strategy with all the skill of a great marshal.

The first step in her campaign, she decided, was a bath. She knew the servants would be heating great caldrons of water for the returning knights. A few copper pennies delivered by Gerda would divert one of the wooden tubs, and sufficient buckets of hot water to fill it, to the ladies' bower.

She had barely stepped into the steaming water, dotted with scattered rose petals, when a knock sounded on the door to the tower room. Madeline sank down in the wooden tub until the scented water covered her shoulders. Then Gerda lifted the latch.

"Aye?"

A gangly page in parti-color hose and a loose knee-length tunic stood on the threshold. His eyes rounded at the sight of Madeline in the tub.

"Don't ye be gawking at my mistress, lad," Gerda admonished. "What do ye want?"

"I have a message for the Lady Madeline de Courcey from Ian, Lord de Burgh."

Water sloshed over the sides of the tub as Madeline plucked a linen towel from the stool beside the tub to cover her breasts and swiveled to stare at the page. What? Was the battle between her and the earl to be joined so soon? "Well, what is it?"

"Your pardon, lady, but Lord Ian requests your presence immediately."

Madeline felt her jaw sag at the imperious summons.

"He awaits you in the solar just behind the great hall. I'm to lead you to him."

She waved a wet, disdainful hand. "Inform the earl that I'm otherwise engaged. He may seek me out after the banquet this eve if he desires discourse with me."

"But, my lady..."

"Shut the door, Gerda. The draft chills the water."

A satisfied grin curved Madeline's lips as she slid back down, letting the warm water wash over her shoulders once more. She rested her head against the rim of the tub and wished she could see de Burgh's face when he received her response.

She regretted that wish mightily not ten minutes later. She was on her knees, head bowed for Gerda to rinse the soap from her hair, when the wooden door to the tower room crashed open.

Gerda shrieked and jumped back. The jug she'd been using to sluice water over her mistress slipped from her hands and shattered on the floor.

Madeline sloshed around in the tub, pushing through the curtain of hair that cascaded over her face. Soap stung her eyes and blurred the figure who stepped into the chamber.

"My lord, ye cannot come in here!" Gerda's dismayed warble had Madeline scrabbling for a linen towel.

"Get you gone. I have business with your mistress."

"Are you mad?" Madeline swiped the soap from her eyes, then clutched the linen frantically over her breasts. "Get out of here!"

De Burgh ignored her, addressing the maid. "You may wait outside and attend your lady when I have said what I will to her."

Gerda sent Madeline a helpless look.

"Go," she ordered. "Go and summon the king's guard."

When the maid scuttled from the chamber, de Burgh turned to face Madeline. His blue eyes surveyed her coldly, from the soap-filled mass of hair that tumbled over her shoulders to the swell of her breasts under the wet linen.

He must have come straight from the tourney, she thought furiously. He'd removed his great helm and the greaves that protected his shins, but under his mud-spattered tunic he still wore the heavy mail shirt and padded gambeson. The added weight made him look huge and formidable and altogether too fearsome.

Madeline ground her teeth at being caught on her knees before this man, but she could not rise without baring more than the towel could cover. Still, she refused to cringe before him.

"In the future, lady, you will attend me when I summon you."

Her chin lifted. "In the future, sir, you are not likely to issue any summons. You will be dead when the king hears of this!"

His lips curled in a slow, predatory smile that sent chills down Madeline's bare back. "I think not."

"If not dead, then blind," she spit out. "I'll see your eyes put out with hot pokers! How dare you intrude upon my privacy!"

He strolled forward, his spurs scraping the rushes. Madeline fought the urge to shrink back against the far rim of the tub. Shivers raced down her spine, caused in equal part by the cold air wafting on her back and the fury that sizzled in her veins. Angrily she flung her hair over her shoulder and glared at him.

He seemed to find her defiance amusing. "A woman who defies her lord is not entitled to privacy.

If he so wished, he could strip her before all and inflict what punishment he would upon her."

"You took one too many sword blows to your helm this day, sir. You are not my lord, nor have you any say in what punishments I may or may not incur. I am in the king's keeping."

"No longer, lady."

The flat assertion made her clutch her towel in suddenly tight fingers. "Wh—what? What say you?"

"You are mine now, as are your lands and revenues. To hold and to use as I will, until I decide where to settle you."

Her voice sank to a disbelieving croak. "Yours?"

"Aye. I won you in the tourney." A sardonic gleam flared in the blue eyes hovering over her. "You, my lady Madeline, are the Lord John's ransom."

Chapter Four

Ian felt a grim satisfaction as the lady's eyes widened to huge, mossy pools and she sank back into the now-scummy water. With her face scrubbed clean of all paint and her body stripped of rich silks and furs, she looked younger than she usually did—and far more vulnerable. Deciding from her dazed expression that she was sufficiently cowed, Ian straightened.

"You have an hour to dress yourself and see that your belongings are packed."

"Packed?" She swallowed painfully. "Wherefore packed?"

"Now that you are in my keeping, I will see you properly housed. You leave today for the north."

"The north? Today?"

He strode toward the door. "You have an hour. Bring with you only what you need for the journey. The rest may follow with the baggage train."

"Wait!"

The stupor that seemed to have locked her limbs

loosened. She knelt upright in the tub and glared at
him.

"Wait. You cannot be so thick-skulled as to think I
can leave Kenilworth within the hour. There's too
much that needs doing. And I'm expected at the banquet this eve," she finished on a shrill note.

And Ian had thought her cowed! He turned and
advanced on her once again. She blinked, but refused
to shrink back as she had before.

"'Twould appear you've held a favored position in
the king's wardship for far too long," Ian said softly.
"You've become lax in the respect due those above
you."

"But—"

"You will call me 'lord' when you address me."

Her jaw clamped shut.

"And you will be ready within the hour." His voice
lowered dangerously. "Do not make me lesson you,
Lady Madeline. You would not enjoy it."

Nay, she would not, Madeline thought in simmering fury, but no doubt he would, the cur. The varl. The
whoreson knave. Her whole body shook with the need
to launch herself at him and scratch and claw. She
wanted nothing so much as to add more bruises to that
marking his lower lip. She, who had always won her
way with smiles and merry laughter! She, who had
enchanted one husband with her wit and enthralled
another with her body! Never in Madeline's life had
any man spoken to her thus, nor raised such violence
in her soul.

Shaken by the force of her unaccustomed blood
lust, she curled her hands into fists under the surface
of the water. As angry as she was, she had yet the sense
to know that she could not win in any physical en-
counter with this broad-shouldered, muscled man.

Taking her smoldering silence for acquiescence, the
earl nodded once, then turned and left. The wooden
door slammed behind him. It opened again almost
immediately, catching Madeline half out of the tub.
With a gasp, she sank back into the chilled water.

"Ooh, milady," Gerda cried, "I couldna bring the
guard! His lordship's men blocked the corridor!"

"It matters not. Just help me with my hair. Quickly.
Quickly!"

Bending over the tub so that Gerda could rinse the
last of the soap from her heavy fall of hair, Madeline
twisted it into a tight rope to wring it free of excess
water, then tugged on the shift she'd discarded just a
short time ago. She pushed aside the stained red robe
she'd worn to the tourney to find her jeweled girdle.
Her fingers fumbled with the flap of the embroidered
pouch attached to it.

"God's teeth," she hissed, as clumsy in her haste as
Gerda ever was. Finally she wrenched the pouch open
and extracted a handful of copper pennies. She
pressed them into the maid's palm, folding her plump
fingers tight over them.

"Get you downstairs immediately and find out
where Lord John is. Give these coins to a page and ask
him to tell the king's son that I desire urgent speech
with him. If it please his grace, I would meet with

him . . ." She searched her mind frantically for a place where she might have private speech with John. "I would meet with him in the chapel. Go! Go quickly!"

Without Gerda's help, Madeline lost precious minutes fumbling into her robe and pulling the silken laces tight. Not wanting to take the time necessary to braid her hair, she grabbed a thin wool mantle and flung it over her wet, tangled mane. She stuffed her bare feet into her boots, then raced out of the tower room. Unconcerned for her dignity, she sped through the corridors, following the same route she'd taken just that morning on her way to mass.

Sweet Mary, was it just this morning that she'd traveled these same corridors? Just a few short hours since she'd stumbled into the earl's arms and then taunted him with her mocking smile? It seemed days, nay, years, ago. She could not believe that she'd been so secure in herself this morn, so secure in her position at court. Now de Burgh had turned her world upside down. Picking up her skirts, she ignored the surprised stares of a pair of pages and ran the last few yards to the chapel.

Panting, she gazed around the small, dim hall. The vaulted nave where the lesser ranks stood during mass was bathed in silent shadows. Her eyes searched the wooden upper gallery that circled the chapel like a monk's tonsure, but found no occupant. Madeline drew in a shuddering breath, scarcely noticing the heavy scent of myrrh that lingered in the air, and leaned back against one of the stone pillars. Please, John, she prayed, please come.

He did, as he always had come for her.

When the door swung open, Madeline started, then held out both hands. He took them in his strong grasp.

"You've heard, then?" he asked, his dark eyes taking in her disheveled appearance and distraught manner. "I'd hoped to tell you myself."

"Lord Ian came straight from the lists to inform me," she replied bitterly. "How—how could this happen?"

John's mouth hardened. "I swear, Madeline, I had no idea that he would demand such a ransom, nor that my father would grant it."

"Why did the king do so? You told me that you had spoken to him and that he'd agreed to give me say in arranging my future."

"And thus I reminded him! But de Burgh pointed out that the lands your first lord dowered on you march with those he holds in his youngest brother's name. Were he to garrison your castles, as well as those of his brother, he could guarantee a strong line of defense against attack by Welsh raiders."

"I see. I'm to be handed over once again for another man's gain!" Madeline tugged her hands free, knowing it was useless to rail against her fate, but too angry and hurt to still her words. "So much for Angevin promises!"

A flush of hot anger stained John's cheeks. "You forget yourself, Lady Madeline."

She realized immediately she'd gone too far. By the saints, this was indeed her day for letting her tongue slip its hold. For all their friendship, Madeline never let herself forget that John was as much an Angevin as any of his clan. She had often seen him fly into one of his rages, as awesome as his father's, although she had learned long ago not to let it intimidate her.

"Your pardon, my lord," she said stiffly.

"Granted." John let out his breath on a gust of air. "In truth, I wish I could aid you, but the king is adamant and de Burgh too powerful. There's naught I can do. Not now, at least. Mayhap soon, though. Mayhap soon things will change."

For the space of a heartbeat, hope flared in Madeline's breast, followed quickly by a new, dangerous worry. Her voice lowered to a whisper. "Oh, John, you don't listen to Richard and those who plot with him against the king, do you? You mustn't. These barons would play you brothers against each other, and you both against your father, all for their own gain."

He hesitated, as if debating whether to speak further. For a moment, the only sound that disturbed the chapel's stillness was the unsynchronized rhythm of their breathing, hers quick and shallow, his heavy and slow.

Madeline saw the doubt in his eyes. With a perception honed by years of closeness, she sensed that John hovered on the brink of some momentous decision. Fear for him clutched at her heart. He courted disaster. She felt it in her very bones.

"Of all his sons, the king loves you best," she told him quietly. "Were you to turn against him, his rage would be ungovernable."

Despite her anger with the king at this moment, Madeline knew that John had not the strength to defy him, not without losing his soul to the greedy barons who would use him.

He stared down at her, his dark eyes unfathomable, then shifted his shoulders, as if pulling at a garment that was too tight for him. "Come, do you think because I could not turn the king's decision to give you into de Burgh's keeping that I plot some mischief?"

"My lord..."

He waved aside her concern. "You were ever one to let your imagination run away with you, Maddy."

She bit her lip, knowing it was useless to press him when his eyes took on that hard, black glitter.

"Look you, 'tis not so bad," he said, with an attempt at reason. "You're not being forced to marry the man. He but holds you in keeping."

"Aye," she acknowledged with a sigh. "Would that it were any man other than this one."

"I don't know him well, but he has a reputation for being fair and evenhanded with those in his care."

"Oh, so? He threatened to beat me but a few moments ago."

John's black brows flew up in astonishment. "Lord Ian?"

"Aye, Lord Ian."

"What start is this? You can twist any male old enough to wear braies around your finger with your lightsome laugh and slanting, sloe-eyed looks. I've seen you do it often enough."

"'Twould appear the earl cares not for my laugh, nor for my looks!''

John appeared thoroughly taken aback for a moment. Then he curled one knuckle under Madeline's chin to lift her face to his.

"If he does not, I do."

Madeline felt her breath catch at the dark, lambent flame that flared in his eyes. Not for the first time, she wondered why she didn't give in to the invitation John issued each time he touched her of late. She was no stranger to desire, for all that she'd tasted it briefly enough in her short marriages. She'd seen it more and more in the looks the prince gave her since she'd returned to the king's ward this time. From the way his finger now moved softly on the skin of her underjaw, Madeline knew she had just to smile, to give the barest nod, and he'd take her to his bed. As the court believed he already had.

The thought flitted into her mind that if she lay with John, mayhap he would try again to convince the king to give de Burgh gold or some other rich widow as ransom. As quickly as the thought came, she dismissed it. She had little enough control over her life, but she had her own sense of honor. Were she to whore with John—whatever the troubadours chose to call it—she would lose that small part of herself she held dearest.

In that tiny corner of her soul, the one she kept private, Madeline knew she wanted more than what John offered. Much as she loved this friend of her heart, she felt no passion for him. No shivers raced down her spine at his glance. Her blood didn't leap in her veins when he pressed his lips to hers in greeting. She experienced none of the wild tumult at John's touch that she had in de Burgh's rough embrace. Feeling as though she were about to take the first step down some unknown path, Madeline slipped her chin free of John's caressing hold.

"What," she teased, "such sweet words from the one who put a beetle down my back that time your lady mother came to inspect the maidens' progress with the bow?"

Accepting the gentle rebuff, John let his hand fall and stepped back. "You know you have but to call me, Madeline, and I will come to you."

"Aye, my lord," she said softly. "I know."

He gave her a twisted grin. "Just smile that way at de Burgh, and you'll soon have him dancing to your tune."

"But for now," she admitted, resignation threading her voice, "I must dance to his."

"If I know you, 'twill be a merry dance."

"Well, a lively one, at any rate."

Madeline hesitated, reluctant to say farewell, yet knowing she must. A wrenching sense of loss filled her. Somehow this leaving seemed more final than when she had left the king's ward—and John—before.

"I must go, my lord," she said finally, forcing a smile. "The accursed man gave me but an hour to ready myself. I leave this very afternoon."

"Get you gone, then. And God be with you, Maddy."

"And with you, my lord."

Madeline swept him a deep curtsy, elegant despite the wet hair that tumbled over her shoulders and the bare ankles that showed over her boot top.

John bowed, then opened the chapel door for her. He stood unmoving for long moments, watching her slight figure disappear around a bend in the high-ceiling corridor. The hand resting on his jeweled belt tightened until the stones cut into his palm.

The journey did not begin auspiciously.

By dint of frenzied effort, Madeline was almost ready when a page knocked on the door and announced that the earl awaited her in the bailey. With a last, resigned glance at the garments still spilling haphazardly out of the wardrobe, Madeline directed her second serving woman to bring them later and slammed the lid of a small trunk.

De Burgh had said to take with her only what she needed for the journey. It would've helped considerably in her packing if she'd known just how long a journey she faced, and to where. As it was, she'd stuffed clean linens, two extra robes, her jewel casket and a small case with her pots of cosmetics, her combs and the silvered mirror her first husband had given her into the leather trunk.

Signaling to the page to shoulder the trunk, Madeline sat down to pull on an extra pair of stockings, then laced up her boots. She stood and smoothed the skirts of her warmest robe, a fine merino wool dyed a rich crimson and adorned with tabard sleeves that draped nearly to the floor. With her now neatly braided hair caught in cauls of woven silver yarn and covered by a silken veil held in place with a guirlande of beaten silver, she felt ready to face the earl. Gerda handed her a hooded cloak, silvery gray in color and lined with marten fur. Wherever their destination, Madeline decided, she would be warm enough for these cold days.

With the maid clumping behind her in thick-soled boots, her own bundle of possessions clutched to her breast, Madeline led the small procession through Kenilworth's halls and out into the bailey. She stopped abruptly on the steps that led down from its main entrance.

"What is that?"

The squire who'd stepped forward to guide her down the worn, treacherous steps, glanced around uncertainly.

"What, my lady?"

"That!"

Madeline jerked her chin toward the wheeled vehicle with two horses harnessed in tandem that waited below. Its rounded roof was ornately carved and hung with thick curtains.

The squire looked completely baffled by her question. "'Tis . . . 'tis a litter, my lady. My lord arranged it for your comfort on the journey."

Madeline shuddered at the thought of being enclosed within those smothering curtains. Lifting her skirts, she descended the rest of the steps. A tall figure detached itself from the group of men who waited beside the horses and strode toward her.

"Are you ready, my lady?" de Burgh said, courteously enough, as though he'd not mauled her in her bath but an hour since.

The knowledge that she was in this man's power ate like a worm inside her belly, but she would, perforce, have to go with him. The manner of her going, however, was yet to be decided.

"Aye," Madeline replied, lifting her skirts. "I'm ready. But I would..." She trailed off in surprise when he stood immovable before her.

"Aye, *my lord,*" he corrected softly.

Heat flooded her cheeks. For a long moment they faced each other, she and de Burgh, green eyes locked with blue. The stamping of the horses as they shifted on the hard cobbles and the murmuring of the men behind them went unheard. There was only this lean, unyielding man filling her vision, his breath brushing her cheeks.

One of the horses teamed in harness shivered in the cold and stepped back, causing the litter to shift and rattle on the cobbles. Madeline caught the movement from the corner of one eye.

She swallowed, and swung her gaze back to de Burgh. "Aye, my lord, I'm ready."

He had half turned away when her low voice stopped him.

"But I would ride my palfrey, if it pleases you."

He frowned and gestured toward the litter. "You will be more comfortable within."

Desperate, Madeline sought some means to sway him. She would not, she could not, climb into that box. Even if she traveled with the curtains drawn open as far as they would go, the tight confines would choke her. Nor could she admit the fear that had haunted her from childhood to this man and give him a weapon he might use against her.

Of a sudden, Madeline remembered John's assurance that she could make any man dance to her tune did she but try. She wet her lips and forced them to curve in what she hoped would pass for a smile.

"I'm well horsed, my lord. My mare was a gift from my first husband, and I...I would not leave her here."

He hesitated.

Hating herself, but driven by a fear that made sweat bead between her breasts, Madeline stepped forward and laid a mittened hand on his arm. Tilting her head, she slanted him a look that had brought courtiers stumbling over their feet to do her bidding.

"Come, sir, I will need my mare wherever it is I go."

"You go to Cragsmore, lady."

Well, at least she knew her destination, although it meant little to her. One of the baron de Courcey's lesser keeps, Cragsmore had come to her as part of her widow's dower and been managed by castellans appointed by the king during her wardship. It sat close on the Welsh border, she knew, and provided her with a steady, if somewhat meager, income in timber and wool from long-haired mountain sheep. Madeline had visited it only once, as a young bride, and had a vague memory of lichen-covered stone walls and drafty corridors. At this moment, however, he had more immediate concerns than the journey's end.

Swallowing the pride that lodged in her throat like a crust of dry bread, she pressed lightly against de Burgh's mail-clad arm. "If I ride, mayhap we can have discourse during the journey and ease this... disharmony between us."

He looked down at her hand, his brows lifting. When he met her eyes once more, Madeline could not quite interpret the look that crossed his face. Whatever he would have said to her was lost in the clatter of booted feet.

"My lady."

Madeline snatched her hand back. Will strode across the bailey, leading her bay mare. The silver bells on the palfrey's halter tinkled as it danced to a halt a few feet away.

Will's golden hair was spiked with dried sweat, and his cheeks yet held the grime of the tourney, but none of that detracted from the huge grin splitting his handsome face. "When Ian told me that the king had given you into his keeping, I could scarce believe it!"

"Nor could I," Madeline replied.

"I was even more surprised when he told me that you leave today for the north."

"Not half as surprised as I."

William blinked at her dry response, apparently recognizing that she was less than overjoyed at her change in circumstances. "I know 'tis a somewhat abrupt departure, but I—I'm glad you're in my brother's care. He'll hold you safe."

Madeline flashed him a startled look, but before she could ascertain why he thought she needed safekeeping, he smiled shyly.

"I leave for the north soon myself. Mayhap I will find reason to journey to Cragsmore."

Over his shoulder, Madeline saw the earl stiffen. The lad would not come to Cragsmore, she knew, not if de Burgh had anything to do with it.

"I had not time to find a suitable farewell gift," Will continued, "but I beg you accept the barding that I won in the tourney this morning."

He tugged the mare's reins, causing her to skip in a half circle on her dainty hooves. Madeline's eyes widened at the rich caparison that covered her mount from neck to haunches. Embellished with a wide border of gold and silver threads woven in a strange cursive pattern, the viridescent trapping gleamed in the winter sunlight. Madeline ran a hand over the smooth, shining fabric, marveling at its tight weave and shimmering thickness.

"'Tis from the East," Will told her. "The knight who ransomed it said he won it at the siege of Jerusalem. He swears he had it of Saladin himself."

"But you should keep such a treasure!"

A tide of red crept up his neck. "Nay, I want you to have it. 'Tis the color of your eyes, though not as deep or as verdant. And the sheen is naught to that which shimmers in your...in your..." He stumbled, searching for an appropriately shimmering portion of her anatomy.

Madeline bit her lip, then thanked him gravely for his gift. When he looked as though he would launch into paeans once more, the earl gave a snort of disgust and stepped forward.

"'Tis too cold for us to stand here while you mangle verses, clunch. Make your farewells and help the lady to mount."

Will grinned, and the earl turned away to mount his huge sorrel stallion.

Relief at having won a reprieve from the litter swept through Madeline, and she accepted the youth's farewells with something close to her customary charm.

Watching the play between them, Ian felt his jaw tighten. If the lady had not just turned her winsome smiles on him, he might have believed her show of sweetness to Will genuine. She was an accomplished jade, he'd grant her that. For a moment there, when she laid her soft hand on his arms and turned those liquid eyes up to him, he'd felt himself respond. Now he wanted nothing so much as to get this journey done.

He signaled impatiently to one of the men-at-arms to help the plump maid clamber into the litter. Mouth agape, she sat in solitary splendor amid the furs and pillows Ian had procured at no little expense. 'Twould not be long before Lady Madeline retreated to the litter's comfort and warmth, Ian wagered.

In that, at least, she would prove him wrong.

* * *

Kenilworth's red walls fell behind them, and they soon gained the old Roman road that cut, straight as a staff, across the winter-browned valleys and limestone ridges of the West Midlands. The small cavalcade of knight, lady, squire, now-grinning maid and platoon of pikemen merged with the flow of pilgrims, itinerant merchants and mendicant friars traveling the road.

Having ridden since she was old enough to demonstrate to the king's master of the stables both her endurance and her skill, Madeline let her body take the rhythm of her palfrey's gait while her mind churned.

Holy Virgin, how had she come to this coil? Not a few short hours ago she'd held a favored position at court, friend to the king's son and ward to the king himself. While she had known that her circumstance would change when Henry bestowed her in marriage once again, she'd been certain that she'd have some say in that disposition. Now she rode in the train of a man who made no secret of his low opinion of her.

As the miles passed, Madeline came slowly to terms with the anger and displeasure that roiled in her stomach over this disruption of her life and set her mind to working how best to address the animosity that had sprung up between her and the earl.

Address it she must, she acknowledged grimly. Her halfhearted attempt back there in the bailey to win him over had not met with notable success, but she could do better. She must do better. Much as she might despise him for it, de Burgh had gained almost absolute power over her. Although laws protected heiresses and widows from abuse by their guardians, the interpretation of these laws depended much on the guardian himself. Reminding herself once again of John's advice, she took another bite of her pride and brought her palfrey up beside the earl's stallion.

"Why have you chosen Cragsmore for me...my lord?"

De Burgh turned toward her, his tawny hair ruffling in the stiff breeze. Although he still wore his mail under a long, fur-lined surcoat, he hadn't fastened the hood. It lay back against his neck, the metal folds forming a heavy coif around the strong column of his neck. Above the coif, the lean planes of his face were washed with color from the bite of the wind. His eyes, a shade darker than the deep lapis of his brother's and far more piercing, lingered on her face. If he did not always scowl at her, Madeline thought sourly, he would be passing pleasant to look upon.

"Why Cragsmore?" he answered. "For the simple reason that 'tis as far away from the king's court as any property you own."

"From court, or from your brother?"

"From both, my lady."

"Yet Will says he soon comes north."

"He'll not come to Cragsmore," de Burgh stated flatly. "He'll be too busy with his own concerns."

Madeline nodded. "I thought as much."

He cocked one brow, as if surprised that she didn't rant or rail.

"You've worn your way in this," she replied with a small, stiff shrug. "What's done is done, my lord. I've not yet had time to adjust to the change in my situation, but I shall perforce try."

"You must do better than try, lady."

"The task would be easier were you to try, as well," she suggested tartly.

His brows snapped together, and Madeline heaved a sigh. "Look you, sir, I think I told you once before that I am neither timid maiden nor lacking in intelligence. I know well why you claimed me in ransom, although I will admit I liked not the manner of your claiming."

His scowl eased a bit. "'Twas not how I would have handled the matter, had you given me a choice," he admitted after a moment. "I don't usually accost the women in my care while they're at their bath."

"I'm much relieved to hear it."

Her dry response brought a reluctant smile. "Come, lady. As you say, what's done is done, and 'tis no use to fash it further. We've a long journey yet ahead before I see you settled comfortably. Shall we cry *pax?*"

Reassured by this offer of a cessation in the hostilities that had dogged them from their first meeting, Madeline nodded slowly.

Mayhap they would contrive, she and this man who held her life in his hands. Mayhap when she had a chance to know him, and he to know her, they could overcome the ill will that had grown between them from their first meeting. Having much to think about, she tugged on her reins and fell back to ride beside the squire.

Mayhap they would contrive, Ian thought, his keen eyes scanning the road ahead in a warrior's unconscious scrutiny while his mind ranged free. Mayhap, now that she was away from Will and from the prince who lusted after her with every glance of his dark eyes, she'd seen that her future lay not with either of them, much as they desired her in their different ways. Moreover, she would be safe at Cragsmore. Ian would see that she was kept close and had no visitors, at least until the rumors about her faded and the king's son turned his attention elsewhere. Then, Will's youthful passion will have given way to the pleasures and responsibilities of marriage. When the time was right and a suitable candidate presented himself, Ian would arrange a marriage for the lady, as well.

With some surprise, he realized that the thought of another man taking Madeline in marriage sat ill with him. His stomach tightened at the idea of another tasting her lips or stroking the small breasts and slender flanks, revealed in precise detail this morning by the sodden towel.

He shifted on the hard wooden saddle at the remembrance of her wet, bare flesh. What was it about this woman that distracted him, he wondered irritably? She had not the lush curves of the women he normally took pleasure with, nor the meek, submissive nature of the women of his household.

'Twas her hair, an inner voice mocked, hair that tumbled like water-slicked sable down her back. And her eyes, her jewel-toned eyes that glittered like the rarest gems when she shed the practiced airs of court and speared him with her glance.

Sweet Jesu, Ian muttered under his breath as heat shot through his loins. He was as bad as Will! He'd best stop thinking of the wench as anything but the responsibility she now represented. He has taken her into his care, and he was not a man to abuse those over whom he held power.

Or so he thought.

Chapter Five

Ian pushed open the door to the rough inn where they'd been forced to take refuge for the night and stood for a moment, letting his eyes grow accustomed to the gloom. Over the hack of winter coughs and murmur of conversation in the dim, crowded room, he heard a trill of merry laughter.

"Nay, sir, I believe it not!"

Slowly, disbelievingly, Ian turned toward the sound of Lady Madeline's voice.

She was seated beside a dark-haired, travel-stained knight. Even as Ian watched, the man's black mustache lifted in a roguish grin.

"Aye, my lady, I swear 'tis true." With one blunt finger, he stroked the fabric of her sleeve where it spilled across the table's width. "'Tis worms who spin the silk for garments such as these. I saw them and many other strange wonders when I was in Palestine."

"Did you take the cross, then?"

The mustache tilted. "Nay. I hired my sword to a rich baron who did."

Absorbed in their exchange, neither heard Ian approach the rough-hewn wood table where they sat. He stopped just behind them.

"Take your hand from her, or I'll skewer you where you sit."

Madeline gasped at the cold, flat order and twisted around on the bench. More deliberately, the knight beside her swiveled to rake Ian with a hard look.

"I but sought discourse with the lady."

"Do you speak then with your hands?" Ian drawled, menace unmistakable in his tone.

The knight's eyes, as gray and as hard as hammered damascene steel, narrowed. He bore the scars of combat on his weathered face, Ian noted dispassionately, and on the nicked mail shirt he wore. Ian knew his kind, even if he didn't know his name. A younger son, he guessed. A mercenary who hired himself out, hoping to win enough booty in battle or in the tourney to buy himself lands. Or win himself a wife who brought them with her.

And if he couldn't win such a wife, he wouldn't hesitate to steal one.

"Nay," the knight drawled, rising to answer Ian's question. "I speak not with my hands. Neither do I leave the women in my care alone and unattended. If you will be so careless with the lady, you should not be so jealous of her honor."

Challenge radiated from his words and from the way his booted feet spread wide on the dirt floor. One hand rested casually on his sword belt, not far from the hilt of the heavy broadsword that hung from a scarred, leather scabbard. The noise and bustle of the inn died away slowly as one after another of the travelers taking shelter from the foul weather outside turned to gape at the two knights.

"My lord." Lady Madeline's skirts rustled in the stillness as she rose. "We but exchanged news of the roads while you saw to your men."

Her voice was stiff, as though it went against her grain to explain herself or her actions to anyone. Ian set his jaw, knowing she spoke the truth but damning under his breath her foolhardiness in encouraging such a man. Could she not see the hungry gleam in his eyes when he looked on her rich raiment and silken veil?

Nay, likely she could not. Having spent most of her years in the king's ward, with only brief forays into marriage, she would not recognize the desperate desire for a prize such as she in a knight whose surcoat bore rough patches. One whose sword went to whatever side would pay the most.

Not for the first time, Ian cursed the series of mischances that brought them to seek shelter for the night at this roadhouse instead of within the thick stone walls of Ilchester Abbey. Not an hour after their departure, his squire's mount had set its hoof in a half-frozen rut, wrenching its fetlock. By the time the youth had transferred his gear to a spare horse and Ian had arranged with a nearby crofter to care for the animal until it was claimed, they'd lost a good hour of daylight.

Ilchester had still been a good five leagues distant when they found their way blocked by a bridge that had fallen in, its timbers a victim to rot and years of neglect by the baron whose responsibility it was to maintain that stretch of the king's highway. The stream the bridge had spanned was swollen with the melt of winter snows. They'd had to detour some miles to find a spot shallow enough for the pikemen to ford.

They'd been halfway across when one of the horses pulling the litter took violent exception to the bloated carcass of a boar that swept downstream and knocked against its hocks. Before Ian could control the curvetting, snorting horse, the maid, who'd poked her head out of the curtains to see what was amiss, had tumbled into the stream. By the time he'd hauled the thrashing woman out of the water, he'd been as soaked as she.

When he finally got his party across, icy wet had weighted down the padded gambeson Ian wore beneath his mail shirt. He'd dared not remove his armor in that open, unprotected spot. And so he'd waited, tight-jawed, for the maid to change her sodden skirts and his men to rub themselves and the horses dry.

Ian couldn't blame Madeline for these unexpected delays, but he could and did feel a tight knot of anger at the way he'd found her sitting next to this threadbare knight. He'd left her for a few moments, safely installed with her maid in a small, dark room hastily vacated by the innkeeper's family, and come back to find her rubbing elbows and laughing with a ragtag knight.

His anger tightened at her haughty look as she faced him now, not the least repentant for her incautious behavior.

"Get you to your room, lady. I will attend you there."

Her eyes flashed, and for a moment Ian wondered if she would be so foolish as to defy him. He met her look with a hard one of his own. "Get you to your room."

Gripping her skirts with fists that showed white knuckles, she turned and made her way through the gaping crowd. Ian waited until the wooden door closed behind her, then turned to face the still, watchful knight.

"Do not make the mistake of thinking that she's unprotected."

The gray eyes measured Ian. "Is she your lady wife?"

"She has my protection. That's all that need concern you."

The knight's gaze rested briefly on the golden hawk set against the field of blue and white on Ian's surcoat. "And is the protection of Lord de Burgh so infallible that another knight may not attempt the prize?"

"He may attempt it, and suffer the consequences."

"So he may." The bedraggled mustache lifted in a grin. "So he may."

Ian said nothing for long moments, eyeing the jagged scar on the man's left cheek. "Did you take a lance at Châteauroux?"

"Aye."

"Fighting for or against King Henry?"

"Against." The mustache lifted. "This time."

"Then mayhap I gave you that cut."

"Mayhap."

Despite himself, Ian felt a glimmer of amusement. For all his tattered appearance, the man made no apologies for his state and looked upon the world with a bold eye.

"I took a blow from a mace midway through the battle," Ian said slowly. "To this day, I know not how we turned Philip's routiers. What say you we share a flagon of ale, and you can tell me what I missed of the battle?"

The knight rubbed his whisker-darkened jaw. "The ale here tastes as though 'twere brewed in a pigsty, but 'tis wet and strong."

They sat across from each other on the pine planks that served as benches, their legs stretched out under the trestle table. Ian took a long swallow of the foaming brew the innkeeper's wife poured into cup horns, grimaced, then wiped the froth from his lips with the back of his hand.

"Do you have a name?" he asked. "One that the world knows you by?"

"I am called Guy Blackhair."

So the knight was a bastard, claiming neither house nor lord's surname. He'd likely won his spurs by the strength of his arm, raising the necessary costs of investiture in battle. Ian considered bastardy no shame to the son, although he had little respect for a father who would not claim his get.

Warily, like two great cats circling each other, the warriors settled back to take each other's measure. In the way of soldiers the world over, the two men, who had been before and might well again be enemies, soon achieved a sense of companionship in tales of battles won and lost.

By the time he knocked on the smoke-stained door and entered at the lady's curt call, Ian was feeling the effects of several brimming flagons and a full day in the saddle, first in the tourney and then on the road. He wanted nothing so much as to strip off his damp, cold mail and tumble to a straw pallet. Or, better, to lose himself in the silken limbs and flushed heat of the woman who now faced him, her chin tilted at an impossible angle and a slow green fire burning in her eyes.

He shook his head to clear it and glanced about the small, rude chamber. The maid, worn out no doubt by her long ride in the well-cushioned litter, snored softly in one corner. A thick pallet fashioned of clean straw overlaid with the Lady Madeline's furred mantle awaited in the other. Not for the lady, Ian noted, the flea-ridden bed the innkeeper and his family slept in.

"Do you have what you need for your comfort?"

"Aye," she replied stiffly.

Ian eyed her rigid shoulders for a long moment, then drew in a long breath. He was in no mood to cater to this woman's ill humors, but long years of seeing to his mother and his sisters forced him to make the effort.

"Look you, lady, I know I spoke harshly earlier, but 'tis not meet for you to discourse with strangers."

Even in the dim light cast by a low, flickering peat fire in the stone hearth, Ian could see the red that stained her cheeks.

"I see." Of necessity, she kept her voice low, so as not to wake the sleeping maid. "This morning you must needs school me in the proper mode of address. Now you tell me I'm too forward with strangers. It appears my training has been sadly lacking."

Ian stifled an impatient oath. "I meant only that 'tis not safe. You're a rich prize, one a knight such as that would snatch in a moment if he could. He now knows better than to dangle at your sleeve."

Her mouth dropped, then shut with a snap. "Do you think the only reason a man would dangle at my sleeve is because of my estates?"

He'd pricked her vanity, Ian realized belatedly. Christ's bones!

"Nay, of course not. You know you're winsome and most skilled at this game of smiles and sighs. I would you did not play it with a knight as hungry as this one, 'tis all."

If he thought his words would smooth her ruffled feathers, he soon saw his mistake. Her chin lifted another notch.

"You are a master of these side-handed compliments, sir. Come, let's have it clear between us. Am I not to speak or smile at another man while I'm in your keeping, lest you think I play with him?"

By the saints, she was as prickly as a hedgehog, Ian thought in exasperation. Where was the charm that Will had rhapsodized over? Where was the winning manner she used with all men, it seemed, except him? He raked a hand through his hair.

"'Twould do your reputation no harm to show a little more reserve in your manner," he replied testily.

"Ah, yes." Her breath eased out in a slow hiss. "This reputation you hold in such low esteem."

"Lady..."

"I am mistress to the king's son, or so you believe. I seek to entrap your precious brother and place on him a pair of cuckold's horns, or so you believe."

"Lady Madeline..."

At Ian's low growl, the maid roused and sputtered incoherently. Her limbs twitched for a moment, rustling the straw on her pallet. She mumbled something into the cloak that covered her, then subsided once again into sleep.

Madeline swung back to face him, taking up the cudgels once more.

"Now you accuse me of tempting this ragtag knight with my siren's ways." Her lips twisted in a parody of the smile she had given Guy Blackhair. "'Tis obvious you think me little better than a whore."

"'Tis your word, lady, not mine."

"We may as well be blunt with each other!" She flung the words at him, her ire well and truly raised now. "No wonder you assaulted me so roughly that day in the garden, if that's what you think of me."

"If it's blunt speaking you want, that was no assault. A rough kiss, mayhap, but don't pretend you did not—"

"You all but ravished me!"

"If I had meant to ravish you, your little love bite wouldn't have stopped me."

"Love bite!" she sputtered. "Love bite! You clod, do you dare to touch me again, you'll feel more than my bite."

Ian smiled dangerously. "A challenge, lady?"

"A promise, sir!"

Ian felt his weariness seep away, to be replaced by a sharp, coiling heat, low in his groin. His muscles seemed to harden of themselves. He wanted nothing so much as to sweep her into his arms and take up her reckless challenge. This time, he swore, she would not bite, nor fight in any way. This time—

He clamped his jaw, resisting the physical need that clawed at his belly. She must have seen something of the struggle in his eyes, because she took a small step backward.

"Nay, you need not fear me," Ian said heavily. "I'll not insult you thus again, not while you're in my keeping."

Madeline stared at him, ashamed of the disappointment his words wrought in the secret recesses of her soul. Her blood pumped with the suddenness of what she'd seen in his eyes. She was woman enough to recognize desire, and female enough to be piqued at the easy way he mastered it. She could not seem to control her own hammering senses so easily.

"It must be a great burden for you to have charge of a woman with such loose and lowly manners as you think mine," she taunted. "I'm surprised you don't just lock me in a chastity girdle and be done with it!"

His gaze dropped to the swell of her hips. "'Twould greatly simplify the matter," he murmured after a moment.

She gasped, truly horrified by this reaction to her heedless comment. "You would not!" she whispered. "You would not dare!"

She knew, of course, that men of the middle classes used such vile instruments to guard their spouses' virtue. Merchants whose business took them far from home and burghers jealous of their young wives often locked them in a metal framework, a handsbreadth wide, with only a small opening for their necessary, nonsexual functions. Madeline had even seen one once, gilded and set with precious stones, a goldsmith's harness for his errant wife. Madeline's first lord had procured it to satisfy her lively curiosity and she'd examined the contraption in some amusement. She felt no urge to laugh now, however. That Ian would even consider such a despicable device made her throat constrict with dismay.

"Nay, I would not gird you so," he replied at last, reaching out to tilt up her chin with one knuckle. "I'm not a cobbler or a clerk, that I need such devices to guard the women in my keeping.''

Despite his denial, Madeline was sure she detected a note of regret in his words. The knavish brute, she thought, more shaken than she would ever admit by the realization that this man could, if he so desired, subject her to the indignity of a girdle of Venus.

Of a sudden, the smothering closeness of the little room that had driven her out just a short hour ago now seemed far less suffocating than before. Like a rabbit seeking a safe burrow, Madeline took refuge in it.

'''Tis . . .'tis late, my lord.''

''Aye, 'tis late.''

He slid his knuckle down the line of her throat, lingering for the briefest moment at the base, as if to test the pulse that leapt under his touch.

Madeline wet her lips. ''My lord . . .''

His hand dropped to his side. ''God grant you good rest, lady.''

She turned away without another word. When she heard the door thud shut, her knees buckled, and she sank to the makeshift pallet.

Lifting her fingers to her throat, Madeline felt the heat that seared her skin. Sweet Mary, what was it about this man that raised such wild reactions in her? She wanted nothing so much as to see him brought low, to see his power over her broken. And yet her very flesh burned where he had touched it. How could she still shiver from the feel of his hand on her?

Mayhap...mayhap she was indeed the wanton he considered her, Madeline thought in some dismay. Mayhap she'd been too long without a husband, and, in her woman's need, responded to his touch like a dog coming into heat, a bitch that responded to any that would use her.

Nay, she was not so indiscriminate. She knew herself better than that. She was but feeling... disconcerted by de Burgh's overwhelming presence in her life. For all his arrogant ways, he was much a man.

And she was a woman grown, after all, with a woman's needs and urges. A woman who'd not been bedded except by her husbands, and not all that often by them. One had been too old, the other so eager he spilled his seed almost afore he even made it to their bed. His urgent, hurried mounting had brought her little pleasure. Madeline had sensed there was more to be found in a man's touch. Now, with the feel of the earl's hand still on her throat, she knew.

Groaning, she buried her face in the folds of her cloak. Sweet Mother, why had she not taken a lover when she returned to court? Why had she not reveled in the pleasure of a lover's touch! Most of the women around her did, the same ones who believed she was mistress to John.

Ah, John. Her own Jackanapes.

She'd not taken a lover because she couldn't bring herself to hurt John.

That was the bare truth of it, Madeline admitted, turning her face aside to stare into the dim glow of the banked fire. Although she laughed and sang and kept this knight and that hopeful, she couldn't hurt John. She'd seen the desire in his dark eyes, and while she could not return it, neither would she flaunt a lover in his face. Nor, to be brutally truthful, had any man taken her fancy.

Until Ian.

The thought sprang unbidden into her mind. Until the earl, no man had made her skin burn at his touch, nor made her thighs clench together at the jointure of her womanhood at the memory of his lips on hers.

Thoroughly disgusted by her own traitorous flesh, Madeline pulled her cloak up over her ears. He would never know, she swore! The man she so heartily despised would never realize that he held more power over her than he dreamed of. The sooner they came to Cragsmore and she was quit of his company, Madeline decided grimly, the better 'twould be.

Outside her door, Ian had much the same thoughts. He sat with his back propped against the entry to the women's room, his sword close to hand. His squire snorted gustily a few feet away, wrapped in his cloak. The youth's raucous breathing merged with the sounds of men settling gradually into sleep. Although he'd told his equerry that they'd take turns at watch, Ian knew he'd get little rest this night. Not with a hungry wolf of a knight sleeping lightly just across the room, dreaming, no doubt, of the rich prize so close at hand.

And not with the feel of Madeline's flesh still prickling the nerves in Ian's fingers. He rested his head against the rough planed wood. The memory of her flashing eyes haunted him, driving all thought of sleep from his mind.

Jesu, those eyes. A man could lose himself in them. Wide and fringed with thick sable lashes, they seemed to frame the lady's soul. Ian's lips relaxed into a small smile as he recalled how those same eyes had widened in dismay when she thought him serious about a chastity girdle.

Mayhap the burghers had the right of it, Ian thought wryly. Mayhap their overzealous protection of their wives was not as much a matter for scorn as he'd always considered it.

Here, in the quiet of the night, Ian could admit to the fierce emotion that had swept him at the sight of Lady Madeline bending her smiles on this rogue Guy Blackhair. 'Twas jealousy, swift and fierce, as much as anger at her foolhardiness in encouraging such a man. Reluctantly Ian acknowledged that he much disliked the sight of Madeline bestowing soft glances on any man.

Including his own brother.

Here, in the solitude of his vigil, Ian could admit that. He'd been jealous of Will, as well as worried for him. The admission shamed him mightily.

Bending one knee, he rested an arm across it and stared into the shadowy darkness. The sooner he got Lady Madeline to Cragsmore and left her there, the better.

Chapter Six

"I'll not stay here!"

Lady Madeline stood in the great hall of Cragsmore's keep, indignation radiating from every line of her slender body. The hood of her mud-stained traveling cloak had fallen back, revealing a face flushed with anger.

Ian shoved back his mailed hood and raked a tired hand through his hair. "You'll stay if I say you will."

"You cannot mean it!"

"'Tis not well tended, I'll grant you."

"Well tended! 'Tis as foul-smelling as a dungeon!"

Ian took a deep breath, struggling to hold on to a temper worn thin by three days of travel plagued by icy rains, near-impassible roads, and a lady who stubbornly refused to retreat to the litter he'd procured for her. On more than one occasion he'd been tempted to haul the stubborn female from her saddle and toss her inside the damned wagon. Only the fact that she had not once complained nor asked to rest had stayed his hand. But if she'd voiced no complaint on the road,

she had not been so reticent when they finally rounded
a bend in the road and spied their destination rising
out of the cold March mists.

Perched high on the rocky prominence that gave it
its name, Cragsmore was protected by a deep ditch and
surrounded by two concentric rings of high stone
walls. Its three-story square keep, buttressed by corner towers, rose high above the walls. Bleak and for-
bidding when viewed from a distance, it had earned a
slow hiss of dismay from Lady Madeline.

When viewed from inside the walls, Cragsmore had
been discovered to be even more discomfortable.

The knight appointed by the king to act as castellan
of Cragsmore had died some weeks ago of a bloody
flux of the bowels, Ian was informed by the man he'd
sent ahead with word of their arrival. 'Twas just as
well, Ian thought grimly, looking about, else he might
have skewered the man on the spot for his misuse of
the king's trust. 'Twas obvious that the castellan had
stripped Cragsmore of every copper in revenues and
put not a single one back into its upkeep. The outer
yards were in shambles, with sheds tumbled into the
dirt, livestock rooting in the garbage and overflowing
privies giving off an unhealthy miasma.

The interior of the keep was little better. The great
hall where Ian and his ward now stood had been
stripped of all finery. No tapestries hung on the dank
stone walls to block the drafts. No banners decorated
the dark timbers that formed an arc high above their
heads. Even the glazed glass was gone from the narrow windows—sold, no doubt, to line the castellan's

coffers. The only furniture in the vast hall was a carved wooden chair that tilted precariously on a broken leg on the dais where the lord and lady would normally take their meals, a few long benches, and the stained trestles shoved up against the walls. Long cobwebs hung like beards from the blackened timbers overhead, which were filled with birds' nests and spotted by droppings. The rushes beneath their feet were filthy and gave off an odor of spilled wine, rotting food and dogs.

Looking about the dark, cavernous hall, Ian cursed himself for not having ascertained the condition of the keep before bringing Madeline here. He debated within himself whether to leave her in such squalor.

"Lady..." Ian began.

"I will not stay here," she repeated.

"We will discuss this later."

Mayhap once they got some food in their bellies and dry clothes on their backs, the place would not appear so discomfortable, Ian thought.

"Tell me straight," she demanded. "Is this a residence you've brought me to, or a prison?"

Her belligerence decided the matter. Ian liked Cragsmore's state no better than she, but even less did he like her open challenge to his authority.

"It will be your residence until I decide otherwise. Enough, lady."

She opened her mouth, then caught his warning look and shut it with an audible snap. Gripping her arms with both gloved hands, she turned and swept the vast hall with a scornful glance. Her gaze lighted on the group of castle servants huddled at the far end of the hall. Even from this distance, their wretched condition was apparent. They'd been as much abused as the keep itself. The senior man-at-arms, a tall, gaunt man in a tattered tunic, blanched at her look.

As well he might, Ian thought grimly. With the steward dead, the next man in authority must bear the burden for Cragsmore's mismanagement. Ian would deal with him shortly.

"I know 'tis not what you're used to," he said, "but the keep's defenses are sound and will keep you safe."

"Safe?" she mocked, swinging around to face him.

"Aye, safe. I'll see it set to rights and provide you the comforts due your station before I must leave. There is a knight in my service I'll bring in to serve as castellan for you."

"To serve as jailer, you mean."

"If necessary."

She stood unmoving for long moments, absorbing the import of his words.

"Am I lady here, or prisoner?" she asked slowly. "I would know my state."

Ian paused, weighing his words. "You are lady of Cragsmore, and you will reside here until I decide otherwise."

"Or until something occurs that changes my circumstance," she told him angrily. "For all that you act it betimes, you are not God. You do not order the universe."

"Nay, but I order you, Lady," he reminded her, then heaved an irritated sigh. "Come, let's be done with this brangling. There's much work that needs doing if you're to eat or sleep in comfort this night. Why don't you warm yourself by the fire while I set the varls to working?'' He raised a hand to summon the cowering servants.

"Wait!" She squared her shoulders in the sodden cloak. "As you remind me, I am lady of this dismal pile."

"You are."

"Then 'tis my responsibility to see it set aright."

Ian frowned, thinking of all that had to be done. As tired as he was from the damnable journey, Madeline had to be just as weary.

"Come, sir, don't scowl at me. While I was in the king's ward, I had little say in the management of my dower lands. But if I'm to live here, even for some little time, I will be chatelaine."

She saw the doubt on his face. "What, do you think me incapable of ordering a household?"

His glance dropped from her face to her fur-trimmed cloak and rich, if mud-bespattered, robe. Doubt became outright skepticism. "You'll need more than smiles and songs to set this pile aright."

"You have not much opinion of me, do you?" she snapped, then waved an impatient hand. "Never mind, I know the answer to that already."

Madeline turned away, tucking her hurt within her heart. Aye, she knew well enough his opinion of her. He'd made no secret of it, after all. He thought her frivolous, and but a half step above a whore, if even that. Well, she could not govern what he thought, but she could of a certainty govern this slovenly keep.

"You!" she called to the senior man-at-arms. "Attend to me!"

The tall man, as thin as a cadaver rolled from its coffin by grave robbers, swallowed and stepped forward.

"What is your name?"

"Ralf, milady."

"Did you come to Cragsmore with the scabrous knight who misused my property so?"

His Adam's apple bobbed like a feathered ball caught on a string. "Nay, milady. I was born here. My father was in service to your lord husband, and his father before him."

She skewered him with a hard look. "As one born to the keep, why did you not stop the knave's depredations?"

"I tried."

"You did not try hard enough, 'twould appear!"

He met her look with a dignity that belied his tattered clothes and gaunt face. "I served as best I could, without losing my post and all chance to restrain one who had the king's authority behind him." He hesitated, then lifted his hands to waist level, palm down. "As it was, he thought me too lax in my management and oft... encouraged me to do better."

Madeline sucked in a swift breath at the sign of scarred wrists, twisted joints and missing fingers. She'd not seen many men racked, but recognized the signs. She knew better than to show pity or softness, however. If she was to establish her authority, she must do so from the start.

"Nor will I tolerate any laxness! If you show yourself willing to work hard to provide for my comfort and the care of those within the keep, I'll allow you to keep your post."

"Y-yes, milady."

She leaned forward, her expression harsh. "But if you once fail to attend to me, you will lose what's left of your fingers. Do you understand?"

"Yes, milady."

Madeline's gaze ranged the gloomy hall once more. Suppressing a shudder, she reached down to grasp her sodden skirts.

"I suppose if we're to eat at all this night, you'd best show me the cellars and the kitchen sheds."

De Burgh stood aside as she swept past. Out of the corner of her eye, Madeline caught the sardonic smile that lifted his lips.

Jesu, he probably thought she didn't even know her way around the storage cellars of a keep. She gritted her teeth. She'd show him that she was more than the simpering, perfumed slut he thought her. And when she had this dismal pile of rocks restored to her satisfaction, she'd damned well find a way out of it and out of his keeping.

Some days later, Madeline shoved aside the hair that straggled free of her braids, straightened her aching back and pushed open the door to the huge lord's chamber that dominated Cragsmore's third floor.

"We're all but done, milady," Gerda announced. She waved a hand to shoo the squadron of mop-wielding women back to their tasks.

"Aye," Madeline murmured, looking about in no little surprise.

Her bedchamber no longer resembled a vast, dark cave. Wooden shutters were thrown back to allow in the first sunshine they'd seen since their arrival. The crisp air filling the chamber carried the tang of snows melting and rising pine sap. It mingled with the scent of soap rendered from mutton fat and wood ash that the women used to scrub the walls and floors and furnishings. The filthy rushes that previously lined the floor had been dumped out the window and raked in with manure from the stables to use later as fertilizer for the fields. Madeline herself had torn down the tattered wall hangings and bed curtains and sent them away for washing and repair, so that the chamber now was clean and light and airy. Some would consider it stark, mayhap, but it suited her.

"You've done well," she told Gerda.

The maid planted her fists on two rounded hips and looked about her. "Well, 'tisna what you're used to, mistress, but 'twill do. Fer now."

Madeline breathed in the brisk air. "Aye, for now."

"We'll do your solar next," Gerda said, a militant gleam in her eye.

Madeline stared at her in some awe. The clumsy maid, who could not handle a veil without rending it, seemed to relish the Herculean challenge that Cragsmore represented. Her red, chapped hands obviously itched to get at the tower room.

"Start the women working at it," Madeline instructed, pulling a heavy scarlet cloak from the wardrobe. "The huntsmen will be return shortly. I'd better see that there's water heating for them to wash with, and inspect the stable roof, as well." She turned a stern eye on the assembled crew. "I'll be back shortly to check your progress, so do not think to slacken."

Madeline maintained her severe expression until she had gained the winding tower stairwell that led from her private solar down to the great hall, two floors below. Then, out of sight of the workers, she slumped against the curved wall, the cloak spilling over her folded arms.

God's teeth, never had she dreamed this business of housewifery could be so exhausting! During her brief marriages she'd had armies of well-trained servants and stewards at her call. She'd conferred with the cooks, overseen the ladies at their sewing, hunted and hawked, and arranged entertainment for guests. She'd been busy, but never as toilworn as she was at this moment.

For a week now they had worked from dawn to darkness, augmented by serfs from the farms that checkerboarded the valley below Cragsmore. Madeline had put Gerda in charge of inside cleaning, and set Ralf to repairing the outside buildings. With the timorous cleric who kept the castle tallies at her elbow, she'd inspected the keep room by room, from cellars to solar, inside and out. No door was left unopened, no dark corner undisturbed. Everywhere she'd found signs of the previous castellan's mismanagement, as well as a few surprises. The dark hole of the oubliette in the dungeon had made her shiver, and the small, secret room built into the wall halfway down these very stairs had made her curious as to its use. Deciding that some long-dead occupant had used it to house his treasures, or mayhap his leman, Madeline had hooked its key on the heavy ring that hung from her girdle.

While she busied herself with these tasks, Ian had seen to Cragsmore's defenses, drilled the men-at-arms who guarded it, and organized hunts to replenish its depleted stores. He'd visited the outlying farms, assessing their condition and instructing serfs and freedmen to bring their grievances to the castle on Justice Day for settlement. He'd also sent messengers to summon the vassals who provided knight service to Cragsmore. They would renew their oaths to Madeline, and through her to him and the castellan who would govern in her name.

Madeline rested her head against the curved wall of the stairwell and sighed, thinking of all that had to be done before the feast and the homage ceremony. And of the castellan who would stand behind her during the oath-giving.

Sir Thomas should arrive this day or the next, according to Ian. He'd relieve Madeline of much of the burden of Cragsmore's restoral and hear grievances in her name, should she wish it. His wife would provide companionship, as well, or so Ian had assured her.

Madeline stared down at the dirt-smeared hands clutching her cloak and wondered why the new castellan's imminent arrival didn't fill her with relief. Why she didn't go to the small, dank chapel and light candles for his safe and speedy journey.

Because, her thoughts mocked her, when this Sir Thomas and his wife arrived, Ian would leave.

Pah! she thought, pushing her shoulders off the wall and continuing down the stairs. Why should she care that the earl would soon depart? She would be glad to see him gone, she told herself resolutely. They'd barely spoken to each other these past days, so busy had they been at their separate tasks. The few times they'd sat together at high table, the talk had all been of the castle and its needs.

'Twas only at night, when she lay exhausted on her lumpy, wool-stuffed mattress, that Madeline let her thoughts roam free. 'Twas only then that she allowed herself to think on Ian's nearness in a chamber on the floor below, to imagine him stripping and readying himself for sleep. To remember the ease with which his arms had held her that day in the gardens at Kenilworth, and to feel again the touch of his hand on her throat.

Sweet Mother of God, why did this man plague her so? What was it about him that raised such wild, contradictory emotions? She wanted nothing so much as to see him brought low, to see his power over her broken. And yet, whenever she was in his company, her heart seemed to double its beat of its own accord. She could not even look upon the man in the jerkin he wore to the hunt without noticing how snugly the leather fit across his broad shoulders and how the fabric of his braies clung to his muscled thighs. Just thinking of him now made Madeline's own thighs clench, and a slow, liquid heat curl in her belly.

'Twas all this housewifery! she decided irritably, stepping into the vast hall and slamming the stairwell door behind her. She'd been playing the lady of the castle too hard, and must needs begin to imagine herself with a lord to share the big bed above stairs. 'Twould pass, this foolishness. As soon as Ian left, 'twould pass.

Ignoring the tight ache the thought of his departure left in her chest, Madeline threw her cloak about her shoulders and crossed the hall to exit its heavy, iron-hasped door. She descended the steep, railless outer stairs, then crossed the now-cleaned yards to the stables.

Hands on hips, she tilted her head back to survey the roof. "What say you, Ralf?" she asked the man-at-arms. "Will that hold against the March winds you tell me sweep this place?"

"Aye, milady. It'll hold."

"It had better," she warned. "Else you'll spend your nights out here with the horses!"

"Aye, milady."

His tone brought her head around. "What? Do you not believe me?"

"I believe you," he said after a moment. "Did you not order the boy who turns the spit punished when he allowed that haunch of venison to burn?"

Her chin jutted up. "Aye, I did."

"'Twas most severe of you," Ralf replied solemnly. "Ordering him to take the ruined meat home to his family, as though 'twere great hardship for them to force it down. As though you didn't know they'd not eaten meat, nor anything at all but watery pottage, these past months."

Madeline raised a haughty brow. "I couldn't allow charred meat to be served at high table, could I?"

"Of a certainty, you could not."

Madeline met his eyes. They were still sunk in their sockets but no longer dull with hunger. A smile hovered in their depths.

Ralf knew full well she'd all but stripped Cragsmore of its pitiful stores to feed the castle people and serfs who farmed the valley. She'd waved aside their grateful thanks, informing them she kept a good accounting and expected each man and woman to repay the stores on the days they owed her service. 'Twould not do for them to think her soft—although it appeared Ralf was not convinced.

"The kitchen boy needs strength to turn the spit," she pointed out. "Just because I want to put a little flesh on his bones, don't think that I am pastyhearted."

"I would never think you pasty-hearted, lady."

Madeline tried to summon the scowl she'd assumed this past week. "Come, let's inspect the rest of the stables. Then I must get back and harry the women, lest they think me lax, as well!"

Ralf had done well, she soon saw. The new thatch roof was woven close and tight, and he'd had stones hauled in to construct stalls for the earl's mounts and Madeline's palfrey. The mare stuck her head over the wooden gate at their approach.

Madeline rubbed the black muzzle, feeling the prickle of whiskers amid its velvety softness. "Do you like your new home, my precious?"

The bay tossed its head and danced away. She circled the roomy stall once, twice, whickering.

"I know, Zephyr, I know." Madeline leaned both forearms on the gate. "You feel cribbed, as do I."

"She's a beauty, mistress," Ralf volunteered.

"Aye, she is that, and she runs like the wind she's named for. How I wish I could take her for a gallop."

Even as she spoke the words, Madeline knew that she would do so. The sun shone too brightly, the wind blew too softly, for her to miss this chance. The huntsmen were still out. The women were busy at their tasks with Gerda as vigilant as a goshawk watching its chicks. Madeline would not be missed if she took an hour to sweep the cobwebs from her mind.

"Saddle her for me, Ralf. This lady needs exercise as much as I and more."

The man frowned. "There's no one here to ride with you, mistress. All the men-at-arms not on the walls are in the hunt."

"You may escort me."

"Me?" He swallowed twice in rapid succession.

"What, can you not sit a horse?"

"I've ridden farm animals," he replied uncertainly, then nodded toward a placid dappled gray, "like that old cob. But..."

"But what?"

"But Lord Ian has said you are not to leave Cragsmore without proper escort."

"You are my escort."

"But my Lord Ian..." Ralf's voice trailed off uncertainly. In the way of all servants, those of Cragsmore had already discerned that their lady and the man who held her in ward enjoyed less-than-cordial relations.

"With all that needed to be done," Madeline said haughtily, "my lord has not had time to see that my palfrey is exercised. He won't take umbrage at my doing so."

While she knew that wasn't precisely true, she would not be denied now. "Saddle the mare, man. Or must I do it myself?"

Ten minutes later she led the way across the drawbridge, a reluctant Ralf following behind on the plodding, broad-flanked cob. 'Twas all Madeline could do to hold herself and her frisky mount in hand until they'd picked their way down the rutted track that led to the base of the crag. Passing through the huddle of mud huts that squatted at the bottom of the bluff, Madeline struck out for the fields beyond.

When she gained the rough, open space, the need to leave Cragsmore's looming bulk behind, if only for a few moments, grew too powerful to resist.

"Follow as you will, Ralf," she called over her shoulder. "I'm going to give this lady a chance to work the kinks from her legs."

"Lady Madeline!"

"I'll but run the length of the fields, then back."

Ignoring his protests, she kicked the mare into a canter. Halfway across the first field, she let Zephyr lengthen her stride into a gallop. As eager as her mistress, the sleek little horse grabbed the bit and ran.

Madeline leaned forward, feeling the rough mane brush her face and the horse's pumping withers reverberate against her thighs. Wind stung her cheeks and teared her eyes. Tendrils of hair, already disordered by the toil of the day, worked free of the cauls and whipped about her head.

She laughed, a joyous, exultant whoop of sheer exuberance, and urged the willing mare to even greater speed. Lengthening her stride, Zephyr seemed to barely touch ground as she flew across the fields.

So consumed was Madeline by the wild ride, she didn't notice the small party that straggled out of the woods to her right. But if she didn't notice them, they certainly saw her.

Ian's heart slammed against his chest at the sight of the horse and rider racing across the valley floor. He recognized the palfrey's rich green barding immediately, and Madeline in her bright vermilion cloak. For one breath-stopping moment, Ian thought the mare had run away with her.

And then he saw how she leaned forward, how she seemed to be urging the mount on. How she left behind her escort and headed for the road that lay beyond the fields.

The road that led south.

Away from Cragsmore.

Back toward Kenilworth. Toward John.

With a savage oath, Ian flung off the stag draped across his mount's withers and spurred his stallion. The sorrel thundered into a gallop.

Over the exultant pounding of her own blood, Madeline heard the sound of pursuit. Her hair whipped into her eyes as she twisted around and saw the earl.

She should rein in, she told herself. She should pull up and explain her sudden desire to feel the wind in her face. Having tasted the heady tang of freedom, however, she wasn't quite ready to come to heel like a docile, well-trained whippet.

Her lips curved upward. The impulse to lead the earl on a merry chase was too strong to resist. Leaning low, she crooned to the mare. "Go, my sweet. Fly."

Zephyr soared over a tumbled stone wall that marked the edge of a field. Mud flew up from her hooves, splattering Madeline's cloak as they tore across the unturned earth.

Ian bent forward, at one with his mount as it cleared the stone wall, and kept his eyes on the scarlet figure ahead. She'd seen him. He knew she had. She'd twisted back and seen that he followed, and still she raced away. He'd bring her to rein, Ian vowed silently. And once he did, she'd not try to escape him again.

The broad valley began to narrow. Squinting ahead, Madeline saw a stream swollen with melting snows, and then the valley's neck, where dark pines grew down to form a branching canopy over the dirt track that wound among them. She'd not risk Zephyr's neck—or her own!—racing down an unfamiliar track. But by the saints, while there was yet room to run, she'd show de Burgh the back of her mare's heels. Grinning wickedly, she urged her mount on.

It all happened so fast. If she had not turned to see how far he was behind her, if Zephyr had not sunk a hoof in a bog created by the swollen stream, Madeline might have held her seat. But the combination of unbalanced position and her mount's sudden lurch sent her flying from the saddle. In a flurry of splattered skirts and flailing legs, Madeline landed facedown in the mud. Still frenzied from the chase, Zephyr leapt the stream, regained her stride, and galloped on, riderless and fleeter even than before.

Ian saw the fall. Fear clawed at his belly as he yanked viciously on the reins to turn his mount before it trampled her. The sorrel's neck twisted sideways, and it skittered crabwise to a stop. Ian threw himself from the saddle before the horse had even come to a halt.

Winded, her arms shaking, Madeline tried to push herself out of the viscous, foul-smelling bog.

"Lie still!" The harsh command sounded just above her ear as he knelt on one knee beside her. "Don't move until we know if you've taken serious hurt."

"Nay," she gasped, pushing upward. Her palms sank into oozing mud. "Nay, I've hurt naught...."

He lifted her, supporting her shoulders as he turned her up to face him.

"Naught but my dignity," she finished breathlessly.

Ian's arms trembled with the need to crush her to him. To lift her in his arms and hold her safe. To beat her black and blue for the fear and fury still hammering in his heart.

Madeline lay in his arms, shaken, trembling, intensely alive. She stared up at the earl, her pulses pounding. The sky above his head seemed sharply blue, but not as vivid as the eyes that raked her face. She could see each gold-tipped lash, each lean, angled plane of his face. She waited, breath suspended, for him to speak.

"You could have broken your damned neck!"

"Aye. But I didn't."

A muscle twisted beside his jaw. "I may break it for you."

Madeline gaped at him, then felt a bubble of laughter well up in her chest. So much for imagining that the man was as moved as she by the closeness of their bodies. She struggled to sit up, her lips curving into a grin.

"What? Is the mighty Lord de Burgh so poor a sport? Do you so dislike to lose a race?"

The painful grip on her shoulder tightened for a moment, then fell away. "A race? This mad run was but a race?"

"Aye, what else?" Her grin widened. "And I would've beaten you, too, had I not fallen from my saddle like the veriest clunch."

He rested his arm across his bent knee and regarded her for a long moment. "Had you not fallen, most likely I would have beaten *you*. With a birch branch. Soundly. As I will if you ever try such a trick again."

Madeline was in no mood to take his threats to heart, not with her blood still racing from the wild ride. Not with Ian's breath sounding as short and as tight as hers. Not with him leaning so near to her that she could smell his heady scent of leather and sweat and male.

"You know, my lord," she taunted softly, "you should learn to take defeat more graciously."

"Think you so?"

"Aye." She tilted her head, driven by the same reckless mood that had made her urge Zephyr on and on. "And I think, as well, that you should learn to take yourself less seriously."

"Do you?"

"Aye." She lifted a hand filled to overflowing with thick, sludgy mud. "'Tis time and past that you descended to a level with the rest of us mere mortals."

He eyed her cupped hand. One blond brow rose infinitesimally. "You would not," he stated calmly.

"I would, my lord. In fact . . . I think I shall."

He could have pulled back. He could have reached out and knocked her hand aside. But he did neither, clearly not believing she would dare.

She dared.

By the saints, she dared!

Her eyes gleaming wickedly, Madeline brought her mud-filled hand smack up against his cheek, then let it fall. Leaning back on both palms, she gave vent to the laughter welling in her chest.

Ian knelt as if turned to stone, his eyes narrowed in disbelief. A great glob of mud slithered down his cheek, gathered on his chin, then fell to the ground with a soft plop.

His jaw rigid, he fought to control his rioting emotions. He couldn't believe this was the same woman who'd kept half the king's men dangling at her fingertips. She was filthy and disheveled, with her hair straggling down her back and her skirt rucked up about her knees. Her veil was gone, as were her gloves. Mud clung to her face and smeared her front. Yet her laughter sounded like molten silver and the gleaming lights in her eyes made his breath catch somewhere in the vicinity of his breastbone.

Ian wanted her.

He wanted her with a need so fierce it drove out all conscious thought.

He wanted to roll her back into the muck and cover her body with his. He wanted to take her mouth, to tear the filthy cloak from her body. To throw up her skirts and plunge into her depths with all the force of his being.

She must have seen the stark desire on his face. The laughter faded from her eyes, to be replaced by uncertainty, and then by a leap of feminine satisfaction so quickly gone that Ian almost missed it.

By the saints, she played with him! Even here, with her bottom planted in four inches of bog and the stench of rotting vegetation rising all around her, she played with him.

Although his aching body protested violently, Ian forced himself to rise.

"Well, madame, now that you've demonstrated that I'm on the same level with other mortals, I suggest you get your backside up before it freezes there. You've a long walk back to the keep."

She sat up straighter. "Walk?"

"Aye, walk." Ian strolled to his mount. "You have no horse that I can see."

"You cannot be serious! 'Tis three miles and more back to the keep." She pushed herself awkwardly to her feet, dragging her skirts out of the clinging morass with some difficulty.

"So it is." Ian threw the reins over the sorrel's head and swung into the saddle. "While you trek it, I'll go search for your mare."

She stood with both feet planted wide, hands on hips. "De Burgh, you wretch! You would not leave me here!"

"Aye, lady, I would." He leaned a forearm on the pommel. A slow grin sketched across his mouth. "As you pointed out just moments ago, I've not yet learned to take defeat gracefully. Remember that the next time you think to play with me."

Chapter Seven

Mud squishing from her boots with every step, Madeline trudged nearly a mile before she met Ralf coming from the opposite direction.

Wide-eyed at her sorry state, he slid off the cob and cupped his hands so that she could mount, then clambered back aboard himself. Madeline spent the rest of the slow ride back to Cragsmore alternately cursing the earl and biting back bubbling, rueful chuckles.

The knave! The scoundrel! How could he ride off and leave her like that? Madeline suspected that he'd only done so because he'd seen Ralf in the distance. Ian had known that she'd not have to slog the whole distance. Nor would he have abandoned her without protection. But even so, to leave her standing in the mud!

Her ignominious return from her wild ride didn't bother her, however. She would have endured far worse, just to see Ian's face when she'd smeared it. By the saints, he'd been so astonished. So deliciously human. Madeline lowered her chin into the folds of her soiled cloak to muffle her chuckles, then immediately lifted it again to drag in a breath of clean air. Holy Mary, she smelled as though she'd rolled in manure!

Laughter rippled through her once more, causing Ralf to glance back at her over his shoulder, then shake his head in bewilderment. Tales of her strange ride would soon circulate throughout the castle, Madeline was sure, but she couldn't bring herself to worry yet again about her image as chatelaine.

Lifting her face to the sun, she drank in the last of its golden light. Sweet Mother, it felt good to laugh again. And it felt good—nay, wonderful!—to have shocked Ian out of his customary control, if only for a brief moment. She'd seen the desire that flamed in his eyes when he held her. She'd felt the tremors in his arms and heard the pounding of his heart. A heady sense of feminine power shimmered in her veins. It thrilled her that she could cause such a reaction and made her eager to test her power over him once again. Like a challenger in some contest that involved only the two of them, she looked forward with mounting anticipation to their next meeting.

It came sooner than she'd expected. As the cob plodded over the drawbridge and ambled toward its stall, Madeline saw Ian in the shadows that now crept across the yards.

He leaned one shoulder against the stable wall, stroking Zephyr's muzzle. Ian's long legs were still encased in the tight leather braies he'd worn in the hunt, but he'd shed his soiled tunic. Despite the nip in the air as the sun sank behind the castle wall, he wore only a wool shirt dyed a deep blue and belted at the waist. The ties that held it at the neck had fallen open to reveal the thatch of golden hair curling below the strong column of his neck.

As he straightened and came to greet her, Madeline saw with some satisfaction that he hadn't washed his face. For all that he strode toward her with the unconscious arrogance of a warrior, he had the dirty face of a boy.

He lifted her down easily, his hands lingering on her waist. "You didn't walk far, I gather."

"Far enough."

The farm horse's broad rump swayed, pushing Madeline against Ian. She put her hands on his forearms to steady herself, discovering the hard, tensile cords of sinew and muscle beneath her fingers. The feel of his firm flesh shot through her stomach like a bolt loosed from a crossbow. Startled, she raised her eyes to his.

As if from a distance, she heard Ralf dismount and lead the cob toward the stalls. It snuffled faintly as it clopped across the hard-packed dirt, or Madeline thought it did. Her senses registered nothing except Ian's face. The lean cheeks, with just a faint blond bristle beneath the remains of the mud. The blue eyes gleaming down at her. The lazy smile she hadn't seen since their first meeting and hadn't known how much she missed until this very moment.

"I found your mare in the copse at the edge of the fields. She's not the least repentant for having run off."

Tilting her head in a way that would have brought a dozen knights running to her side at the king's court, Madeline smiled up at him. "Why should she be? 'Twas a glorious run."

He arched one brow. "Nor does her mistress seem at all penitent that she rode without proper escort, despite my orders to the contrary."

"'Tis a failing of ours," Madeline admitted. "Neither Zephyr nor I responds well to a heavy hand on the reins."

She'd meant to tease him. The words had spilled from her tongue lightly, with the ease of one who had exchanged a thousand sallies with a hundred men or more. But as soon as she spoke them, she saw Ian had taken them at their worth.

"So it appears. But you will not ride like that again, either of you."

"What? We may not gallop with the wind? Surely you'd not condemn either Zephyr or me to a sedate trot upon occasion?"

"I mean you will not leave Cragsmore. Not without proper escort."

"I thought we had this out already. Am I lady of Cragsmore, or prisoner, that I may not ride when and where I will?"

She would have pulled away, but the hands at her waist held her still.

"Don't make this more difficult for yourself than it needs to be," he told her, his voice quiet. "Accept that I'm thinking of your safety. I will not have you leaving the keep unless I—or Sir Thomas, when he arrives—see you are properly escorted.''

The brightness of the afternoon seemed to dim, then fade away. All that was left of Madeline's exuberant ride and heady sense of womanly power was a gathering disillusionment.

''I see. I am to be accountable to the knight who by rights should be accountable to me.''

''Thomas of Lorchester is a reasonable man, and very loyal. He'll serve you well in all matters.''

''As long as those matters coincide with your wishes.''

The hands at her waist tightened, drawing her up, almost into the curve of his body. ''Madeline, I would—''

''You've made your point, my lord,'' she said icily. ''Release me.''

Ian stared down into green eyes now flat and cold. He thought of how they'd gleamed with laughter when she teased and taunted him with that handful of mud. More than all else, he wanted to rekindle her warmth, to hear her laugh or see the sudden awareness that had flushed her face when they both sprawled in the bog. Instead, he released her and stepped back.

''A messenger arrived while we were out, bringing word that Thomas is but a few hours distant. He and his lady wife should arrive before the boards are laid.''

She drew in a deep, quick breath, and let it out slowly. ''Then I'd best go cleanse myself. If I'm to be subject to this man's whim, I don't want to give him a disgust of me at first meeting.''

* * *

Two hours later, Madeline slammed down the lid of the silver chest that held her precious pots of cosmetics and jars of perfumes. Angling her head to catch the light of the oil lamp, she stared at her reflection in the gold-backed mirror propped on the table. She'd not bothered to paint or primp since coming to Cragsmore, but tonight...tonight she felt the need for all her armor.

The woman who stared back at her held little resemblance to the one who'd arrived home filthy and unkempt. This creature's cheeks held a high color, due only in part to skillfully brushed rouge, and her eyes glittered with an iridescent gleam. Soot had shaped her brows into dark wings and formed her lashes into soft, thick crescents. Her hair, left unbraided after a hurried bath, flowed down her back in a river of golden brown. She would not tame it into braids tonight, but leave it loose and covered only by a light silk veil anchored with a circlet of gold.

"Will ye wear the blue gown, mistress?" Gerda asked, fumbling at the tall carved chest that held Madeline's robes.

"Yes. No. The green, I think."

"Oooh, mistress, 'tis yer best. 'Tis far too fine for this place."

Madeline suppressed a wince as Gerda's work-roughed hands stroked the emerald-colored foulard silk. "It'll do. Here, let me have it while you untangle my girdle."

Ducking her head, Madeline pulled on the robe and smoothed it over a fine linen shift embroidered with mythical animals at neck and hem. The gown's sleeves were trimmed in dark marten fur, and so long they almost dragged the floor. Additional fur edged the V-shaped neck, providing a dramatic frame for the heavy necklace of gold and sapphires she'd decided to wear. Madeline waited impatiently while Gerda clucked and fussed with the gold links of her gem-encrusted girdle. She finally brushed the maid's hands away to fasten it loosely around her hips. The ends of the jeweled belt dangled below her knees and swayed provocatively when she walked.

She tested their movement, gliding the length of the room and back in graceful steps. The scent of sandalwood, light and fragrant, followed her.

Gerda clasped her hands at her breast. "Ye look so fair, milady. Lord Ian will nay be able to keep his eyes from yer face."

Madeline tossed her head. "'Tis not him I want to bedazzle tonight."

"So you say," Gerda replied with a little snort.

"And so it is."

"Aye, milady."

Madeline ignored Gerda's knowing smirk and made for the door to the winding tower stairs.

God's teeth, she thought savagely, why would the maid suppose that she primped and painted herself for Ian? He'd be gone tomorrow, or next day at the latest. The vassals he'd summoned had begun arriving this afternoon, hard apace with this Thomas of

Lorchester. The rest would arrive by noon tomorrow. The homage ceremony was planned for midafternoon, with a feast to follow. The men would confer with Ian, compare the strengths and weaknesses of their outlying manors, reaffirm their knight service fees in terms of men and equipment, then disperse. Only she would be left here at Cragsmore. She and her keepers.

Madeline paused at the foot of the stairs and drew in a deep breath. Well, if this Thomas and his wife were to be her warders in Ian's stead, she would have to ensure that they properly understood the mettle of the woman they guarded. Forcing her lips into a smile, she walked into the great hall and approached the couple who stood talking with the earl. Ignoring Ian, Madeline gave Thomas of Lorchester her hand.

He was a bull of a man, broad-shouldered and red-faced. He bowed over her fingertips with a singular lack of grace and gave her a respectful, if obviously rehearsed, greeting. When Madeline told him she'd heard much of him from the earl, his ruddy color deepened to an alarming shade, and he stammered out a response.

Instinctively Madeline slipped into the role she'd learned from earliest childhood. Her smile became fuller, more welcoming, which seemed to disconcert him no little bit.

His wife was his opposite in every respect. Small and ferretlike in appearance, Lady Catherine nevertheless managed to cast an avid eye over Madeline's jewels and gold-stitched robe. Madeline disliked her on the instant.

"I'm sorry I wasn't in the bailey to greet you when you arrived," she said coolly. "I hope your apartments are to your liking."

Lady Catherine sniffed and glanced about. "They'll do, although I must say this is a dismal place."

Two days ago, even two hours ago, Madeline might have heartily agreed with her. Now she lifted her chin and gave the other woman her most haughty smile. "Some might think so."

Her tone implied that only those with small, narrow minds would see aught amiss in a hall bare of all ornamentation and lacking the most basic amenities. Lady Catherine's almost lashless pale gray eyes blinked, and a slow color rose in her sallow face. Satisfied, Madeline turned her attention once more to the lady's husband.

Ian frowned, recognizing that his ward and the woman he'd thought would be companion to her were off to a less-than-cordial start. His frown deepened when Madeline tilted her head in the way she had, showing a fall of silken hair under her gossamer veil. She listened while Thomas described his journey, as though it were a topic of the most consuming interest.

Jesu, Ian thought wryly, just because the wench floated into the hall looking like the lady of every man's dreams and then proceeded to ignore him, that was no reason to feel this tightening in his gut. Just because her gown dipped provocatively in front, hint-

ing at the shadowy valley between breasts covered by
a near-transparent linen, should not cause him to want
to take her arm, spin her about, and march her out of
the hall. Her smiles were wasted on Thomas, Ian
knew. Even if the man's loyalty had not proven itself
time and again in battle and in service, Lady Catherine would keep him under close watch.

Still, Ian liked not the way she summoned up so
easily the soft glances he'd seen her use at the king's
court and spent them on Thomas.

"Come, lady," he said when Thomas paused in his
description of the journey to Cragsmore. "'Tis time
that you meet the vassals who have gathered to renew
their oaths to you, and through you, to me."

Her eyes flashed at his unsubtle reminder of his
power over her, but she allowed Ian to escort her
around the hall and introduce the knights who had
gathered so far. They were a motley lot, Ian had discovered, some battle-scarred veterans, some obviously more farmer than warrior. They guarded the
steep hillsides and verdant valleys that comprised
Cragsmore's demesne properties and did knight service according to their various holdings.

Madeline greeted these rough men easily, repeating
their names as if cataloging them in her mind and
asking questions that surprised Ian with their perspi-
cacity. For all that she'd not been given management
of her lands during her wardships with the king, the
lady had a neat grasp of what was due her.

Ian felt his back stiffen when one scarred old warrior held her hand longer than was either necessary or

polite. The man leered down at Madeline, as though
she were a tasty morsel just served up on a silver platter instead of his liege lady.

As much as Ian disliked the man's rudeness, however, even less did he care for Madeline's response.
Where another woman might have drawn back in
fright or affronted dignity, Madeline gave a low,
throaty laugh such as Ian had not heard since he'd first
met her at Kenilworth, and thoroughly captivated the
old reprobate. The crusty knight followed her around
like a well-trained boar hound for the rest of the evening, reminding Ian all too forcibly of his brother Will
at his most slavish.

He was being churlish. Ian knew it, and yet he
couldn't seem to rid himself of the tendrils of possessiveness, jealousy and desire that curled in his stomach. Every time Madeline laughed, it grated on his ears
like the rasp of a sword drawn across a stone. Each
time she slanted a sideways glance at another man, he
had to fight the urge to wrap an arm around her waist
and haul her up against his side, warning all men off.
Hell and damnation, even the kitchen boy turned
page, who'd been devoted to Madeline since she'd sent
him home with a haunch of charred meat, raised Ian's
ire with his reverent manner and adoring eyes.

Ian lifted his pewter cup—the best that had been left
of Cragsmore's ravaged housewares—and emptied its
contents in one long swallow. The thin, fruity wine slid
down his throat with satisfying ease. He stared at the
cup in his hand in some surprise, thinking that Cragsmore's hillsides yielded a fine harvest in grapes. Sig-

naling to the page to refill his cup, he settled back to do some serious drinking.

'Twas all he was likely to do during the endless meal that followed, he realized. Lady Madeline studiously avoided him throughout the meal and showered all her attention on the red-faced Sir Thomas. Lady Catherine sat at her husband's other side, picking at her food and frowning every time her lord stammered out a gruff reply to Madeline's skilled probing.

Resting one elbow on the table, Ian studied his ward's profile. She was still too slender for his taste, he told himself. Her jaw was too firm, as well, and bespoke a willfulness he had yet to curb. He liked his women softer, more compliant.

So why did his fingers tighten around the stem of his cup when she lifted a hand to brush back an errant lock of golden-brown hair? Why did he have to fight the urge to bury his fist in that thick, rippling mane and bring her face around to his? To force her to acknowledge him and his possession of her?

Because he did not possess her, Ian admitted bitterly. Not in the way he wanted to. He took another long swallow. Christ's toes, would this night never end!

The dairykeeper, pressed into service as singer for the evening because of the astonishing purity of his voice, entertained the guests. Madeline listened to his tale of the heroic deeds of some long-deceased lord of Cragsmore, sipped delicately at her wine and allowed none of her inner turmoil to show on her face.

Holy Mother, would this night never end? she wondered. 'Twas not the bare hall, devoid of any of the luxuries she was used to, that disturbed her. 'Twas not the plain fare, boasting no peacock tongues roasted with pine nuts or dishes spiced by costly cloves or precious cinnamon. Nor was it the rough garb of her servants, with nary a bright tunic or long-toed felt slipper to distinguish them from the serfs who worked farms.

Nay, it was the man next to her who distracted her so much that she couldn't enjoy the food or the entertainment, improvised as it was. Ian's long legs sprawled too close to hers. The strong, blunt-fingered hand holding his goblet rested too close to her plate, so that she couldn't even reach for a sweetmeat without her sleeve brushing against it.

In desperation, Madeline turned once more to Thomas of Lorchester. Laying a light hand on his arm, she directed his attention to Ralf, seated at a trestle below the high table. She leaned forward to suggest quietly that Thomas use the man-at-arm's knowledge of the area to aid him in his duties, and thus missed the angry glare Lady Catherine gave her.

Ian didn't miss it, however, nor did he miss the way Madeline's white hand rested so negligently on Thomas's brawny arm.

He stood, his chair scraping the stones under the rushes as he pushed it back. Madeline turned to stare up at him in surprise. The singer's liquid, silvered song died away.

"'Tis late, lady. You are no doubt tired from your walk this afternoon, and wish to retire."

Madeline raised one brow. "My *ride* did not tire me in the least, my lord. Nor would I be so discourteous as to retire before my guests are finished with their meal."

"They're finished," Ian announced, holding out his hand. "Come, I'll escort you to your chamber."

Heat rose to stain her cheeks, but whatever she might have said was lost in the clatter of Thomas's chair as he pushed it back.

"My pardon, lady! I'm a thoughtless clod to keep you at the boards so long. You'll need your rest for tomorrow, for the oath-taking and ceremony."

Ian could see that Lady Madeline liked the inference that she was so delicate that she needed to be abed with the hens as little as Lady Catherine liked her husband's oversolicitous concern. He would have to have a frank talk with Thomas before he left, Ian decided.

Her face rigid, Madeline rose and put her hand over his. Ian could feel the anger in the tremors that shook her fingers. His own temper, scored all evening long by her flirtatious ways, took wing.

They spoke not a word to each other during the walk down the length of the hall, although Madeline returned her vassals' wishes for a good rest with a semblance of composure. When they reached the central staircase, she snatched her hand away from his and lifted her skirts for the climb to the third floor. Chin high, mouth pursed, she led the way to her chamber. Pushing open the massive wooden door, she stepped inside and turned.

"I would pray that God grants you good rest," she told him, "but I cannot bring myself to do so. In truth, my lord, I pray you find your mattress infested with fleas and the straw so lumpy you cannot close your eyes!"

With that, she slammed the door in his face.

Or tried to.

Ian caught it with one fist, and forced it open. She stumbled back, and he shut the heavy panel behind him.

"Get you gone," she said angrily. "I don't wish to speak any more with you this night. Or any night. 'Tis as well you leave tomorrow. At least I'll be spared any more of your heavy-handed manners."

"Before I leave, madame, there are things that need to be made clear between us."

"There are many things that should be made clear between us, but not tonight."

"Aye, tonight."

She folded her arms across her chest. "Do you know how much I mislike this arrogant way of yours?"

"As much as I mislike seeing you simper, no doubt."

"Simper! I do not simper."

Ian waved an impatient hand, unwilling to admit, even to himself, how much it irritated him that she'd practiced her graceful gestures on every man present tonight—except him. "You'll not get around Lorchester with pretty pouts and sweet smiles."

"Oh? Think you not?"

"I know not. I'll see that he understands your ways before I leave."

Her arms dropped. "My ways!"

"Aye."

Her eyes took on a dangerous glitter. "My loose ways, you mean?"

Ian shrugged. "The ways you learned at the queen's skirts. Your husbands may have allowed you to play with men as you do, and twist them to your wishes, but I will not."

"But you won't be here to allow or not allow it, will you?"

Her taunting reminder that he must leave her seemed to hang between them both. Ian set his jaw.

"I will be back, lady, in good time. Until I return, Lorchester will hold to my orders where you are concerned, however much you smile and sigh upon him."

"And just what are these orders, my lord?"

"To keep you safe and close, until such time as I find a proper husband for you. Lorchester will see that these rough vassals don't sniff at your skirts, like hounds after a bitch in heat. They're not for you, Madeline, however much you play with them."

Her face drained of color, leaving only bright spots of red high on each cheek. "What a pretty opinion you have of me, my lord."

She flung her head back, her bosom rising and falling rapidly under its covering of silk and linen. The possessiveness that had gripped Ian all evening rose like a slumbering dragon prodded suddenly from its sleep. It swept over him, gripping his loins in a hard, hot hold.

"I think you a most desirable woman, Madeline de Courcey, and well you know it."

At his blunt admission, her stomach clenched. Emotions, sharp and painful, gripped her heart. He wanted her. He made no secret of it. The knowledge should have rekindled the secret sense of power she'd felt earlier this afternoon, riding home from the valley. 'Twas something she'd learned to use young, this woman's unique power over a man—with her husbands and with the men who danced around her at the king's court.

But Ian neither danced at her fingertips nor wanted her to wife. He would find her a husband, in his own good time, but until then he found her desirable. Spurred by an aching, piercing hurt, Madeline approached him.

"So what is it that you want from me, my lord?" she asked, her voice low and husky. "Should I turn my . . . my smiles and sigh on you instead?"

"Madeline . . ."

"Should I lay my hand on your arm, like so? Do you wish me to bring my body next to yours, like so?"

A muscle quivered on one side of his jaw.

"What?" she queried. "Does that not please you? What is it you want of me, my lord? Shall I raise my skirts and—"

He wrapped an arm around her waist and hauled her up against his chest.

"Ah..." she breathed. "Now we come down to it, this game between us."

He slid his other hand behind her neck and used his thumb to tilt her chin up. "Nay, Madeline, 'tis no longer a game. Whatever else it is between us, 'tis no game."

Madeline's pulse hammered as he brought his head down and took her lips.

Ian felt her tremble in his arms. His mouth slanted over hers, plundering, claiming. She was all that he'd remembered and more. So much more. She tasted of tangy meats and fruity wine and warm, delicious woman. No, not woman. Not just any woman. She tasted of Madeline. Only Madeline. The fragrant scent of sandalwood teased Ian's senses, and the feel of her slender, silk-clad body burned against his chest, his thighs, his groin.

He tightened his arm, bringing her full against him. Her breasts flattened into soft mounds, their peaks barely discernible through the layers of clothing separating them. Ian shifted, hungry and swiftly hard. The hand circling her neck came down to palm the tops of her breasts, then settle over one. He kneaded it, shaped it, felt its small, ripe weight through the heavy silk.

Her lashes lay like shadows against her cheeks. A breathless moan, half sigh, half sob, sounded against his lips. Ian growled, far back in his throat, and widened his stance. His hand left her breast to cup the firm flesh of her bottom. He brought her into the juncture of his thighs and measured her firmness with his.

Her lids fluttered upward, revealing eyes as hard and lustrous as any polished gemstone.

"Is this what you want, my lord? Shall I play the whore with you?"

Chapter Eight

He should have taken her.

The thought charged through Ian's mind like a spurred and angry war-horse for the next two days, thundering into his consciousness whenever he saw his rigid and unsmiling ward.

It hammered in his head as he left Cragsmore in the dank, misty dawn, with Madeline's cold farewell speeding him on his way. The portcullis clanged shut behind his troop, and Ian swore viciously to himself.

He should have taken her. He should have swept her into the huge bed and buried himself in her white, soft flesh. He wouldn't have been the first to lose himself in her. She was no timid virgin, as she herself had pointed out on more than one occasion. She was a woman grown, twice wedded and many times bedded, if the rumors about her were to be believed.

That was the rub, Ian admitted, his eyes on the road ahead, but his mind on the woman he'd left behind. He couldn't reconcile the Madeline he now knew with the rumors that floated about whenever her name was mentioned. Despite the evidence of his own eyes, despite her offer to play the whore with him, he was finding it harder and harder to believe her wanton.

True, she had offered to lift her skirts for him. But Ian had seen the glittering hurt in her eyes when she taunted him. And, true, she had an easy, beguiling way about her, one that men responded to. Looking back on her exchange with Thomas, however, Ian could admit that when she laid her hand on his arm and smiled so prettily, she'd not been bent on seduction.

Ian was no fool. Now that his jealousy had cooled, he was coming to realize that Madeline's coquettish gestures and curving smiles bespoke a potent combination of natural liveliness and learned feminine arts. Yet for all that he could understand and explain and rationalize his behavior toward his ward and hers toward other men, Ian wished he had taken her. She was much a woman, this Madeline de Courcey, and he wanted her as he'd never wanted any woman. 'Twas as well the heavy responsibilities of his own lands demanded his attention. If he stayed another week, or even another day, he might have given in to the raging need he felt for her. Ian had never yet abused a woman in his keeping, and he would not do so now. Nor would he destroy Will's trust in him.

But that didn't ease the ache in his loins. He flung one last, disgusted look over his shoulder at the bleak, towering keep that was Cragsmore and wished savagely that he had taken her.

* * *

He should have taken her!

Madeline stood at one of the narrow, slitted windows that pierced the thick walls of the west tower, shivering in the icy mists that had replaced the false spring of just a few days ago. Her heart as cold as the slick stones under her fingertips, she watched the distant line of men-at-arms snake away along the road, then fade into the drizzle.

Damn him, he should have taken her.

If he had, Madeline could hate him with a clear conscience. She wouldn't feel instead this cringing sense of shame whenever she thought of how she'd taunted him so crudely two nights ago. Of how she'd offered him her body, and he'd refused her.

Nor would she feel this searing sense of loss. God help her, had Ian said yes, had he swept her into his arms and kissed her again, she doubted she would have pulled away. Despite her hurt, despite her anger, she might have returned his kisses with the passion that built within her whenever she was near him.

Damn him to the depths of perdition.

She lifted her skirts and climbed the winding stone stairs to her private solar, taking refuge for a few moments in its stark, unadorned grandeur. Madeline wanted to fling herself across her bed and weep. Or scream with frustration. Or... or she knew not what! Instead, she clenched her hands and stood still in the center of her empty chamber.

She had to get away from him. She couldn't bear any longer the pain of his scorn, the shame of his rejection. Her mind searched for some way to break his hold on her. There must be some means to force him to relinquish the prize he'd won. Madeline was not so foolish as to believe that she would ever have complete control of her life, but she would, she must, find some way to free herself of his hold!

The sounds of the keep intruded upon her bitter thoughts. Across the hall, Lady Catherine's shrill voice chided the maids, warning them to have a care setting up her embroidery frames. A door slammed, and Sir Thomas's deep voice called to his squire to mind his step, reminding him that there were stones loose on the stairs.

Madeline squared her shoulders. She had to get out of the keep, if only for a few hours. The icy drizzle suited her mood. Mayhap a ride would wash the angry hurt from her mind so that she could think more dispassionately, more clearly.

"Gerda!" Madeline called, reaching into her wardrobe for her fur-lined cloak and boots. "Attend to me!"

When the door opened a few moments later, however, it wasn't the sturdy, red-cheeked maid who entered.

Lady Catherine stepped inside and glanced about with thin, raised brows. "Your pardon, Lady Madeline. If you call for the clumsy wench who thought herself a lady's maid, she's not here. I've sent her to the kitchen sheds to work."

Madeline stared at the narrow, lined face, framed by an unflattering white wimple. "You've done what?"

"The stupid fool nearly scalded me this morn. She dropped the bucket of hot water I bade her bring me to wash with."

"She's somewhat unhandy," Madeline admitted stiffly.

"Unhandy? The woman is oafish beyond words. I thrashed her well for her clumsiness and ordered her not to show her face above stairs again."

A bolt of anger shot through Madeline, white-hot in its intensity. She might have to take such high-handedness from Ian, at least for now, but she did not have to take it from this pinch-faced female.

Narrowing her eyes, she advanced on Lady Catherine. "Listen to me, woman, and listen well. I am lady of Cragsmore. I order the servants here, and only I. You will not change what arrangements I have made, except for your immediate comfort, and then only after you have consulted with me."

"Bu—but—" Lady Catherine sputtered.

"Say me no buts!"

White-faced, the other woman drew herself up. "My husband is castellan here, at Lord Ian's command."

"So he is. And I will deal with Sir Thomas in all matters that relate to Cragsmore. But not with you, lady. Do you understand?"

Queen Eleanor herself could not have been more regal in her tone or have held herself more imperiously than Madeline did. If she'd learned nothing else during her years in the king's ward, Madeline had learned to depress the pretensions of toady women such as Lady Catherine.

"Lady Madeline..."

"Do you understand!"

"Aye, lady."

"You will send word below stairs immediately that I wish my maid to attend me."

The woman's sullen face told Madeline that she'd made an enemy, but she cared not.

"You are dismissed."

Catherine's eyes locked with hers, until the pale lashes dropped and the woman dipped in a curtsy so slight it was barely discernible. Madeline allowed her to depart, then stood rigid for a moment, her fisted hands buried in the folds of her cloak.

Holy Virgin, how had she come to such a place? A dark, dismal keep at the back of beyond, with only a mean-spirited harridan for company? Well, she would not be here for long, Madeline vowed.

Until she found a way to free herself of Ian's bonds, however, she must needs keep busy. As soon as Gerda had been returned and her weepy anger soothed, Madeline sought out Sir Thomas.

March melted into April, and Madeline rode out with the gruff castellan almost every day, as much to escape Lady Catherine's dour company as to find some occupation to pass the time.

As the weeks passed, the snows on the distant peaks dissolved, the winds blew more softly, and the air waxed clear. Moisture was drawn to the treetops, which budded a pale green. Wild roses unfurled among the thorny branches of the hedges that marked the boundaries of the fields in the valley, competing valiantly with the scent of the manure that the peasants spread atop the newly turned earth.

Gradually Madeline found herself drawn into the rhythm of the surrounding countryside. To a woman raised in the crowded confines of a king's household, the impact of nature's cycle on the land and its occupants was astounding. Work, play, even procreation, it seemed, revolved around the season.

With Sir Thomas at her side, Madeline oversaw the distribution of seed and decided which fields were to be planted with spring crops, which with winter, and which to leave fallow. After the ploughing and the planting and the harrowing, she rode into the hills to check the crop of spring lambs. She found herself called upon to settle disputes between shepherds, who, she soon learned, raided each other's flocks with ruthless abandon.

Amid the backbreaking labor that spring brought with it, there was revelry, as well. Madeline presided over the sheepshearing, a smelly, noisy, tumultuous affair that involved the whole village and pens of bleating, shaggy-haired sheep. As lady of Cragsmore, she provided foodstuffs and ale for the entire village when the shearing was done.

At the solemn high feast of Eastertide, she hosted her vassals, and the games that followed the feast. 'Twas during the revelries of Hocktide, the two days immediately after Easter, that the means for her removal from Cragsmore occurred to Madeline.

In keeping with a tradition so old its origins were lost in the mists of time, on Hock Monday the women of the village could seize the men and hold them to ransom. On Hock Tuesday, 'twas the men's turn to imprison the women. Much enjoyment and disorder resulted, as well as feuds between irate fathers and hurried marriages of nubile young women and brawny young men. Madeline tried halfheartedly to impose some order on the villagers' high spirits, but in truth she couldn't help but sympathize with the saucy wenches who teased and tantalized their bound, helpless victims.

She herself would give much to have a certain lord bound and helpless and at her mercy, Madeline mused as she rode up the winding trail from the village late on Hock Tuesday. Her eyes lifted to the silhouette of the keep, dark against the blue of the spring sky. She would demand her release from Cragsmore as his ransom. And his pledge that she would have the right to chose her next lord.

Why not? she thought, sitting up straighter in her saddle. Her fingers tightened involuntarily on the reins, causing Zephyr to toss her head and snort in surprise. Madeline calmed the mare with a pat on her neck, her mind racing. Why not take him to ransom? He had taken her as John's ransom. Why not turn the tables?

But how? How could a woman capture a knight as strong and powerful as Lord Ian and hold him? Her gaze slid sideways, assessing the man who rode beside her. No, Sir Thomas wouldn't help. He was Ian's man, through and through. He hadn't relaxed his vigilance these many weeks, although he treated her with unfailing courtesy.

No, she thought with an inward sigh, not Sir Thomas. Nor any of the vassels who called her liege. They would not risk the wrath of one as powerful as Ian, not when he was well within his rights to hold her where he would. The iron portcullis clanged down behind them, and Madeline forced herself to tuck the delightful image of de Burgh, chained and furious, far back into a corner of her mind.

And there it might have stayed, had not she walked into the great hall the next evening, escorted by Sir Thomas and his wife, and stopped abruptly at the sight of a pair of broad shoulders encased in a tattered, much-patched surcoat. The face above the surcoat sported a luxuriant black mustache. When he saw her surprise, the knight strolled forward, his mustache lifting in a grin.

"Sir Guy?"

"At your service, my lady."

Madeline remembered all too well the roguish light in his gray eyes. She remembered also Ian's anger that she'd even spoken with this knight at the inn where they stopped on their journey to Cragsmore. She gave a brilliant smile of welcome. "What do you here?"

He bowed over her hand. "I've come to beg a night's lodging."

"Of course, and welcome. Are you en route somewhere?"

"I was." The gleam in his eyes deepened. "A fat merchant seeking forgiveness for his sins hired me to provide escort to the shrine of Thomas à Becket at Canterbury. But the old goat stuffed himself at a posting house not far from here and died of a bone lodged in his throat."

"How—how unfortunate," Madeline sputtered.

"Aye. 'Tis to be hoped the good Lord forgave him his gluttony. I surely won't. The dolt expired before he paid me a single silver penny."

Her laughter spilled over, causing heads to turn and Lady Catherine's thin brows to shoot up. Belatedly Madeline remembered her manners and introduced Guy Blackhair to Sir Thomas and his wife.

"So you are without service?" the castellan inquired, giving the other man a shrewd, assessing look.

Guy shrugged. "For now. Rumors are rife that the Lusignans stir rebellion in Poitou. I'll probably hie myself to France. If there is battle, one side or another will need swords for hire."

Madeline's small, swift intake of breath was lost in the general conversation about the uncertain state of affairs on the continent. His sword was for hire! Concealing her sudden, thudding sense of excitement with a coquettish smile, Madeline took his arm.

"Well, until you decide where you go next, you may stay here. Cragsmore is sadly thin of company. Come, join me at table. I would have you finish the tale you started when we met at the inn."

Lady Catherine's lips folded into lines of disapproval as she took in Guy's poorly stitched surcoat and scuffed boots. "Lady Madeline, the high table is not set with a place for him."

Even Sir Thomas flushed at his wife's lack of courtesy. "Then you will sit at the boards, wife, so that Lady Madeline may enjoy her guest's company."

Guy tucked Madeline's hand in the bend of his arm and led her down the hall. "That one would curdle milk still in the cow's udder."

"Well do I know it!"

"Why do you keep her here?"

"She is wife to the castellan my—my warder has appointed."

"Ah, Lord Ian. I wondered if he would still be here."

"No, he is not," Madeline replied shortly, taking her seat.

Guy grinned down at her. "I see you're on no better terms with him now than you were at the inn."

'Twas not the time to speak of Ian, Madeline thought. Not now, with Lady Catherine glaring up at them from her place below the salt and Sir Thomas at Madeline's other side. She needed time to think. To decide if she really dared hire this man for what she had in mind.

"Let us not speak of my warder now," she said, with a smile that gave no evidence of her inner turmoil. "Tell me instead of your travels and what sights you saw when you were in the Holy Land. Is it true

that the men there wear silk trousers and take many
wives?''

Guy Blackhair settled back in his chair, not loath to
entertain the lady of Cragsmore. Christ's toes, she was
a delicious morsel, with her great, green eyes and long,
slender throat. All the while he spun fantastic tales of
eunuchs and flower-strewn harem gardens, he watched
her face.

Long used to living by his wits and the strength of
his sword arm, Guy had learned at a young age to look
beyond the facade most people presented to the world.
He could see that the lady was not happy to be immured in this damp, dark keep, despite her light chat-
ter and easy smiles. Nor was she at all pleased with the
man who held her in keeping. That much Guy had
seen in their brief confrontation at the inn and she now
confirmed by the way she refused to speak of him. His
agile mind leapt to the possibilities the situation offered.

At Lady Madeline's left hand, Thomas consumed
his meal with the same thoroughness he always gave
his trencherwork. His ruddy face was impassive but
his gaze sharp as he studied the knight at his lady's
other hand. Lord Ian had warned him that there were
those who would try to steal Lady Madeline. A rich
widow was too tempting a prize for second sons and
impoverished widowers to resist. He chewed his mutton steak slowly, assessing the potential threat offered
by this Guy Blackhair and ignoring the evil, fuming
looks his wife shot him.

* * *

Madeline could scarce sleep that night. She tossed in her big bed until Gerda muttered grumpily from her pallet that it must be time to change the wool in the mattress, so poorly did her mistress rest. Slipping out of bed, Madeline padded on bare feet into the high tower room that served as her private solar. She leaned both elbows on the sill of a high, slitted window and stared at the dark valley far below.

Guy said the barons of Poitou stirred rebellion. If so, 'twas just a matter of weeks before Ian was called to knight service. He could be gone for months, mayhap a year or more. She'd be left at Cragsmore for all that time, unless he decided to give her in marriage to another lord before he left.

Or unless she wrested from him the promise of freedom. And if she did, would he keep it?

Madeline pressed her forehead against the cool, dewed stone, seeing in her mind the warrior who charged boldly across a tourney field. He was proud and arrogant and more damnably handsome than any man had a right to be. He thought her a strumpet, or worse. Yet Madeline knew that if he gave her his pledge, he'd hold to it. Her mind leapt this way and that, seeking some way to put him in her power. Finding none, she sighed and went back to bed.

She had all but given up all hope when a courier wearing Ian's azure-and-white colors arrived early one morning a week later. The Lusignans had indeed revolted, the messenger announced, confirming the rumors Guy had heard. The rebels were supported in their efforts by the wily old count of Toulouse and King Philip of France. Richard *Coeur de Lion* had taken his forces deep into Toulouse and besieged the impregnable fortress of Tallebourg, holding the rebels at bay until King Henry could assemble his forces.

Lord Ian requested Sir Thomas to gather a force of ten knights and one hundred men-at-arms from those vassals owing knight service to the lady of Cragsmore and send them to Shrewsbury, where they would join his banner and march south. Ian himself would come to Cragsmore within the next few days, if he found time, to see to the Lady Madeline's state.

If he found time! Madeline clenched her fists in the folds of her gown. *If he found time!*

Sir Thomas decided to leave that same day for a circuit of the manors in Cragsmore's demesne. New to his position, he wanted to ensure that the vassals provided trained men, well equipped with boiled-leather haberauks, shields and spears. He came to Madeline's solar to tell her of his plans and seek her concurrence in the ordering of the levies. She reviewed the lists, gave her assent, then listened impassively while he assured her that his second-in-command, a brawny young knight who'd come in his train, would keep her safe.

She voiced a strong protest, however, when Thomas told her that he had invited Guy Blackhair to leave Cragsmore when he did.

"Sir Guy is my guest! He may stay, and welcome."

Thomas rubbed a palm across his bristly chin. "'Tis not my place to govern who you guest at Cragsmore, lady, were I here. But I may be gone a fortnight or more."

He hesitated, and his ruddy complexion took on a deeper hue. "Lord Ian would not wish me to leave you in the company of so... attentive a knight."

Damn him, Madeline thought furiously, her own face flushing. Damn de Burgh. He had lectured Thomas well before he left, it appeared.

"Lord Ian himself arrives within the next few days," she said coldly. "He may decide himself if Sir Guy should stay."

Thomas looked doubtful.

Madeline bit back a sharp retort and forced herself a smile to her lips. "Come, sir, you'd best not delay. You have no need to worry. I'll stay within the keep, I promise you, and have Lady Catherine for company."

At the subtle reminder of his wife's hostile but ever-present company, Thomas bowed and left.

Aye, she'd stay within, Madeline vowed furiously, until she rode out of Cragsmore forever, freed of it by Ian himself. Her skirts swirling, she strode purposefully out of her solar.

She found Guy Blackhair at the stables in the outer bailey. He sat on a bucket, his raven locks ruffling in the morning breeze and his threadbare shirt open at the neck. He was busy rubbing sand into his mail shirt to remove the rust. 'Twas a job his squire should have attended to, had he one. He looked unperturbed by the bustle all around him as Sir Thomas's escort made ready to depart. His own horse was saddled and waiting, apparently, for him to finish his task.

Madeline stopped a few feet away, still spurred by her anger, but racked by sudden doubts. 'Twas no small thing she would ask of this knight, to pit himself against one as powerful as Ian. Could she ask him to risk so much, even for payment?

At that moment, Guy glanced up and saw her. He rose, setting aside the mail and gave her the roguish grin that was his alone.

"Are you come to bid me farewell, lady?"

"Nay, I've come to speak with you. You're not leaving, at least not yet."

His brows rose at her terse reply. When she struggled to find the words to describe what she wanted of him, he smiled and hooked a foot around an upturned pail.

"Here, take your ease and be comfortable while you tell me of this change in my plans."

Madeline sat on the wobbly perch, wondering how to go about hiring a man to kidnap another. She waited until he'd resumed his seat, his back to the stable wall and his long legs stretched out before him, then decided 'twas best just to plunge into the heart of the matter.

"I wish to hire you, Sir Guy."

"You wish to offer me service in your household?"

"Nay. I mean, I would but... but Sir Ian..." She stopped, loath to admit she had not the power to pledge what knights she would to her service.

"But Sir Ian would not approve," he finished for her.

"Nay, he would not," Madeline snapped. "He approves of little that I do."

"Does he not?" Guy murmured, his eyes on her face.

"As you saw at the inn, ours is not a cordial relationship."

"Nay, not cordial, certainly. I would not describe what he feels for you as cordial."

"Aye, well, 'tis for that very reason I wish to hire you." She drew in a deep breath. "I want you to kidnap Sir Ian, that I may hold him to ransom."

He sat very still. For the space of several heartbeats, not a muscle moved. Madeline bit down on her lower lip, feeling her palms grow moist as she awaited his reply.

Slowly, his gray eyes filled with a gleam she could only have described as devilish. "It might be easier than my original plan," he said at last.

"What plan?"

His mustache lifted in a wicked grin. "I'd planned to kidnap *you*, lady."

Madeline's mouth dropped open. "You...you were going to hold me to ransom?"

"Nay, lady. I was going to steal you away, bed you, and wed you—in that order, or any other I could contrive."

"You would not!" she gasped. "You would not abuse me so!"

His rich laughter rolled across the bailey. "Think you not? There's a deserted farmhouse tucked deep in the woods, not two miles distant. I took shelter in it the night before I came to Cragsmore, and had already decided it would be our bridal bower."

Madeline gaped at him. Shock and indignation warred with astonishment that she'd been so naive. She didn't know whether she should call the guard and have this man thrown into the dungeons or clout him between the eyes with his own sword, which rested against the stable wall. In the end, she did neither. Shaking her head at his unrepentant grin, she felt her own lips lift in a rueful chuckle.

"So now you think it easier to kidnap Sir Ian than to take me to wife, is that it?"

"Far easier," he admitted cheerfully. "Had I stolen you, I would've had to guard my back from your dagger while I battled him with my sword. For all your sweet smiles, lady, you're far more dangerous a foe."

"Thank you ... I think!"

While he laughed at her tart reply, Madeline felt a rush of nervous exhilaration.

"Come, let us settle the terms of your employ, and then I will tell you how I want this business done."

Ever after, it seemed to an increasingly nervous Madeline that events moved quickly beyond her control. One minute she was sitting on a bucket in a sunny yard, the next she was pacing her solar in the dark of night, a crumpled parchment clutched to her hand.

Ian would come on the morrow, the brief message said. Lady Madeline might expect him sometime after the noon hour. He came alone, having sent his squire ahead with his war-horses and battle armor. He could stay but one night, and then must rejoin his men.

Excitement, fear, and a wild, reckless sense of reaching out to take hold of her fate rushed through Madeline.

He came on the morrow.

Chapter Nine

As with most hastily contrived plans, Madeline's went awry almost from the moment she put it into play.

She'd planned to be in the bailey to greet Ian when he arrived. She wanted to be the one to tell him of Guy's presence. She would say, truthfully, that the knight had stopped to visit while en route to find service in the south. She would shrug and say, again truthfully, that he had enlivened the high table for herself *and* Sir Thomas these past nights. Ian would not be best pleased to find Guy here, she knew, but there was little he could do about it if Sir Thomas had concurred.

Unfortunately, Ian arrived well before the hour he'd said to expect him, and Madeline was not present to greet him.

She was with Guy in the small, secret room that opened off the stairs to her private solar. He'd managed to extract a pair of rusted shackles from the dungeons, and he was showing her how to work the locking mechanism when Gerda pounded on the door to her bedchamber.

Warning Guy to stay hidden, Madeline hurried up the half flight of stairs to her solar, crossed through to her bedchamber and slid the bolt.

"Why do ye bar the door, mistress?" the maid asked curiously.

"I . . . I was resting and did not wish to be disturbed."

"What? Ye never rest. Why, if ye had your way of things, ye'd be off every day on that horse of yours."

"Aye, aye. What did you want, Gerda?"

"I came to tell ye the master's come."

"The master—?" She gasped. "You mean Sir Ian?"

"Aye, the master."

"Holy Mary! Why didn't you tell me!"

"I be telling ye," Gerda said indignantly. "He's in the bailey now, with none but Lady Catherine to greet him. The old hag," she added under her breath.

Throwing a nervous glance over her shoulder, Madeline shooed Gerda out of her chamber. She could only hope that Guy had heard and had the presence of mind to present himself in the great hall forthwith. She raced down the stairs, her mind working feverishly to come up with a rational explanation for their both having been absent when Ian arrived.

She saw at once that whatever explanation she devised would do no good. From across the dirt yard, Ian's dark blue eyes locked with hers, cold and hard and furious. Lady Catherine stood at his side. The woman's triumphant smile told Madeline that she'd already informed Ian of Guy's presence—and put the worst possible interpretation on it.

Madeline swallowed an involuntary groan of dismay. Burying her shaking hands in the folds of her skirt, she walked forward to where they stood.

"So you are come, my lord."

No smile, Ian saw, struggling to contain his fury. No word of welcome. He hadn't missed the quick swallow when she first saw him, nor the flash of guilt that crossed her face.

So 'twas true, what Lady Catherine had so slyly suggested when she made excuses for the chatelaine's absence. When she sighed and said that the lady of Cragsmore was oft in the company of this Guy Blackhair and seemed to forget herself and her duties.

Ian took in the silken wisps of gleaming brown hair that escaped from the braids looped about Madeline's ears and blew gently across her face. He saw the flush that rose above the neckline of her linen shift, displayed so provocatively by her low-cut violet gown. He stared into the wide, thick-lashed emerald eyes—and he damned himself for a fool.

To think he'd detoured a full day out of his way just to spend one evening in her company! Even now, some two hundred of his men rode south, drawn from his various holdings in the north and from those of his brothers. More would gather to his banner when all his vassals answered his summons. He'd sent them forward under the command of his senior lieutenant while he rode to Cragsmore.

To think he had worried about this woman, Ian
thought savagely, had felt the lash of guilt at leaving
her with only Lady Catherine's sour companionship
in such bleak surroundings. What a fool he'd been!
What a sap-skulled fool! He should have realized that
one such as Madeline would find some man to keep
her company.

His lip curled as he surveyed her, standing so proud
before him, refusing to drop her eyes.

Jesu! To think he'd turned down every offer for this
woman's hand. Half a dozen knights of various es-
tate had presented themselves at Wyndham in the past
weeks with offers for Madeline. One was fat and
bloated with dropsy. Another wanted to wed the well-
dowered widow to his twelve-year-old son. Ian had
turned them down, and all the others, with one excuse after another, until he finally admitted to himself the reason why. He would allow no other man to
take Madeline to bed.

To think he'd come here having decided to wed the
woman himself!

His jaws tight, he nodded in response to her cool
greetings. "Aye, lady, I've come."

If Madeline had had any doubts about her plan to
win some measure of freedom from Ian, he soon put
them to rest. Taking her arm in an iron grip, he escorted her back across the bailey and into the keep.
Lady Catherine trailed at their heels, her pale eyes
glinting with satisfaction.

Guy strolled out of the shadows that made the great hall seem dark and cavernous even in the early morning. He glanced at Madeline's face, then gave Ian an easy greeting.

"So we meet again, Sir Ian."

"Aye, so we do."

"You arrive early."

Ian's eyes were like shards of winter ice, a deep, frosted blue. "Do you make yourself so much to home at Cragsmore, that you know of my comings and goings?"

"Aye," Guy replied softly. "I do."

The gauntlet was thrown down, and the challenge just as readily answered. And none of the four persons present believed for one moment that the conversation had aught to do with Ian's travel arrangements.

Oh, sweet Mother of God! Madeline thought desperately. If that wasn't just like men. The one must needs assume the worst, and the other ruffle his feathers like a bantam cock at the faintest challenge. Did none of them ever think with anything other than their codpieces?

Ian's fingers were clenched tight on her arm, his hard gaze fixed on Guy Blackhair.

Guy returned his look, his stance relaxed but his eyes gleaming with intent lights.

Lady Catherine gave a little snigger, hardly more than a gust of air through her pinched nostrils, but enough to make Madeline want to claw her eyes out.

Perforce, she ignored the woman to concentrate on the two men.

They were so disparate, these two bristling cocks. The one so dark and lean and ragged-looking, the other golden-haired and splendid, his broad shoulders encased in gleaming mail and a fine-sewn tunic of midnight blue that came near to matching his eyes. And yet they were so alike, both warriors, both dangerous.

She drew in a little breath, freed her arm and gave the group a practiced smile.

"Come, why do we stand about like this? Lady Catherine, go to the kitchens, if you will, and have them prepare meats and bread and ale for Lord Ian. He's ridden hard, and must needs refresh himself. Sir Guy, will you take word to the stables that I'll not ride out this morning after all?"

She waited, her heart pounding. Guy slanted her an assessing look, then lifted his shoulders in a little shrug and headed for the door at the far end of the keep. Lady Catherine hesitated, like a thin, avid sparrow waiting for another crumb to drop. Then she caught Madeline's stare, and turned on her heel.

Mayhap if Ian had not looked on her with such cold contempt, Madeline might never have proceeded with her plan.

Mayhap if he had said one civil word to her in the long, agonizing day that followed, she might have sent Guy on his way that afternoon and abandoned the whole mad scheme.

But Ian listened to her outline of the arrangement she and Thomas had made, nodded curtly, then strode away with only the brief comment that she'd best make her farewells to Guy Blackhair, because she'd not see him again after this day. Nor any other man.

So Madeline sat, angry and tight-lipped, at high table that night, with Guy to one side and Ian to the other and Lady Catherine watching them all with malicious pleasure. Sir Thomas's second-in-command sat below them at the boards, stabbing at his beef and mutton and stuttering in awe whenever Ian addressed him.

Under her warder's cold eye, Madeline made a brief farewell to Guy. He bowed and thanked her for her hospitality, saying that he would leave early in the morn, before the dawn.

She and Ian did not speak again. He watched her leave the great hall with no expression on his face.

Only Guy noticed how his hand clenched the silver drinking cup so tightly his knuckles showed white. Under his silky mustache, Guy's lips curved. Signaling a page to pour more wine, he settled back in his chair and set about drinking his taut, unsmiling host into a stupor.

He didn't quite succeed.

When Guy slipped into Ian's chamber in the dark hours before dawn, he found him sprawled across his bed, still in shirt and braies and boots. But Ian's instincts were yet sharp enough for him to leap out of bed, groping for his sword. Thanking the Lord for the absence of any squires or body servants, Guy ended the fight before it began by the simple expedient of bashing his opponent over his head with the stout oak staff he'd provided for himself. Not very knightly, he reflected with a grin, heaving Ian's heavy form across his shoulders. But then, he wasn't much of a knight.

She had caged a lion!

'Twas all Madeline could think as she peered through the opening in the storeroom's door. Enough light flickered from a torch thrust into a wall holder to illuminate her captive's tawny mane and massive shoulders. He sat on the floor, his back propped against the stone wall, one leg bent at the knee. An iron chain passed through a ringbolt beside his head and fastened to the shackles on his wrists.

Madeline swallowed the dryness in her throat. For all his immobility, she saw the tension coiled in his long, muscled body. Of a sudden, she wished she'd not sent Guy away.

He had not wanted to leave, had protested this part of her plan most vehemently. But in a hurried, whispered argument, Madeline had reminded him that 'twas vital that none know she held Ian. Guy *had* to don Ian's helm and surcoat, to mount his horse and leave, reclaiming his own horse at the spinney where Ralf had left it.

Before he left, still protesting, Madeline had twisted a small ruby ring from her little finger and shoved it into his palm. Closing his fist over it, she'd told him to ride south with all speed to find Lord John. John had given her this ring, and would give Guy a place in his ranks, did she ask it of him.

So he had gone. And now Madeline was alone with the lion she had caged. The one that would devour her if she did not handle it right.

Her hands shaking, she fumbled with the keys looped together on a leather thong. One was for the cuffs, the other for the door. She'd tied them together and kept them tucked in her girdle, not daring to leave them where Gerda or one of the other servants might see them.

The iron key slid into the lock. She drew in a deep breath, twisted it, then pushed open the door.

Ian lifted his head at the sound, and Madeline saw the unrelenting fury that blazed in his midnight blue eyes. She saw, as well, the blood that streaked the left side of his face.

"Holy Mary!"

She rushed to kneel beside him, close enough to view the wound, but far enough outside the circle of his reach for safety.

"Did . . . did Guy do this?"

"Aye," Ian snarled. "And he'll live to regret it."

The long gash at his hairline had already crusted, Madeline noted with relief. It should be washed and stitched, but somehow she suspected Ian wasn't in the mood to submit to such ministrations. Sitting back on her heels, she met his furious glare.

"Don't blame Guy Blackhair for this. He but did my bidding. 'Twas my idea to take you, and mine alone."

"Do you think to spare your lover my ire by this touching confession? Save your breath, Madeline. He'll pay, as will you."

"He's not my lover, although I doubt you'll believe me."

"Nay," he sneered. "Of a certainty, I will not."

Madeline told herself she was beyond being hurt by his low opinion of her. She should not even try to defend herself, but the scorn in his eyes goaded her to one more attempt.

"He's a friend, I tell you, and only that."

"'Tis an ever-growing list, is it not, the men who have *befriended* you?"

Madeline flushed. "You're in a precarious position to be flinging insults! I suggest you keep your evil tongue to yourself."

"Or what? You'll call in your lapdog to bash me on the head again?"

"Nay," she replied through set teeth. "I'll do it myself!"

He jerked forward as far as his chains would allow. "You have not the courage, you little—"

A spasm crossed his face, and he leaned back again, breathing heavily. Madeline saw the blood drain from his cheeks, leaving them white with pain.

"Ian! Holy Mother! Here, take some wine."

Her hands shaking, she scrambled for the wineskin she'd brought to the room earlier the morning and pushed it within reach of his right hand. He pulled the wooden plug and held it to his lips.

Ruby-red liquid spilled into his mouth and down his chin. He took his fill in long, thirsty swallows, then rested his head against the wall again.

"Well, at least you don't intend me to die of thirst," he observed after a tense, still moment.

"I don't intend you to die at all," she snapped, more shaken by the way his skin stretched taut across his cheeks than she would admit.

His hard, slashing look pinned her to the stone floor. "Then what do you intend, Madeline? What insanity are you about?"

"I intend to hold you to ransom, my lord."

It gave her great satisfaction to say the words, Madeline discovered. With the saying of them, she felt her nervousness subside. Sweet Mother, she'd done it! Still sitting on her heels, she folded her hands in her lap and waited for his reaction.

'Twas not long in coming.

"You'll get no moneys of me to give that bastard knight of yours, you little slut. Not one copper penny, I swear."

"'Tis not moneys I want of you."

"Then what?"

"I want your pledge."

"Of *what*, woman?"

Madeline didn't care for the impatience that sharpened his voice. Who was prisoner here, after all? Lifting her chin, she stated her conditions.

"First, I want your vow that you will not seek revenge on Guy Blackhair when you are released."

He shook his head, as if disbelieving what he heard. "You dare to ask as ransom my pledge that I won't skewer your lover?"

"He's not my lover." She ground out the words. "And I ask—nay, demand more. I want your vow that I may leave Cragsmore, and that I may have the husband of my choosing."

His reply was hard and flat and immediate. "No."

"What?"

"I'll give no such pledge."

"You will! You have no choice!"

"We all have choices. You made yours when you undertook this mad scheme."

"Fine words, sir. I suggest you think on them, however. I'll keep you fast in this dank cell until you make me the promises I ask, I swear it."

He dismissed her threat with a shake of his head. "You know you cannot. I have to be at Southampton within the week. The king has called me to knight service."

"And if you fail to show for your knight service, the lands you hold of the king will be forfeit, will they not?"

His breath hissed out. "So that's your game."

"'Tis no game, Ian."

"Listen to me, Madeline, and listen well. If it costs me all the fiefs I hold of Henry, you and the man you took as lover will not win at this."

Flushing, she pushed herself to her feet. "He's not my lover!"

"Then why do you want the freedom to wed where you will, if not with Guy Blackhair? What other poor fool have you smiled upon and teased and offered your body to, as you did to me?"

"There is no other man," she spit out, flicked to the raw. "None! But when I choose the man I will wed, 'twill be one I may smile upon without being called to task for it. One I may tease and laugh with and…and lust for with all my woman's passion, without being thought a whore."

"If you do not loose me upon this instant," he growled, "I'll give you to the first man I find who promises to beat you thrice daily, and I'll help him do it."

"Hah! Stay here and rot, then!"

She didn't return until the next morning.

At least, Ian thought it was morning. The torch had long since burned out, leaving him in a blackness that matched his mood. He'd tried the gauge the passing hours, with little success. He knew that he'd spent far longer in this dark, airless cell than he wanted to from the way the pain in his temple eased and his stomach rumbled. And from the way the rats grew bolder. The creatures still skittered down the rank hole that served as a latrine whenever Ian kicked at them. He only hoped they would continue to do so.

He'd tried to free himself. The moment the door clanged shut behind her, he'd hauled himself up and worked at the damned chains. The bolt was sunk too deep in the stone, and resisted every effort to pry or pull it loose. The rusted cuffs scraped his flesh raw, but even the lubricant of his blood failed to ease his hands free of the shackles. Settling back down on the cold stone floor, Ian whiled away the rest of the night devising suitable punishments for the jade he'd been so stupid, so incredibly thick-skulled, as to think about taking to wife.

He'd take her, he decided with increasing savagery, but not to wife. When he was through with Madeline de Courcey—and that wouldn't be for a long, long time!—she wouldn't want to see another man for the rest of her days.

When he finally spotted the flicker of torchlight in the small barred grate of the door, Ian pushed himself upright. The ringbolt through which the chain passed was at waist level. Standing gave him several more inches of reach. He tested the circumference of his stretch, seeing how close she needed to be for him to grab her. The iron cuffs bit into his flesh once more and added to the list of wrongs he would right once he got his hands on Madeline's white throat.

As slight as she was, she had to duck her head to enter the door. When she saw him standing, Madeline stopped abruptly. Holding her torch high, she peered at his chains.

"Aye, you'd best be wary," he drawled. "When I am free, you'll much regret this piece of work."

As he'd hoped, his warning stiffened her spine. She shoved the torch into the iron holder and came closer.

"I can see that a night's reflection has not improved your mood."

"Did you think it would?"

"I had so hoped," she replied tartly.

Ian felt a stab of satisfaction at her testiness. A night's reflection had not done much for her mood, either, it appeared. She looked as though she'd slept not at all. Her face was pale above the brave red gown she wore, square-cut across the bosom to show the embroidered shift beneath, and there were dark smudges under her eyes.

He gave her a small, mocking smile. "You're far off the mark, if you think that a night in a dark cell with only the rats for company improves a man's mood."

"Rats?" She gripped her skirts with both hands and looked about the cell. "Sweet Mother, Ian, are there rats?"

"Did you think there wouldn't be?"

"I...I didn't think."

"No," he taunted, "you didn't. Neither you nor that bastard knight of yours. Where is he? Is he afeared to show his face?"

She threw him an angry glance. "He left afore dawn, in your helm and surcoat. And don't begin again about Guy! I didn't come down here to argue with you further."

"Why did you come, then?"

"To see if you're ready to give me your pledge."

"No."

"You must!"

"No, Madeline."

She took a step closer. Ian kept his hands at his side and his muscles loose.

"Think, man. Think of the lands you hold of the king. You could lose them, and more, if you don't answer his call."

"No."

"You won't be able to explain it away, you know. None would believe that I could hold so fearsome a knight against his will."

Ian took perverse delight in the frustration that showed in her eyes. "No, Madeline," he repeated softly.

She swept him with an angry glance. "If you could but see yourself. In those irons, you look the veriest—" She broke off, frowning at his manacled wrists. "Is that blood?"

Ian shrugged, willing her to take but one more step.

"Ian, is that blood that stains your hand? Holy Christ in heaven, both your hands? It is!"

She whirled and sped back toward the door.

"Madeline!"

"Wait. I'll return shortly."

Ian groaned in sheer vexation. As if he could do aught else!

She came back in a breathless rush, her arms full. Elbowing open the door, she left it ajar as she moved toward the center of the cell. Ian eyed the winding stone staircase beyond the door.

"Where does that lead?"

"To my solar." She dumped her load on the floor and knelt to sort through it. "This room is secreted from the rest of the keep. Some long-forgotten lord of

Cragsmore took his private and perverse pleasures down here, no doubt.''

"So I'm not in the dungeons. That explains why I've seen no guard, nor heard any noises.''

"Nor will you,'' she said absently, clearly more intent on her task than his interest in the only means of escape. "None can hear you, either. The walls are too thick, and cut off all sound.''

She rose and came to stand in front of him, a roll of soft cloth in one hand and a heavy iron key in another. A frown drew her sable brows together as she eyed him uncertainly.

"Tricky, isn't it?'' Ian mocked. "You've caged a beast, and now don't know how to handle it.''

Her eyes gleamed unexpectedly, as though he'd said something to amuse her.

"You must let me attend to you,'' she said. "Those shackles are rusted, and could poison your blood.''

"Nay, Madeline.''

"'Tis not part of my plan for you to die, Ian, nor can you wish to. Don't be so pigheaded.''

"What would you have me do, woman? Sit docile while you tend my hurts, and then let you lock me up again?''

"Aye,'' she replied simply.

He gave a bark of laughter. "You would loose these chains and trust me not to wring your neck?''

She paled a little, but continued doggedly. "You honor the flag of truce that calls a halt to battle. You take pledges of your captives, then let them go home to collect their ransoms. Why is it so impossible that I would have the same trust in you as you do in the men you take?''

'''Tis not the same, Madeline.''

"Why not?" she argued stubbornly. "Because I'm a woman? Will you not honor a vow of truce to a woman as you would to a man?"

"Jesu, I disbelieve this!"

"You know, Ian, it occurs to me that we're at the heart of what caused this war between us in the first place. You disbelieve all I say, either because I'm a woman or because you think I have no honor.''

"Or because you've given me no reason to believe you," he replied softly.

Her clear green eyes didn't waver. "Well, if you have no faith in my honor, I believe in yours. I ask you to give me your pledge, and let me tend your hurts."

Chapter Ten

Madeline drummed her fingertips on the polished oak surface of the table that graced her bedchamber, willing Lady Catherine to be done with her petty grievance against the maidservant who cleaned the garderobe.

"'Tis foul-smelling in there," Lady Catherine complained. "The closet needs to be scrubbed with lime mixed with ash. I would have told the worthless little slut to do it, had you not forbidden me to order your servants."

As Catherine whined on, a sense of unreality gripped Madeline. She could not believe that she stood here, discussing privies with this woman, while Ian awaited her in his dark, airless cell, just a few steps down the winding tower stair. It had been several hours since she'd been to see him. Several long, endless hours since she'd unlocked first one cuff to cleanse his abrasions, and then the other. Eons since she'd left him tight-jawed and uncommunicative and chained once more.

Compounded by lack of sleep and nerves strung so tightly that they hummed, Madeline's feeling of strangeness expanded until she had to lean both hands on the table for support.

Catherine stopped in midsentence. "Are you ill, lady? You look pale."

"Nay..." Madeline bit off the instinctive denial, realizing 'twas just the excuse she needed to keep her chamber door bolted the rest of this day. "I'm...I'm just a little fagged. I did not sleep well last night."

"I would imagine not." Catherine stroked the graying braids that hung below her white wimple and smiled. "Lord Ian took no pains to hide his displeasure yesterday, did he? 'Tis uncomfortable to be at odds with one such as he, is it not?"

She had gone well beyond uncomfortable, Madeline thought wryly. She was now hovering somewhere between distraught and racked.

"'Tis unfortunate he had to leave so early this morn," Lady Catherine continued. "Before the sun rose, even. It gave you no time to speak with him, to regain the ground you seem to have lost."

"I doubt not I'll have the chance to speak with him again ere long," she said dryly.

"Oh, so? He'll be some months in France, you know."

"Mayhap."

If he even went! Ian had been so stubborn, so adamant about refusing to barter his freedom for hers last night. Surely by now he would have seen that she was serious. Impatient to get back to him, Madeline straightened and nodded dismissal to Catherine.

"I'll speak to the maid about the garderobe, lady, after I rest a bit. If you see my serving woman, please tell her not to disturb me."

"Humph! That one! You have no fear she'll disturb you. I saw her slipping out to the stables with the one called Ralf. I misdoubt she'll be lifting her skirts for him ere long, if she has not already."

Madeline escorted Catherine to the door, declining to confirm the fact that Gerda had indeed lifted her skirts for Ralf, several times. Madeline hadn't quite believed it when the maid casually let fall that she was taken with the man-at-arms. Gerda, who was half again as stout as Ralf was lean! She'd laughed at Madeline's openmouthed astonishment, and said that he wasn't so lean between the legs, not by any man's measure—no, nor any woman's, either.

At least Madeline knew Gerda would be well occupied for the next few hours.

Closing the door behind Catherine, she slid the iron bolt home, retrieved the basket of foodstuffs she had hidden from the other woman's prying eyes and headed for the narrow, winding tower stairs.

Once again Ian was sitting with his back to the wall, one leg drawn up. The chain was long enough for him to rest an arm across his knee if he raised the other arm a bit. Madeline saw with relief that there were no new bloodstains on the bandages she'd wrapped around his wrists.

His linen shirt gaped open, the ties undone, revealing tufts of golden chest hair. Black wool braies hugged his hips and showed clearly the delineation of muscle in his thighs. He'd run a hand through his hair, Madeline saw, dislodging the dried blood that had matted it to his skull earlier. He looked so different from the knight she was used to seeing. Less refined. More primitive. Even in chains, he emanated a raw male strength that made Madeline swallow.

Assuming a brisk air of assurance, she entered the small cell and crossed to stand beside him. "Well, my lord, are you ready now to make your ransom?"

He took his time replying, raking her first with a cool glance that left her skin tingling. "I've told you, you'll get no ransom from me."

"You've had time to reflect. Surely you can see that I'm determined in this."

When he didn't answer, she tapped one slippered foot on the stones. "Don't think, because I tended to your wrists, that I'm weakhearted. I won't let you free, Ian, not until you accede to my demands."

"I think you many things, Madeline, but not weakhearted."

The tapping stopped. "Do you start the insults once again?"

"Nay, I'm done with insults. What's in the basket? I hope you brought something more than those stale crusts of bread and old cheese you left earlier. My belly's doing a jig with my backbone."

Eyeing him in some exasperation, Madeline set the basket on the floor and pushed it within his reach.

"You *are* a captive, you know. I had not planned to feed you a banquet."

"You also said that you didn't intend me to starve." He pulled out a cold breast of squab, grimacing. "I hope there's more than this puny thing in here."

Madeline watched with one brow raised as he demolished the bird. His strong white teeth made quick work of the tiny bones and succulent meat.

"You need not stand on ceremony," he said between bites. "Sit down."

"Thank you, my lord." Dripping with false sweetness, she tucked her skirts under her and sank to the floor while Ian poked through the basket in search of more sustaining fare.

The sense of unreality that had plagued Madeline earlier returned in full force. This was not going at all as she planned. In her wildest dreams, she would never have imagined herself sitting on the floor of Ian's cell while he devoured a basket of food, for all the world as though they were on a picnic. She studied his face for some sign that this incarceration was wearing on him. She saw none, except the golden bristles on his lean cheeks and the angry bruise that still darkened his temple.

"Ah, this is more like it." He pulled out a thick, savory pasty and leaned back against the wall, sinking his teeth into the crusty mincemeat pie.

"I don't know how you can eat like that," she said crossly. She'd not been able to force down a single bite.

He chewed in a leisurely manner, then swallowed. "Feeling a bit unsettled, are you? I would be, too, were I in the fix you're in."

"I? I, in a fix? You have it wrong, sir. You're the one in chains."

"But I won't be in chains for long, and you will still have to deal with me when I am out of them."

"If you keep making threats like that, you may never be out of them!"

His deep blue eyes, screened by gold-tipped lashes, swept her face. "Here, have some of this pasty," he offered. "'Twill improve your mood."

Madeline hesitated, then reached out for the bit of pie.

That's it, Ian urged her silently. Take it! Imperceptibly his muscles tightened, like a great cat's just before it springs.

"Nay." She sighed and dropped her hand into her lap. "I could not swallow a bite."

The flaky crust disintegrated under his fingers.

She raised her lids, and Ian was startled to see the mossy eyes gleaming with laughter behind their fringe of thick, black lashes.

"I thought as much! You offered that as bait, did you not?"

"Think you so?" He tried to shrug aside the disappointment lancing through him.

"Aye, I do," she replied, grinning. "'Twas just such a trick as John was wont to play on me when we were young."

Ian discovered he liked her gloating as little as he liked the sound of another man's name on her lips. His own lips twisted. "Ah, yes. The king's son. Another of your... friends."

The laughter faded from her eyes, and she gave a cool nod. "My especial friend."

Ian shifted on the hard stone floor, causing iron to rattle again iron. "You make no bones about it, do you?"

"No. I never have."

He had no answer for that. There was none, he decided grimly.

She pursed her lips for a moment, studying his set face, then shook her head. "I don't know why I do this, but I'll tell you this once, and once only. There's naught between John and me except the friendship you sneer at."

He wanted to believe her. The Lord help him, he wanted to. Seeing her sitting on the stone floor with her robes puddled around her and tendrils of soft brown hair escaping her braids to curl about her face, Ian wanted nothing so much as to believe her. He hesitated, not trusting his own instincts anymore where this woman was concerned.

"Last night I believed you when you gave your pledge, and I loosed your chains," she said softly. "Can you not do the same for me?"

"'Tis not so much that I disbelieve you," Ian began. "'Tis just—"

She cut him off with an angry little wave of one hand. "'Tis just that you prefer to believe instead all those who delight in whispering about me."

"Nay, Madeline, don't put words in my mouth."

"Then what?"

"If you want the truth, lady, I don't believe a man and a woman can be friends in the manner you suggest."

She blinked, taken aback by his response. "Why-ever not?"

"'Tis unnatural."

"Unnatural? Unnatural!" She frowned, then shot him an indignant glare. "What, do you think I engaged in...in perversions? With one who has been like a brother to me since we were children!"

Christ's blood, was she really so naive? Was this the practiced lady of the king's court? The same one who dangled men at her sleeve like trophies captured in battle?

"Nay, woman. I say simply that whatever you and the king's son may have been to each other when you were children, he is now a man. John doesn't want to be friends with you," he said bluntly, "any more than I do. You are not made for friendship, Madeline."

Color flooded her cheeks. "Am I not? What am I made for, then? A good rut? A hard futter in a soft mattress?"

Ian swore, savagely. "Do not misconstrue my words."

Her eyes glittered like the green panes in a stained-glass window when the sun struck full upon them.

"Hah! How could I misconstrue them? Tell me, then, in your own words, what it is I'm made for. Tell me, if you dare."

"Loose these chains," he said softly, "and I will show you."

Her head snapped back, and she sucked in a swift breath. "It always comes down to that between us, does it not, my lord?"

He would not lie to her. "Aye, Madeline, it does. I want you, and well you know it. I did not take you when last I was at Cragsmore, because of my loyalty to Will and the fact that I would not abuse a woman in my keeping." His eyes burned into hers. "But I feel no such restraints now. Now, these chains are all that keep me from you."

Madeline paced her bedchamber, the skirts of her linen shift swirling about her ankles. 'Twas late, well past midnight. Ian's stolen supper sat in a basket on the table, catching her glance each time she made another turn about the room. She'd not been able to bring herself to face him again this night.

She'd decided to let him go hungry, to let him stew in his dank little cell. She'd even disrobed and taken down her hair, telling herself that she would sleep. She had to sleep. She needed her wits about her when she faced him again. But sleep wouldn't come, of course. After tossing and turning, Madeline had finally thrown the covers aside and begun to pace.

Outside her chamber, thunder rumbled. An occasional flash of lightning illuminated the narrow, slitted windows. The turbulence without matched the tumult within, Madeline thought wryly. Her fingers closed about the iron keys clutched in one hand.

What was she going to do about her captive? For two days now had she kept him. And two long, endless nights. Yet still Ian refused to accede to her wishes. He was too proud, too stubborn. Too damned pigheaded to barter his freedom for hers.

She tightened her fist, feeling the uneven edges of the keys cut into the flesh of her palm. How had she gotten herself into such a coil? How had her plan gone so awry? She'd truly caged a beast. She could not tame it, and now dared not release it.

He would take her, he'd vowed. Her heart tripped, then sped up again. Mayhap she should just go down to the cell, unlock his shackles, and be done with it. Let him exact his vengeance and be gone. A shiver raced down her spine, and Madeline tried to tell herself it was fear. Or disgust, that he would use her so. Furious at the sudden tightening of her loins, she paced even faster.

Nay, she could not do it. She could not give herself to him, much as her secret inner being wanted her to. Did she surrender herself to him, she'd never see outside Cragsmore's walls again. At least not in this lifetime.

Sweet Virgin, how was she to—?

A scratching at her chamber door, barely heard over the grumble of thunder, stopped Madeline in midstride. Her heart thudding, she stared at the door. The scratching came again, accompanied Gerda's soft call.

"'Tis me, mistress."

Madeline didn't answer.

"I see the light betwixt the cracks, lady. Be ye ill?" Gerda's voice sharpened with concern. "Is it yer woman's flow that keep you awake? Ye know ye always need a posset when your monthlies comes."

Jesu! Madeline swept across the room and pulled the bolt. The maid stumbled in. Her brown eyes searched Madeline's face.

"Be ye all right?"

"Aye, I'm all right. What are you doing roaming about the halls so late?"

"I couldn't sleep. Nor could ye, I see..."

Her words trailed off as her brown eyes flickered toward the table. When she spied the woven basket, filled with thick slabs of bread and a joint of boar meat, her frown deepened. Planting both hands on well-padded hips, she faced her mistress.

"What's wrong? Ye barely swallowed a morsel at supper, yet have enow here to feed two good-size men."

While Madeline struggled to find an answer, Gerda found her own. Her eyes rounded to huge saucers. She swung around to stare at the rumpled bed covers, then peered into the shadows of the solar.

"Be he here?" she whispered.

"He?" Madeline squeaked.

"Is he in the solar?"

She shook her head helplessly.

Gerda's brown eyes reproached her. "Ye can trust me, mistress, ye know ye can."

"Gerda..."

"'Tis all right, lady. I won't betray ye. Nay, nor Sir Guy."

"Sir Guy!" Madeline sputtered in surprise. "You... you think 'tis Sir Guy I have in here?"

"He's not the one I thought ye'd take to yer bed, but I understand. He's a handsome rogue, to be sure."

"Gerda," Madeline said faintly, "I don't have Sir Guy here."

"Ach, o' course ye do. Did ye not tell Ralf to lead his horse away in the dark of night? Why would you do so, except to make Lord Ian think him gone? Not that Sir Ian would know, of course, since he left without speaking to a soul, riding off as stiff and silent as a corpse. Who else could ye have here, except Sir..."

Her words trailed off. Her mouth sagged open, until she much resembled the stuffed carp that had been served for dinner earlier.

"Nay, lady!"

"Nay, Gerda!"

The denials burst from mistress and maid simultaneously. They stared at one another, consternation writ clear across one face, astonishment across the other.

"Never say 'tis Lord Ian ye have in here!"

"Aye," Madeline admitted, knowing there was no help for it.

"I though 'twas strange that none saw him leave! Well, well!"

"He's... he's been here two days now."

"No!" She glanced around the bedchamber, honest bewilderment replacing her initial amazement. "Why in the name of all the saints be ye sneaking about like this? Anyone could see 'twas naught but a matter of time until ye fell to it, as hot as ye both are for each other."

"*What?*"

"None would fault ye, mistress, he's that much a man," the maid offered. "You being his ward 'an all, 'tis no great surprise."

"I am *not* bedding with Sir Ian! Nor am I...hot for him!"

"Hah! A body has to stand well clear when the two of ye are together, so many sparks do fly."

Lady Catherine was right, Madeline thought indignantly. 'Twas obvious the mistress had been far too familiar and lenient with the maid.

"I'm not bedding Sir Ian," she said in her most haughty manner. "I'm holding him to ransom."

Once more Madeline was reminded of the fish that had graced the dinner table. Gerda's mouth popped opened, then closed, then opened once more.

"Yer holding him to ransom?" she repeated weakly. Her stunned gaze roamed the room, and she dipped slightly to peer beneath the wooden bedstead.

"Oh, for—I'm not keeping the man under my bed!" Madeline unclenched her fist and held it out, palm up, to show the iron keys on their leather thong. "He's in the small storeroom, the one in the tower stairwell."

Gerda crossed herself twice in rapid succession. "God help us."

The stiffness went out of Madeline's spine. "He'll have to," she muttered morosely. "I know not how to get out of this damnable coil."

At the maid's horrified stare, Madeline's shoulders slumped.

"I have Lord Ian caged and chained, and now don't know what to do with him. The bloody pigheaded fool won't pay the ransom I demand. I couldn't even bring myself to go back down there to take him his supper. I get naught but insults every time I set foot within the room."

"Insults?"

"He's . . . not best pleased with the situation."

Gerda's most constant quality, the one that had kept her at Madeline's side through years of torn veils and boots that trod unwittingly on her mistress's hems, edged aside her fear.

"He has no cause to give ye insult!" she declared loyally.

Madeline sighed. "He thinks he does. He calls me a jade, and a strumpet, and is sure I want only to go back to Lord John's bed, when all I want is to win free of this damnable place."

Gerda's plump lips firmed. She, of all people, knew how little her mistress deserved the slander that had been heaped on her over the years. Bristling in Madeline's defense, she gave a little snort.

"If that isn't like a man! He calls ye names acause he thinks ye do with another what he wants to do with ye himself!"

She had the right of it there, Madeline thought.

Stepping forward, Gerda plucked the keys from Madeline's lax fingers. "Here, give me these. Ye'll not have to deal with him no more, mistress. I'll see to the man's needs. And after I'm done with him, he'll beg to pay his ransom and gain release!"

"Nay, Gerda." Madeline stopped her as she turned toward the table. "You must not involve yourself in this. I'll not have you incur his wrath. This is between me and Lord Ian."

"Hush, now. I'm not afeared of him. Besides, he's chained, didn't ye say?"

At the determined glint in the maid's eyes, Madeline felt herself weakening. She'd been strung as tight as a bowstring for the past two days and nights, and she wanted nothing so much as to ease the tension that racked her.

"Just get yerself back to bed. I'll take the food to him, and give him a piece of my mind. Mayhap then he'll be more amenable when you go to see him in the morning."

Mayhap he would, Madeline thought, sagging down onto the bed.

The sound of the maid's boots echoed briefly on the stone stairs. As if in counterpoint, a long roll of thunder filled the chamber.

Mayhap 'twas her own presence that goaded Ian to unreasonableness. If she didn't go to him again until morning, mayhap he'd change his tune.

She heard the faint scrape of the wooden door being pulled open.

Madeline willed herself to relax. She knew Ian wouldn't take out his wrath on Gerda. That was reserved for her alone. The maid was but loyal to her mistress, after all, and he couldn't fault her for that.

With a small smile, Madeline remembered Ian's exasperation during the journey north, when she had insisted on riding while Gerda made the trip in the luxurious litter. He could have ordered the maid to ride, as well, and much increased their speed, but he had not.

And that time when Gerda had fallen into the stream, he'd ordered the troop to halt while she changed her wet clothes. He'd cursed the maid's clumsiness, as Madeline herself had many times, but he'd not punished her for—

Holy Mary, Mother of God!

Madeline shot off the bed like a bolt loosed from a crossbow. Fear slammed against her ribs as she raced for the stairs.

How could she have forgotten Gerda's tendency to trip and spill and tear! How could she have failed to warn her to stay well away from the reach of Ian's chains!

Lightning split the sky. Blinding white light blazed against the narrow window slits, followed by a crack of thunder.

Over the furious roaring in Madeline's ears came the sound of a startled shriek.

"Mistress!"

Iron clanked against iron.

"Aieee! Mistress!"

Her heart in her mouth, Madeline shoved open the storeroom door—and saw she was too late.

Chapter Eleven

'Twas a scene such as she had never envisioned in her worst nightmares, one that would live in her mind forever.

Gerda hopped about like a scalded chicken, the woven basket clutched in her left hand, while the right flapped wildly in the air. A heavy iron cuff banded one ankle. The other, empty cuff was attached to the ringbolt and clanged and clattered with each frantic step.

"Flee, mistress!" she screeched. "Flee!"

Ian was halfway between Gerda and the door. He held the keys clenched tight in one fist. A feral light gleamed in his blue eyes, and his lips curled in a smile that raised the hairs on the back of Madeline's neck.

She didn't stop to think.

She didn't try to soothe the savage beast.

She whirled and ran.

He caught her on the third step. His hand snagged the hem of her shift, yanking her to a stop. Madeline twisted and grabbed the cloth, tugging frantically with both hands against his hold.

"Oh, no, you little witch. You're not getting away this time."

He wrapped the fabric around his fist, once, twice.

She pulled with all her might, her feet scrabbling for purchase on the slippery stones, made wet by the rain that now pelted in through the open windows.

He wrapped the cloth one more turn. Relentlessly, inexorably, he brought her closer.

Madeline arced away, panting. Her foot slid out from under her, and she landed painfully on her hip.

He leaned over her, one hand still fisted in the linen shift that now rode halfway up her thighs, the other planted on the stone step behind her head. He was so close Madeline could smell the musky odor of the cell on his skin, see the golden bristles that bearded his cheeks and the mottled, fading colors of the bruise to his temple.

She flattened herself against the stone steps.

He leaned closer still, until the broad planes of his chest pressed against her breasts.

"Aieee!" Gerda's shriek bounced off the narrow stone walls. "Harm my mistress, and yer a dead man! Lady! Lady!"

The edge of a step cut into Madeline's buttocks, another pressed at her back. "No, Ian," she panted. "No! Not here! Not like this! Don't do this!"

Chains banged against stone. "Lady!" A long screech filled the night.

Ian flung a look back over his shoulder at the open door. Madeline knew that Gerda's cries would not rouse anyone. The walls were too thick, the stairs too close, for sound to carry beyond her own solar, just a few yards away. But she used the momentary distraction to shove against his chest with both hands.

He didn't move, not so much as an inch. Until he chose to. Then he took both her wrists in one hand and used the other to push himself up, yanking her up with him.

"Ian . . ."

Whatever she would have said was lost in another ear-rattling yell.

Swearing, Ian hauled Madeline back down the few steps and reached for the storeroom door. The heavy panel slammed shut, cutting Gerda off in midscreech.

Without another word, he turned and headed back up the stairs. Madeline stumbled after him, her wrists still caught in his iron hold. He strode through her solar into the bedchamber and flung her on the bed.

Like a cat, Madeline twisted to her knees and scrambled backward, toward the far side of the bed.

"Don't try to run from me," he warned her, his voice low and dangerous. "Even if you should make it as far as the door, I'll bring you back. This time we settle what is between us."

He grabbed the hem of his shirt and pulled it over his head in one quick movement. His skin was golden in the flickering candlelight, in stark contrast to the white linen that bandaged both wrists. When his hand moved to the ties of his chausses, Madeline swallowed convulsively.

"You would rape me, then?"

He jerked at the strings. "There'll be no rape."

"You expect me to...to just lay here and let you use me?"

"Nay, I expect you to show the same idiotic courage you showed when you unlocked my chains."

"What?"

"You gambled greatly, Madeline, and lost. Now you'll pay your debts."

He loosed the ties and shoved his chausses and braies down over long, muscled flanks. Madeline took one look at his erection, then moaned and hunkered down to bury her face in the coverlet.

Naked, rampant, and pulsing with the knowledge that he would have the woman he now wanted with a need so primal, so raw, that he burned with it, Ian strode to the bed. He stood for a moment, studying the head pressed against the wool-stuffed mattress and the rounded bottom that stuck up in the air.

"Madeline, look at me."

She moaned again, the sound muffled by the covers.

"Look at me."

Her head moved from side to side. As did her rear. Ian's loins tightened painfully as the linen shift stretched tight across the fullness of her bottom cheeks, shaping them for his eyes to feast upon. His palms felt slick with the need to stroke that curved flesh.

"Lift your head, Madeline. Unless you wish me to mount you from behind," he added after a moment.

That got her attention. She jerked upright. "Ian, we cannot do this!"

We, he noted with a rush of satisfaction, not *you.* He reached for the ties that held her shift at the neck. Her hands came up to cover his, holding them still.

"Think of Will," she pleaded.

"'Tis too late for that."

"Think of how you swore that you would not abuse a woman in your keeping!"

"'Tis too late for that, as well."

His fingers pulled at the strings. "At this moment I can think of nothing and no one but you, Madeline."

The ties came loose.

Her hands fell slowly to her sides.

She would not fight him, Ian saw with a leap of fierce male triumph. Although it caused white lines of strain to bracket his mouth, he resisted the urge to throw her on her back and have her then and there. He'd waited too long for this moment to end it with a quick thrust and a hurried spend. Instead, he set about turning her reluctant acquiescence into willing participation.

Near sweating with the effort, he schooled his hands to gentleness and brushed the wet linen off her shoulders. It peeled down to drape across her breasts, catching on the upturned peaks. Ian followed its path with the back of one hand, his knuckles caressing the creamy flesh. Taking hold of the linen, he drew it down farther.

Her breasts were small and proud, he saw, like Madeline herself. His palm cupped one rounded mound, shaping it, claiming it. His other hand slid under her heavy, silken mane to cradle the back of her neck. He drew her forward until she was stretched up on her knees, but inches from him.

"Put your hands on me."

Biting her lip at the low, growled order, Madeline stared up at his eyes. In the flickering candlelight, they were a deep, dark blue, lit from within by the heat of desire. They willed her to lift her hands, to take an active part in what was to come.

"Put your hands on me, Madeline. I would feel your touch, as you'll feel mine."

She had no choice, she told herself. The time for reckoning between them had come, whether she willed it or nay. And, God help her, she willed it. She willed it with all her soul.

Her hands shook as she raised them. Her fingers trembled as she laid them lightly on his forearms, just above the makeshift bandages. A thousand sensations bombarded her senses at the feel of his flesh under hers. His skin was warm, the golden hairs that furred it crinkly. Under the layer of supple flesh, muscles banded, flexed. She slid her fingers along his forearms, over the crease of his elbows, up his biceps. Their smooth, rounded shape tensed under her fingertips.

The only sound that disturbed the thundering stillness between them were Gerda's faint, muffled cries and the splat of rain against the stones. And their mingled breathing, harsh and fast and ragged.

Ian was on fire with the need to have her. He stepped closer to the bed, using his hold on the back of her neck to draw her up against him, until his rigid shaft pressed against her belly. He closed his eyes briefly at the sensation, willing himself to control. Muscles corded with the effort it took to hold back. Tendons strained.

In the midst of her own mounting need, Madeline could yet marvel at his restraint. When she imagined their joining, during the dark, secret hours of the night, she'd imagined it hard and fast and furious. She'd thought that the tension that had built between her and Ian would explode into mindless passion. Never, in all her private dreams, had she thought that he would hold back and let her explore the contours of his body with her hands, nor allow her own desire to fan itself into flames.

She felt him pressed against her from knee to breast. His rod probed her stomach, leaping when her muscles clenched in involuntary reaction. Her hands glided up, across his shoulders, measuring their breadth. An old scar had left a ridge of flesh along his collarbone. She felt its roughness, and ached to kiss it. She moved her hands upward, tunneling her fingers in the hair at the back of his neck.

Her head seemed too heavy for her neck, and lolled back into the support of his warm, callused palm. He slid his thumb along the side of her jaw, then used it to tilt her head back farther.

Ian sucked in a swift, hard breath at the sight of her flushed face. Her lips were parted, her eyes were wide and gleaming with green fire.

"Ian..." she began hesitantly.

"Nay, Madeline, the time for talk between us is past. Now there is only this."

He bent his head and took her lips. This kiss held none of the anger that had marked her in the gardens at Kenilworth, none of the hurt that had seared her when she'd taunted him before he left her at Cragsmore. This kiss was hard and sure and hungry, the kiss of a man who would have the woman he held. Madeline surrendered without conscious thought, wrapping her arms around his neck to bring herself even closer into his body. The golden whiskers scraped her chin, adding to the needles of fire that shot through her.

She strained against him, her own need spinning, spiraling. His hand left her neck, the other deserted her breast. They planed down her sides, over the swell of her hips, and cupped her bottom. He lifted her, crushing her against his hardness.

She was panting as fast as he when they tumbled to the bed. Her hands helped lift the wet, tangled shift and draw it over her head. Her hips shifted and fitted themselves to his.

When he bent his head and took her engorged nipple in his mouth, Madeline arched under him. He was less restrained now, rougher, more urgent. He nipped at the tender peak, using one hand to plump and push her flesh. His tongue laved the stinging little hurt, adding its rasp to the sensations streaking through her breast.

She didn't need his low, husky order to open herself. Her legs had already drawn up of their own accord, cradling his lean flanks. She hooked one ankle around his calf, drawing him even closer.

"Ian!" She half cried, half moaned his name, and arched under him.

"No," he growled. "Not yet, sweeting. Not yet."

Fierce, unrelenting need gripped him, but Ian forced himself to put some space between them. Just enough to ease his hand between her smooth belly and his. Enough to slide his palm down her mound and probe the slick, hot flesh at her center.

Parting the folds that guarded her womanhood, he explored her satiny core. Using one finger, then two, he stretched and primed her. His thumb rubbed the hard nubbin at the jointure of her legs until she gasped and cried his name again.

Clenching his jaw against his own desire, Ian continued to stroke and thrust his fingers deep within her. He knew that if he mounted her now, he'd spend himself long before he brought her to pleasure. Only after she had groaned, far back in her throat, and strained upward, convulsing around his fingers, did he roll atop her shuddering body and sink himself to the root.

Bracing himself on both elbows, he buried his hands in her hair and anchored her. His hips slammed forward. Hers rose to meet them.

The fire between them fanned once more into flames, and consumed them both. Fisting his hands in her hair, Ian bent his head and ravaged her lips while his seed pumped into her.

After they had sprawled, spent and lifeless, for what seemed like hours, the sparks smoldered once again. This time the taking was slower, the giving more generous.

And then, when a cool, fresh breeze blew away the last of the rain, the embers glowed once more.

Drained and replete, Ian lay in the wide bed and watched the blackness outside the shuttered windows gray with the coming dawn. Madeline sprawled at his side, one arm outflung across his chest, her head a dead weight on his shoulder.

He'd have to leave, he knew, and soon. 'Twould take two days and a night of hard riding to reach Southampton, where his men waited. He only hoped that his armor and his sorrel stallion, bred more for speed and stamina than the barrel-chested destriers he took into battle, awaited him at the deserted farmhouse where Madeline said Guy Blackhair had promised to leave them.

At the thought of the rogue knight, Ian felt his languor slip away. He glanced down at the face so close to his own, seeing only the crescent of black lashes against one cheek and the tip of a short, saucy nose. Stiffly he lifted his hand to brush a tangled strand of glossy brown hair from her forehead. His hand stilled when he saw the rash of red where his whiskers had marked her.

She murmured in her sleep, her lips pursing in irritation at the disturbance, and snuggled closer into his body warmth.

Had she lain with Guy Blackhair? Ian wondered. Had she given herself to him with the same abandon she'd shown last night? Had she moaned and writhed under him when he plumbed her depths? Had she panted and arched and cried his name just before the muscles at her core tightened and she spasmed with her release?

Ian waited for the surge of rage such imaginings should bring. But instead of a wash of white-hot, burning jealousy he felt only cold, steely determination. Whomever she had lain with before, whatever she'd been before, Madeline was now his. She would touch no other man the way she'd touched him, kiss no one else.

Ian had a score to even with Guy Blackhair, and he would settle it in his own way, at his own time. But for now he had to rejoin the world he'd left so abruptly two—nay, three days ago. He uncurled his arm from the smooth shoulders resting so close to his.

"Madeline, rouse yourself."

She mumbled and flattened her nose against his chest, burrowing deeper into his warmth.

"Wake, sweeting," he insisted. "I must go."

At the shift of muscles under her cheek, her deep, steady breathing hitched for a moment, then resumed its rhythm.

Jesu, the woman slept the sleep of the dead. Ian didn't know whether to be more flattered or amused. He'd suspected from her wan looks and the shadows under her eyes that she'd not rested easy during the long hours she held him in chains. He knew, moreover, that their wild couplings had drained her of every ounce of strength she possessed. The last time he'd taken her, she'd been more than half-asleep, and she'd protested grumpily. At first.

To his considerable surprise, his shaft stirred at the memory. For a moment he contemplated rolling over and burying himself once more in her soft, unresisting flesh. He glanced at the narrow window across from the bed to judge how much time was left until the dawn.

Not enough, he decided with a wry twist of his lips. He suspected 'twould take far longer for him to gain release this time than it had before, as depleted as he was.

Easing himself out from under her weight, Ian stood and stretched. By the saints, it felt good not to have the weight of chains on his wrists. He smiled briefly, wondering how the doughty maid fared. Her muffled shouts had died away sometime after he and Madeline tumbled to the bed. Well, he'd best go find out.

He pulled on his clothes, grimacing at the odor that clung to them, and cast the lady one last glance, then turned and headed for the stairs.

The storeroom door creaked in protest when he opened it, but not enough to disturb the maid. She sat on the floor, her back to the stone wall, her plump chins folded one atop the other as she snored. The basket was still clutched in one hand, although the foodstuffs had fallen out and lay scattered around the cell. From the look of them, they'd provided a banquet for the rats.

Ian shut the door behind them, not wanting her screeches to jerk Madeline into wakefulness. As if they could!

Hunkering down on his heels beside the maid, he shook her shoulder.

She started, her brown eyes wide and unfocused. "Wh—wh—?"

When she recognized him, however, recognition, fear and anger flooded all at once into her brown eyes. In a swift, sure movement that would have done a well-seasoned warrior proud, she swung the basket up and whacked Ian on the side of the head.

He grunted, more surprised than pained, and rocked back on his heels.

"Ye bluidy bastard, if ye have harmed my mistress, I'll bash yer head in!" All thoughts of rank and the consequences of her actions forgotten, she lunged at him, the basket swinging.

Ian toppled backward under her assault. "Hold, woman!"

"I'll hold!" she yelled, thumping him yet again. "I'll hold ye till the entire castle wakes and hears me shouting!"

Christ's toes, if Ian didn't disarm this rotund little amazon, and soon, he'd soon be back in chains.

"Hold!" he roared, and grasped her flailing arm. Without the basket pounding him about the head and ears, he managed to get up, bringing her with him.

"Jesu, if ever I need fighters to augment my ranks, I'll send for you and your mistress. The two of you could take down King Philip's entire army."

"Niver mind yer armies and fighters! How fares my lady?"

Ian stared down at the red, round face and snapping brown eyes. "She was asleep when I left her," he answered truthfully.

"Did ye harm her?"

That one he couldn't answer quite as readily. "What was done, was done of her free will."

"Harrumph!" She glared at him a few moments longer, and then the fight seemed to go out of her. She looked tired and rumpled and disgruntled. "Ach, well, 'twas bound to happen sooner or late, as hot as ye were for each other. Aye, and 'tis time she tasted a bit o' lust in her life," she added, as if to herself.

Ian had no time to probe that interesting remark further.

"Here," he said, tossing her the keys. "You may release yourself and tend to your lady after I'm gone. Tell me where these stairs lead."

She set her lip mulishly.

"Come, wench, don't make me force it out of you. You'd best tell me the way out of this tower, or your lady will have to come up with some embarrassing explanations."

She eyed him for a moment longer. "The stairs lead directly from my lady's solar to the great hall, two floors below." She hesitated, then added, "The senior man-at-arms, Ralf, sleeps on a pallet just outside the door. He'll help you steal away."

If anyone had told Ian that he'd be creeping down a narrow, dank staircase to steal out of a keep that was, by rights, his to command, he would've laughed in his face. Or ordered a physician in to tend the poor fool's deranged mind. He shook his head in the darkness, wondering how in hell he'd come to such a pass.

The iron hinges grated when Ian eased open the door at the bottom of the stairs. He stood still and silent for long moments, letting his eyes adjust to the greater gloom of the hall. As the maid had said, a long, gaunt form was rolled in a pallet just a yard or two away.

Ian knelt on one knee in the rushes beside him and placed a hard palm over his lips. Ralf grunted, then came swiftly awake. His eyes widened when he saw whose hand was clamped across his mouth.

"Outside," Ian hissed, "and quietly."

The storm that had thundered above them the night before had washed the bailey clean. The odors of a busy, crowded keep were missing. No scent of manure gathered from the stables lingered on the air. No trace of kitchen smoke drifted across the yards. There was only the crisp, clean bite of cool morning.

As soon as they had gained the shelter of the stone stables, Ralf swung to face Ian.

"How did you leave my lady?"

"You'd do better to worry how I will leave you, man," Ian retorted. He wondered in some exasperation whether he'd have to fight off another of Madeline's loyal retainers. "Were you part of this mad scheme?" he asked harshly.

Ralf met his look without flinching. "I suspected that something was afoot when she told me to take Sir Guy's horse to a tumbledown farmhouse. I knew for sure when I went back the next day and saw your own horse and armor left there."

Relieved though he was that Guy hadn't absconded with his precious mail shirt and sword, Ian nevertheless felt a surge of anger at this man.

"Yet when you found my gear, you did not sound the alarm, nor alert anyone else."

"Nay, my lord."

"I could have you hanged for that."

"Aye," he said simply.

Ian decided that his hours with Madeline must have turned his brains to mush, as well as his manhood. He knew he ought to gut the man where he stood, but could not summon the will for it. Shaking his head in disgust, he let him off with a promise.

"I have not the time to attend to it now, but you may be assured that when I return you will pay a suitable penalty. In the meantime...continue to give your lady as true service as you have done so far."

"Aye, my lord."

"Come, let's get the horses saddled and devise some excuse for the guards to lower the portcullis as soon as the dawn breaks. I must retrieve my gear and get myself to war."

Chapter Twelve

"He gave you no message for me? None at all?"

Gerda sighed and twisted the thick skeins of Madeline's chestnut hair into a fat braid. "Nay, mistress, none at all, as I've told ye many times these past four days."

"But he must have given some indication of his intentions toward us . . . toward me."

"'Twill come," the maid predicted glumly. "Ye can't expect to treat a lord of his rank as ye did and not suffer fer it. We'll all suffer fer it, most like, in his own good time."

Madeline winced at an overhard tug, not sure it was entirely accidental. For all Gerda's fierce defense of her mistress the night of Ian's escape, in the cool light of day she'd had a few words to say about the folly of putting great lords in chains.

Taking the braid from her maid's hands, Madeline twisted it deftly into a coil and covered it with her second-best caul, a woven net of silver and gold threads that matched the embroidery on her honey-hued surcoat. Anchoring a silken veil in place with a circlet of silver, she rose and moved toward the wardrobe.

"We'd best hurry, or we'll be late for mass," she told the maid, declining to address Gerda's dire forebodings. In truth, she had little to counter them.

Flinging a light mantle over her shoulders, Madeline headed for the tower stairs. Halfway there, she stopped abruptly, and Gerda almost tripped over her heels. She muttered to the maid to watch her step and wheeled about. Since Ian's surreptitious departure, Madeline couldn't bring herself to use the narrow stairs that took her past the dank, airless storeroom. Ignoring Gerda's raised brows, she marched through the main bedchamber and out into the upper-story hall.

All through mass and the quick meal that followed, Madeline found it difficult to concentrate on the matters at hand. She mumbled automatic responses to the prayers and ignored Lady Catherine's whining complaints while they broke their fast with breads and ale, then took herself to the rear of the keep to oversee the replanting of the herb garden. Feeling the need to find some occupation for her hands, as well as her mind, she was soon on her knees beside the workers. While she dug in the soft composted earth and the tangy scent of mint and tansy seedlings teased her senses, one refrain kept running through her mind.

Sweet Mary, four days! Four whole days since he'd left! And nary a word to tell her what the consequences of her rash act might be. Both rash acts! Not only had she held the man in chains, but she'd given herself to him like the wanton he believed her to be.

At moments like this, when the sun shone bright and people chattered around her, Madeline could almost convince herself that she had imagined those desperate days when Ian was within that little cell. That those tumultuous hours after he'd won free were naught but a bad dream.

A dream, mayhap, her inner voice mocked, but not all bad. A slow heat rose in Madeline's cheeks at the memory of Ian's hands and mouth on her body. Even their last, languorous coupling, when she'd been too exhausted to do more than lie like a corpse and let him play with her, was enough to put her to the blush. The tender green of the garden dissolved, to be replaced in Madeline's mind by a dimly lit bedchamber and two sweat-slick bodies.

A wave of embarrassment washed over her as she remembered the way she had moaned and writhed under his skilled hands, for all the world like a seasoned strumpet. He could not know—and she would die rather than admit it—but she had never before felt a pleasure that could arch her back and curl her toes into the mattress. Nor had she ever known a man to hold back, as Ian had, until she had come to her own release. Even her first lord, as gentle as he'd been with her young innocence, had lacked either the skill or the stamina to hold himself in check. And in his eagerness, her second lord had all but spilled himself afore he got his braies off. But Ian had wrung responses from her she'd never dreamed she was capable of. Re-

sponses that shamed her and, she knew, damned her
in his eyes.

She sat back on her heels, wiping the back of a
grubby hand across her forehead. No wonder he'd
ridden off without a word. In a single night, she'd
proven the truth of all the rumors about her. He must
think she . . .

"My lady!"

Madeline blinked and looked up to find the little
page she'd raised from the kitchens standing before
her. His hair stuck straight up at the back of his tow-
head, and he almost danced from side to side in his
excitement.

"My lady, didn't you hear me? A troop approaches."

"What?"

"A troop approaches. They're almost to the gates
of the barbican. They wear Lord Ian's blue and
white."

With a rush of excitement, Madeline thrust herself
up and ran for the outer yard.

By the time she gained the wooden rampart that
circled the walls, the frantic flutter in her heart had
given way to more sober reflection. 'Twas not Ian, she
knew. He would have sailed for France by now. But
whoever approached bore his colors and, she didn't
doubt, word of her fate. She would now pay the price
for her madness in thinking she could barter for her
freedom.

For a wild moment, Madeline considered ordering
the knight beside her to refuse entry to the advancing

company. She could say, truthfully, that they'd had no warning of this troop's arrival and that this might be a ruse.

She dismissed the notion almost as soon as it occurred to her. 'Twould only delay the inevitable, and Madeline was not one to run from adversity. Still, her palms dampened as a lone knight detached himself from the main body of the mounted force and rode forward. When he drew up in front of the gate and pulled off his helm, Madeline gasped. There was no mistaking those bright golden curls.

"Will!"

Gathering her skirts, she rushed down the wooden stairs to greet him. The young knight dismounted awkwardly, using only his left hand. The right, she saw, was bound to his chest under his surcoat.

"Lady Madeline!" He swung around to greet her, a wide grin on his handsome face. When he caught full sight of her, the grin slipped. A look of dismay seized his features. "Lady? Are things so desperate here?"

"What?" Sweet Mother, what had he been told?

He gestured helplessly with his good arm. "When I rode up, I thought this a cheerless place, but that it should have such an effect on your bright beauty..." His voice trailed off.

Of a sudden Madeline realized that the picture she presented after her hours in the garden was far different from the sophisticated lady of his youthful fantasies. How strange, she thought ruefully. When the elder brother saw her tumbled in the bog and streaked with mud, the sight had filled him with lust. The

younger could scarce conceal his shock at seeing her
with dirt on her face. Pushing aside such traitorous
thoughts, Madeline gave a gay laugh.

"Cragsmore is beyond dismal, I'll agree, but this
dirt is come by honestly. I've been grubbing in the herb
garden."

He swallowed, obviously having difficulty recon-
ciling his ladylove with this earthier Madeline.

"Never mind about me," she said, smiling. "What
are you doing here? And what happened to your
arm?"

His grin crept back. "'Twas the damnedest bad
luck! I was helping load the war-horses on the trans-
ports when one of the stupid beasts took exception to
a swooping sea gull. It lashed out with a hoof and
caught me squarely in the arm. My sword arm, yet!
Ian said 'twas too bad I wasn't kicked in the head,
where it would've done less damage."

So Ian had made it to Southampton in time to take
ship with his men. Madeline didn't know whether she
was more relieved or piqued that her great scheme had
come to naught. Shrugging off her disquiet, she smiled
up at Will.

"So now you'll not be able to take part in the battles. How disappointing it must be for you to miss all
the fun."

"Aye, more than disappointing, but there's a good
side to the coin. It gave me the chance to see you
again."

"'Tis kind of you to stop here. Does . . . does Ian
know you come to Cragsmore?"

"He sent me."

"Ian? Sent you?"

"Aye." Will's grin widened. "He said that since I was so clumsy as to take myself out of the action, I might as well make myself useful. I'm here to escort you to Wyndham."

Madeline gaped at him. "To Wyndham?"

"Aye."

"To Wyndham?"

She felt like the veriest dolt, repeating herself so stupidly, but she couldn't believe what she was hearing.

"My brother charged me to tell you that he would accede to at least one of your demands, seeing as how you'd pleaded your case so passionately."

Hot color flooded Madeline's cheeks. "Oh, he did, did he?"

"I knew once you and Ian got to know each other better, you'd come to terms," Will continued, plainly in blessed ignorance of the true state of affairs. "You had but to smile upon him, I'm sure, to get him to realize this dreary keep is no place for one such as you."

Madeline's face burned when she thought of how much more she'd done than smile upon Ian.

"Is that what he told you, that we'd come to terms?" she managed stiffly.

"Nay, he said that things were yet unfinished between you." Will paused, and for a moment his eyes held a keenness that belied his youth. "It appears I have a rival for your affection in mine own brother, lady."

Madeline could've told him that it was not her affection his brother wanted, only her body. He'd made no secret of it, after all, nor pretended otherwise. But she couldn't bring herself to tell Will what had occurred, any more than Ian had been able to, apparently.

"You'll like Wyndham," Will assured her when she made no comment. "My mother, Lady Elizabeth, resides there."

"Does she know that I come?"

"Ian sent word to her. He said to tell you that she'll give you far closer company than Sir Thomas's wife. He . . . and I . . . wish our lady mother to know you."

Madeline suspected that this sudden turn of events had little to do with any desire on Ian's part for Lady Elizabeth to make her acquaintance. Rather, he must have realized Will would come to Cragsmore on his own. By charging his brother to take her to Wyndham, Ian was putting them both under his mother's watchful eye. Bleakly Madeline wondered if she was about to exchange one prison for another.

"I mislike rushing you, lady, but must ask you to—" he cast a quick eye over her hair and face "—to ready yourself and have your things packed as quickly as possible. If we leave within the hour, we might make Chester tonight, and raise Wyndham by week's end."

With much to occupy her mind, Madeline rode north beside Will at a steady pace along the ancient road laid out by the Romans. Gerda, grumbling at having been wrested from Ralf's arms, rode pillion behind one of the men.

Their route took them through the crags and valleys of the rugged Cumbrian Mountains. Never having ventured so far north, Madeline could only marvel at the uncompromising beauty of the terrain. 'Twas a place of sharp contrasts, this land of meres and mountains.

Like long inland seas, the huge meres nestled amid rocky peaks, the tallest in all of England. Tumbling streams and waterfalls fed hundreds of smaller tarns that sparkled like jewels flung by a careless hand across a misty gray-green landscape. Tall pines grew right down to water's edge, their greenery reflected in the still, silvered surfaces. Small villages clung to the steep mountain slopes and lined the shores, while hardy Herdwick sheep—thought to be the native sheep of Britain—grazed in almost vertical fields delineated by centuries old stone walls.

Wyndham was strategically located in the shadows of towering Skiddaw peak, close to the north shore of Derwentwater, a three-mile-long mere. A solid fortress built of blue-gray Lakeland stone, Wyndham had long served as a bulwark against marauding Scots. As Will proudly informed Madeline, the keep had withstood a long siege by King William, the Lion of Scotland, when he sided with King Henry's sons in their abortive rebellion some fifteen years ago and swept south to ravage the English countryside.

Of course, Will added with a grin, the raids were not all one-sided. Ian owed his Scots name to the blue-

eyed, fiery-haired lass his grandfather had taken in a
foray across the border. The widow had threatened to
geld the English warrior with his own dagger did he
dare to touch her without the blessing of the kirk, at
which point he'd carried her, kicking and cursing, to
the chapel and wed her forthwith.

As they passed through Wyndham's massive barbican and rode across the bridge over its broad moat,
Madeline well believed the keep could withstand any
siege. Crenellated towers stood strong and bold against
the sky, their clean lines and gray-blue hues a part of
the landscape itself. A well-tended outer bailey housed
stables and mews and dovecotes. A second gatehouse, at an off-angle from the first to prevent a
straight line of attack by besiegers, opened onto a
cobbled inner bailey. The keep itself was built around
a flagged central courtyard, which Madeline guessed
would offer welcome protection from the rough ex-
tremes of the Cumbrian weather.

'Twas in this central courtyard that Lady Elizabeth
met them. She came hurrying out of an arched doorway, a generous smile on her lovely face. Behind her,
what appeared to be the entire population of the castle spilled out to welcome the lord's brother.

"Will! I had not thought to see you afore you took
ship with the king!" Lady Elizabeth called in greeting. "What do you here?"

Almost as soon as the words were out, she caught
sight of Will's bound arm. The young knight dismounted and stood in good-natured patience while
Lady Elizabeth exclaimed over his injury.

"Didn't you get Ian's message?" he asked, when she was satisfied he was not mortally injured.

"Nay, no courier's arrived in a week or more."

It wasn't an uncommon occurrence for messengers to be waylaid by the brigands who preyed on travelers or to meet with some other disaster. Madeline hoped no harm had befallen Ian's man, but wasn't sorry that his missive hadn't arrived. There would be time enough for Lady Elizabeth to discover the reasons Ian had sent her to Wyndham.

"I'm sorry you had no word of our coming," Will said with his engaging smile. "I've brought you a guest."

"So I see." Lady Elizabeth sent a friendly nod in Madeline's direction. "Bring the lady forward, so I might meet her."

Will strode back and reached up with his good arm to assist Madeline from the saddle. When her booted feet touched the cobbles, she drew in a deep breath, then stepped toward the curious circle of faces.

"God grant you good greeting, Lady Elizabeth. I have heard much of you from William. I am Madeline, widow to the baron de Courcey and, of late, to Sir Arnould of Berchester."

Like a petal falling from a withered rose, the older woman's smile faded. After a long moment, she acknowledged the greeting with a stiff nod.

"I have heard much of you, as well, Lady Madeline."

* * *

Ian propped a foot on a gunwale and stared across the swells of the sea. A thick, wet fog hovered a few feet above the rolling waves, blocking all sight of the horizon. For two days now had they lain off the coast of Normandy, waiting for the fog to lift so that the shipmasters could warp their way into the quays of Cherbourg.

By now, Ian mused, Will should have Madeline safe at Wyndham. He could picture her amid his boisterous family, charming them all, holding his vassals in thrall, much as she was used to doing at the king's court. He should have sent her to Wyndham when he first took her in wardship, Ian admitted to himself, ashamed of the anger that had led him to isolate one such as Madeline at Cragsmore. Mayhap if he had not immured her in such bleakness, she might not have been driven to such desperate measures as to try to hold him to ransom.

He glanced down at the angry red marks that still ringed his wrists and smiled slowly, wickedly. Nay, he could summon no regret for her rash, impetuous act. Although he'd cursed her during those hours he was in chains, and sworn dire revenge, he now looked back on those days and nights with as much wry amusement as chagrin.

Not for the first time since he'd met up with Will in Southampton, he wondered if he should have told the lad what had occurred during those lost days at Cragsmore. At first, there'd been no time. Ian had arrived at the shipyards just as the horses were being loaded. Worried at his brother's delay, Will had sent riders back along the route to look for him and had taken charge of the disposition of the men who would fight under their banner. In the noise and confusion of a great army embarking for war, the brothers had had little time for much more than a quick, relieved reunion. And then, just hours later, Will had been kicked into the scum-filled harbor by a panicked war-horse. They'd hauled him out, cursing, broken-armed, and bedecked with the garbage that floated at quay-side.

Since Ian had already decided to send Madeline to Wyndham, Will's accident provided a ready-made escort. There were few men he would trust with her, Ian had realized with a start, and Will was one. Only now, when he had time to reflect on it, did he recognize that trust for what it was—an implicit belief that his brother would not forsake his vows to his betrothed any more than Madeline would tempt him to.

When had he come to this belief in her? Ian wondered, staring out at the sea. Had it been when she looked up at him with those devastating eyes and told him that she had faith enough in his honor to unlock his shackles? Or when she told him that there was naught but friendship between her and John?

Mayhap it had been when she lifted her hands and put them on his naked arms, her touch so tentative, so light. 'Twas not the touch of a wanton. Nor were her kisses those of a woman who gave them freely. They were warm and passionate and incredibly rousing, but not practiced, not calculated. Ian had enough experience with women to trust his instincts in such matters.

And those instincts had caused him to send Madeline to Wyndham. He'd given his brother an abbreviated account of his visit to Cragsmore—a very abbreviated account!—and sent him off. With just moments before the ships set sail, he'd scribbled a quick private message to Lady Elizabeth. See to the Lady Madeline, he'd asked, because when he returned he intended to make her his.

Chapter Thirteen

'Twas no easy matter to live with a woman who believed you'd seduced two of her sons.

Madeline sat alone in Wyndham's enclosed courtyard, her brilliant-hued silk skirts spread across a stone bench in the shade of a huge, twisted cypress tree. She'd donned the bright turquoise bliaut and exquisitely embroidered chainse as much to show how little she cared for the frowning looks sent her way as to bolster her own spirits.

Summer had at last found its way so far north, and no trace of any cooling afternoon breeze lifted the ends of her gauzy veil. The heat lay oppressively on Madeline's brow, making her feel sluggish and uncharacteristically tired. With all her heart, she wished she could order Zephyr saddled and ride out with Will to explore Derwentwater's shoreline, as she had during her first few days at Wyndham—before Ian's courier arrived.

Before Lady Elizabeth, rigid with fury, had summoned Madeline to her private solar and read her the contents of her son's curt note.

Before Madeline had admitted what she could not deny. That she had bedded with Ian, and he now thought to make her his mistress.

If, in the secret recesses of her soul, she'd harbored any hope that Ian might want her as something other than a bedmate, Lady Elizabeth had soon laid that false dream to rest. Had she her wish, she'd stated frigidly, no son of hers—nay, nor daughter, either— would come within a mile of a woman such as Madeline. 'Twas only at Ian's order that Lady Elizabeth kept her at Wyndham, and she would watch her like a cat staring down a rat. Madeline would not leave the women's quarters after the candles were snuffed, nor escape the confines of the courtyard for the duration of her stay. She'd not practice her loose ways at Wyndham, not if Lady Elizabeth had aught to say about it.

When Ian returned, it would be up to him to decide her future. And to explain to Will how he, too, had fallen into her wicked snares. Lady Elizabeth could not. Would not.

Madeline sighed and picked at the bright-colored threads that formed themselves into flowers and vines on the cuff of her sleeve. So much for the songs of the troubadours, she thought. Those melodic odes to bravery and chivalrous love, in which ladies gave themselves to their true knights with much glory and the full blessing of other sophisticates, held little basis in reality. Reality was one man, one woman, sweating and straining together, locked in a need that had little of glory in it... but much of passion. And desire. And, mayhap on one side at least, the first stirrings of love.

Madeline tugged irritably at a loose thread, causing the delicate linen to pucker. Bah! What did she know of love? For all that half the world believed she lifted her skirts for any man who came within arm's reach, the sorry fact was that she'd tasted this passion, this desire, but once in her whole, miserable existence.

Well, mayhap twice.

Nay, three times.

Ian had taken her three times that night, although she could scarce recall the last. She'd been so sated, so boneless, so damnably exhausted. And if he strode into the courtyard this very day, her heart told her mockingly, she'd fling herself into his arms and beg him to do so again.

Bah! She yanked at a long blue thread, completely destroying a delicate embroidered periwinkle.

"Lady Madeline?"

She glanced up at the small figure who stood before her. "Aye, Lady Alicia?"

"May I speak with you?"

Madeline hesitated, sure that Lady Elizabeth would not approve. Will's mother had sent for his betrothed soon after he'd arrived at Wyndham, obviously determined to remind him of his responsibility to the girl he'd been pledged to since childhood. Although Will had made no public remonstrance, Madeline could tell the lad was not best pleased with this interference. His cool reception of Lady Alicia had only added to the wrongs his mother laid at Madeline's door.

"I'm sure Lady Elizabeth would wish you to take company with the younger maids," she replied diplomatically, "or with Will."

The girl's small, rounded chin wobbled. "Will's gone out. As he has each day since I arrived."

Madeline had no answer for that. She'd be gone each day, too, were she able. She needed exercise to rid herself of her weariness and languor of spirit.

Alicia clasped her hands nervously in front of her, nibbling on her lower lip.

Taking pity on the girl's timidity, Madeline swept her skirts aside and patted the bench. "Here, why don't you sit for a few moments and enjoy the shade?"

Alicia sank down gratefully on the stone, still worrying her lower lip. Madeline tilted her head and studied the girl. Nay, not a girl. But not quite a woman, either. Although 'twas obvious from the way her gown hugged her chest that her breasts had budded into fullness, she carried herself with the shy awkwardness of one embarrassed by the weighty protuberances. From the snippets of conversation Madeline had picked up in the women's quarters, she knew Alicia had begun her monthly flow and thus was ready for bedding. She'd heard, as well, however, that the girl had begged her father not to set the date for the solemnizing of her marriage to Will. In disgust, her irate parent had been only too happy to send the girl to Wyndham at Lady Elizabeth's urgent summons.

Madeline had studiously avoided Alicia since her arrival. She knew it wouldn't take long for the whispers about her to reach Alicia's ears. She had no desire to "taint" an innocent young girl, nor to make her more unhappy by letting her see that Will harbored an ill-concealed passion for another woman. Still, she found herself unable to resist the unspoken plea in Alicia's violet eyes.

"Is there aught that troubles?" she asked, resigning herself to the tearful scene she was sure would come.

"Aye," the girl replied hesitantly, "there is."

"Will you tell me? Mayhap I can help."

The pansy eyes, really quite remarkable in their striking color, searched Madeline's face. "Would you? Help me?"

"If I can." Madeline took the small, fragile hand that trembled on the stone beside her. "Come, tell me, what is it that you wish of me?"

"I would like you to show me . . . to teach me your ways with men."

"What?" Madeline dropped her hand as if scalded and jumped up.

"I know 'tis much to ask of you," Alicia said earnestly, "but I beg you to grant me what moments or hours of your time you will. Just share with me what you wish."

"Do you taunt me, girl?" Madeline asked coldly, drawing herself up.

"No! Oh, no! It's taken me days to work up the nerve to approach you!"

"As well it should have!"

"Lady Madeline, 'tis unseemly, I know, to beg a woman of your poise and sophistication to have aught to do with a mouse such as I. Please, please, forgive my boldness, but I'm—I'm desperate."

Tears welled in wide purple eyes, and Madeline's affronted fury slowly abated. Holy Virgin, the girl was serious! Was she so unhappy in her betrothal, Madeline wondered with a rush of pity? Did she think that she could ensnare another man with bolder ways?

"You don't have to tell me all your secrets," Alicia pleaded when Madeline didn't answer. "I'd not know how to use them, in any case. I just want to know enough to... to..."

Torn by conflicting loyalties to Will and to the young girl who begged her help, Madeline sank back down on the bench. "You want to learn enough to what?"

Alicia drew in a shuddering breath. "Enough to make Will look at me as he looks at you."

Madeline stared at her, openmouthed. "But... but I thought you objected to your betrothal?" She shook her head, collecting her wits. "Forgive me, but I had heard that you begged your father not to force you to wed Will."

"I did." She drew in a small breath. "I would not bind him to me when he has eyes only for you."

The girl's simple dignity touched Madeline's heart. "Ah, child, could Will but see you now, he'd have no eyes for me, nor for any other woman. You're not such a mouse, Lady Alicia. No woman who has the courage to ask what you do could ever be thought a mouse.''

''But I'm not beautiful as you are, nor self-assured, nor able to laugh away my pain as you do.''

Madeline's brows rose.

''I may be timid, Lady Madeline, but I'm not stupid. I see that it hurts you, what they whisper about you in the women's quarters. I see how you shrug aside Lady Elizabeth's stern looks, but...but your smile has a hard edge. Even then,'' she finished quietly, ''tis a smile that sets Will's blood to rushing.''

Silence stretched between them. From the outer bailey, Madeline could hear the faint sounds of the blacksmith's hammer and the distant honk of a goose paddling in the pond. Closer at hand, in the upper story, overlooking the courtyard, two servants laughed and flapped a sheet out a window to air it. But between this girl who wanted Will's love and the woman who wanted it not, there was only silence.

Madeline leaned her head against the scaly tree trunk at her back, thinking how much she used to pride herself on her merry smiles and ready jests. How easily she had held a string of men dancing at her fingertips. And yet the one man she wanted, the only one she had ever wanted, scorned her. He craved her body, but he scorned her. As ye sow, so shall ye reap, she thought with a weariness that seemed to leach the youth from her bones. Sitting up, she turned to study Alicia's earnest little face.

''I have no tricks to teach you, lady, none that you have need of.'' She held up one hand at the girl's in-

voluntary protest. "But if you'll trust me, I'll show
you that Will's infatuation is just that, and nothing
more. 'Tis not the love a husband brings to his wife,
nor even the respect a man shows his betrothed. 'Tis
only the wistful yearning of a boy who knows he must
soon become a man and wants to play a while yet."

"I would as soon he played with me as with you,"
Alicia said, somewhat tartly.

Madeline's trill of laughter went far toward easing
the ache in her heart. "He will, lady, he will. Just trust
me."

Madeline took special pains with her appearance
before she went to take supper that night. While Gerda
grumbled as she hunted through boxes for this shift
and that caul, a certain ring and a special bracelet,
Madeline opened her little silver casket of cosmetics.
Frowning at the wan image in the mirrored lid, she
painted her cheeks and brows with a lavish hand, then
rubbed dried rose petals across her lips to give them
color, as well.

When at length she was satisfied with the glowing
face staring back at her, she shed the linen chainse
whose embroidered sleeve she'd all but destroyed and
donned instead one so thin and sheer it was almost
transparent. The soft material clung to the slopes of
her breasts, clearly delineating them above the low,
square neckline of her best bliaut, a costly gown of
gold cloth. Disdaining a veil, Madeline set a circlet of
gold on her forehead, to which Gerda attached the
golden cauls sewn with seed pearls and emerald drops.

"Ooooh, lady," Gerda breathed, "ye looks as fine as any woman that ever graced the king's court!"

"Think you so?"

"Oh, aye," the maid assured her, then added slyly, "I wish Lord Ian could see ye tonight."

"I misdoubt he'd enjoy seeing me this night," Madeline murmured to herself, strolling out the door of the small chamber she'd been allotted in the women's quarters. "Not when I'm about to seduce his brother."

'Twas an amazing simple process.

When Madeline swept into the great hall, Will's eyes widened in a flattering combination of masculine appreciation and youthful adulation. He rushed to her side like a bee drawn to nectar. Within moments of her arrival, Madeline had gathered about her a circle of grinning vassals, shy squires and those knights too old or, like Will, too infirm to go to war. Her gurgle of merry laughter vied with the notes played by the strolling lute player who graced Lady Elizabeth's boards with music in the evenings.

'Twas as though the wretched woman who had doubted herself but a few hours previously had never existed.

Will was delighted with this return of the sparkling beauty who had won his heart at the king's court. This was the woman he remembered, the one he cherished in his dreams. He'd hoped to further his acquaintance with Madeline during their ride north and these weeks at Wyndham, but she'd been strangely quiet. Of a sudden, she seemed to have blossomed forth.

Lady Elizabeth watched these proceedings with tight-lipped disapproval. Her soft brown eyes, usually so gentle and filled with maternal affection, shot daggers at Will when he made so bold as to suggest that Lady Madeline join them at high table.

"Oh, no, Sir William," Madeline protested with a slanting smile. "Would you remove me from these gallant gentlemen who would share my trencher?" She indicated the avid circle around her with a wave of one beringed hand. "Go, sit with your betrothed. She's of higher rank than I, who am a mere baron's relic."

"Nay, lady," one doughty would-be gallant exclaimed. "Never call yourself a relic. Why, your sparkle lights fires even in these old bones."

Madeline's laugh was bright and gay. "You see, Sir William? Mayhap I'll find among these lusty men my next husband. 'Tis a while, after all, since I tasted the delights of the marriage bed."

Will looked a little startled as he glanced at the men, whom he'd known all his life. Old Sir Alymer, who'd been liege man to his father, was sixty if he was a day. He all but drooled on Madeline's bosom. Young Piers de Montiel was a squire in training, and hardly older than Will's youngest brother. Yet the lad gazed at her face with a heat that said he was well on the road to becoming a man.

Reluctant to leave this revitalized Madeline, Will nevertheless took his seat at high table and dutifully speared the choicest morsels for Lady Alicia from the many dishes passed.

"She's beautiful, isn't she?" Alicia commented quietly after the buttered prawns swimming in a lentil sauce had been followed by a haunch of venison seasoned with garlic, pepper and verjuice.

"Aye," Will responded, his eyes on the spirited exchange down the boards. "Well, most times. 'Tis not so much that she is beautiful as that she's so...alive."

"Aye."

Although Will's heart might have been with the boisterous group surrounding Madeline, he was a wellmannered lad. Alicia's small response caught his attention. Turning away from the somewhat disturbing sight of Lady Madeline nibbling on the bite of stuffed peacock that Sir Alymer held to her lips, Will courteously carved up a capon breast with his eating knife to share with his betrothed.

And so was set the pattern for the next weeks. While Lady Elizabeth's lips thinned to a tight line, Madeline flirted and teased and tormented with a gay impartiality. Will dogged her steps whenever she allowed him to.

If this was not as often as he would like, he shrugged and told himself that she was much a woman. 'Twas natural that other men would want her company, as well. When the occasional thought came that mayhap she smiled *too* freely on this knight or that, he dismissed it as dog-in-the-manger disappointment that 'twas not him she smiled on. If mayhap her bodice was just a bit too low and showed more of the shadowy cleft between her breasts than he would wish, he reminded himself that Lady Madeline was used to the ways of court. She couldn't know that these rough north-country men might mistake her display of her charms for lack of modesty.

Alicia, in whom he had found a most unlikely ally when it came to defending Madeline from all criticism, seconded his praise of the lady in every respect. Will was much struck by this sign of maturity in the girl he'd previously thought of as a timid little wren, and took to spending more hours with her when banished from Madeline's immediate circle.

'Twas only natural that he would solicit Alicia to ride with him on these fine summer days, since Madeline kept close to the keep at Lady Elizabeth's request. And 'twas only to be expected that the fresh air and exercise would put a sparkle in the girl's eyes and a bloom in her cheeks.

Will was a healthy young man of direct appetites, and it didn't take him long to notice how Alicia's figure had ripened since last he'd seen her, nor how she seemed to reserve her smiles for him alone.

June passed into July, hot and bothersome. By day Madeline was merry and fulsome in her pursuit of the innocent pleasures of dance and song and impromptu archery contests. By night, she lay abed exhausted and yet sleepless, telling herself 'twas only the heat that sapped her strength, not the role she played. 'Twas second nature to her, after all. She'd been taught by Eleanor herself, known throughout the world as the queen of love.

She would not have to play the role much longer, Madeline thought as she lay abed one stifling summer night. Already Will made excuses for her conduct and forwardness with other men. Already his eyes rested on her thoughtfully on occasion, until she laughed and teased him and brought him to heel again. Already he seemed to find relief from Madeline's vibrant personality in Alicia's quiet, steady presence. She should feel pleased with her progress, Madeline told herself, lifting one hand to brush the sweat-dampened tendrils of hair off her forehead.

'Twas only the heat that took the enjoyment from her game. This damnable heat. It had to be the heat. It could not be because she'd grown weary of the charade. Or that she'd now gone two full cycles of the moon without her woman's flow.

Ian raised the peaked visor on his great helm and lifted a corner of his tunic to wipe the sweat from his eyes.

The air around him was hot and still and heavy, with the brooding tension that comes right before a summer storm. A storm would soon break, he knew, but it would not be one caused by nature. In this case, the clouds of war were about to rain down on the keep that sat on a small rise a hundred yards away. The lightning would be the crack of deadly projectiles flung by the siege engines at the crumbling outer walls. The thunder would be the pounding of a hundred destriers' hooves as they charged the breached walls.

Why didn't the fool surrender? Ian thought wearily. He was caught in a deadly vise between Duke
Richard's forces pressing up from Aquitaine and King
Henry's armies sweeping down from Normandy. Ian
had sent a herald under a flag of truce to inform the
besieged knight that peace talks had already been
called for. The bastard had trumpeted out that he believed not such trickery and put a crossbow bolt
through the herald's throat, thereby sealing his own
doom. Still, if he surrendered now, Ian would see that
his death was relatively quick and painless.

Ian stretched in the saddle, trying to ease muscles
strained almost beyond endurance. After two long,
bloody months of battle, he was ready for it to end.
He slipped off his mailed gauntlet and rubbed the heel
of his hand against his eyes. Jesu, he felt like he hadn't
slept in weeks. Nay, in months, ever since the king's
forces had landed. No one had, Ian thought wryly.
Once Henry set foot on land, he'd moved with the
same demonic energy that had marked his reign for
over twenty years. Without pausing to eat or sleep,
he'd charged across Normandy, regaining the castles
in Maine and Anjou that Philip had taken.

The wily French king had fallen back and rein-
forced only those keeps that Ian suspected had been
his targets all along. Châteauroux, which had been
fought over so bitterly just the year before, was lost to
the French. Along with it went most of Berri. But in
all else, Henry prevailed. In a brilliant encircling maneuver, he'd sent John to flank left, while he and the
rest of the army flanked right. The two thrusts had

swept around the French king's forces and all but cut them off from their main ally, the count of Toulouse. To give credit where credit was due, John had fought fast and hard and brave these weeks. His forces were now only a few miles distant, according to the scouts, subduing another of the last holdouts.

Ian squinted up at the hazy sun and saw that it had reached its zenith. The deadline he'd given for the surrender was now past. Lifting a hand, he signaled to his lieutenant to start the final bombardment.

By the time the sun hovered just above the horizon that evening, the keep was in a pile of tumbled stones and smoldering ruins. The dead knight's lady and children had been sent to Rouen, to be held until ransomed back by their French king. Those of the defenders who'd survived the final, brutal assault had paid the price of their lord's folly.

Ian had removed his hot, heavy helmet and was directing the disposition of salvaged treasures when a rider galloped toward them. Drawing rein on the lathered, huffing beast, the soldier flung himself from the saddle.

"Sir Ian, my master fights to take Ballieu keep, just over the hill. We've breached the walls and stormed the outer bailey, but found the place manned by a double force of routiers. If you can spare any men, my master bids you send them right away."

Too experienced to commit his forces to an unknown engagement, Ian snapped at the man, "Who is your master, and what sign does he fight under?"

"His shield bears a black bar across a white field. He is known as Guy Blackhair."

"Guy Blackhair! Guy Blackhair asks me to come to his aid?"

"Aye, my lord. He says if you help him take this keep, he'll let you take a swing at his head afterward, to right the score between you."

The weariness slipped from Ian's shoulders. He gave a shout of laughter and strode over to where his squire squatted, cleaning the blood and filth from his sword. Ian snatched up his weapon and rammed it into his scabbard. Setting the heavy helm atop his head, he reached for his blue-and-white chequy shield.

"Lead me to him, man. This is one fight I much look forward to."

It took less than twenty minutes of hard riding to close the distance between the keeps. Ian had brought with him every mounted warrior he could spare from his own prize. He soon saw that they would be needed.

The battle for Ballieu raged fierce. The barbican and outer walls had been breached, but shouts from the bailey told Ian the defenders still battled valiantly to hold the inner yard. As he galloped toward the fray, a bright arc of liquid fire poured over the inner walls. Men screamed and threw down their weapons, beating about their heads and shoulders to put out the leaping flames. Bodies lay strewn everywhere, and Ian could only pray that those his horse trampled in its charge were already beyond pain.

Using his destrier as a weapon, he barreled to the aid of a knight surrounded by foot soldiers who slashed and hacked at him. The knight's frenzied stallion lashed out with front hooves and back, keeping the attackers at bay while its rider swung a mace in a vicious arc. The man's surcoat was so covered with blood that Ian could barely see the plain white patch with a black bar across it sewn to the shoulder.

It took three hours of hacking, slicing battle before Ballieu was taken. Darkness had fallen, and the leaping flames of torches illuminated a scene of destruction and death. By the time it was over, Ian was hoarse from shouting, and his arms ached so fiercely from swinging sword and shield that he could hardly lift them. Stinging sweat poured into half a dozen sword cuts and the wound on his temple. His sides heaved as he struggled to draw air into his starved lungs. Stepping over the bodies in the great hall, he went forward to meet the blood-stained knight who descended the wooden stairs.

Guy Blackhair lifted off his helm and hitched it under his arm, wincing with the effort. "The last of them...just went out...the tower window...." he reported in a raw, tortured voice.

Ian nodded and reached up with a shaking hand to remove his own suffocating headgear. The great helmet slipped from his slick, bloodied gauntlet and clattered to the stone floor. "It took you...long enough."

"Aye, well..." Guy panted. "You know how paid mercenaries are." He paused to suck more air into his throat. "They fight without conscience...for either side, but . . . once they pledge their swords, they give fair value else . . . else no one would hire them.''

Ian grunted.

The knight's mustache twisted in a parody of a grin. "So, Sir Ian, you've done your duty to the king by coming to my aid. Now . . . now you may take that swing at my head. Or try to."

Ian's own lips lifted. "I'll do more than try, Guy Blackhair." He hefted his sword, ignoring the fiery protest that shot all along his arm and back.

Guy brought his blade up, as well. He took a half step forward, then stopped, wavering. His black brows drew together.

"Well, hell and damnation . . ." he muttered, then crumpled to the ground in an untidy heap.

Chapter Fourteen

Madeline shoved the wooden bucket aside and sat back on her heels. The sour taste of bile filled her throat. For long moments she remained unmoving, willing her rebellious stomach to right itself.

"Here, mistress, I'll take that."

Gerda swept the odoriferous bucket away and left the small bedchamber to dump the pail's contents down the hole in the garderobe. When she returned, Madeline was still on her heels, her eyes trained on the glazed glass window that overlooked Wyndham's central courtyard.

"Now, now," the maid clucked. "'Tis nay so bad. Yer not the first lady to find unwanted fruit in her basket, nor will ye be the last. Here, I brought ye some water to wash yer face with."

Using the side of the bed for leverage, Madeline pushed herself unsteadily to her feet. She dampened the end of one long sleeve in the water and dabbed her flushed face with the cooling, soothing moisture. In a few moments the nausea had passed, and she felt energy flowing back into her limbs like sweet, honeyed wine.

"Be ye all right now?" Gerda asked.

Madeline drew in a deep breath. "Aye, I am."

And she was. 'Twas strange, this business of being with child. First, those weeks when she'd been so drained, so lethargic, and blamed it on the heat. Now, this nausea that swept over her with the suddenness of a summer thunderstorm, violent while it lasted but leaving her cleansed and revitalized after it had passed.

"'Tis not too late, ye know," Gerda said matter-of-factly. "I can ask among the kitchen wenches for the name of the local herbswoman. I used such a posset myself once, when I were twelve. 'Tis not so bad, after the first few hours."

"Nay," Madeline replied emphatically. "I want this babe."

"Well, 'twould be good if ye had a husband to go with it!"

"I shall."

Gerda's brown eyes widened. "What, do ye think to take that big lump of a lad? Sir William? He'd have ye in a minute, his mother be damned, if ye didn't keep driving him back to the company of that little Lady Alicia with yer 'come hither, get ye gone' ways."

Madeline smiled as she tucked the stray wisps of hair around her face back into her cauls. "He *is* starting to tire of the game, isn't he? Nay, I won't take Sir William."

"'Tis just as well. Sir Ian wouldn't allow it, in any case, not when he knows about the babe. He'll want to claim his child."

Madeline shrugged to hide a sudden shaft of hurt. "He won't believe it's his."

"Likely not," Gerda huffed, "the way ye've been spreading yer smiles of late, and dressing like yer going to the king's table fer every meal. 'Tis the talk of the kitchens, ye know, the way the men here hang on yer every word."

"Not just of the kitchens," Madeline admitted, thinking of the sly glances and whispered comments from the other ladies in residence at Wyndham.

"Well, what will ye do? Surely ye·don't intend to take any of the wheezers who dance about ye here at Wyndham to husband?"

"Nay. We shall go back to the king's ward, Gerda, at least for the next month or so, until I find a man to my liking." At the maid's doubtful look, Madeline nodded. "'Twill be settled when Lord Ian arrives home next week, you'll see. I have it all planned out."

"It seems to me, mistress, 'twas one of yer schemes that got ye into this predicament in the first place."

Madeline disdained to respond to this pert statement and left her chamber to rejoin the women in the weaving room. She sent Alicia a small smile as she slipped back onto the stool she'd vacated so abruptly not fifteen minutes ago. Ignoring Lady Elizabeth's sharp glance, she pulled her wooden embroidery frame closer and plied her needle with every evidence of contentment. In truth, 'twas not really a facade.

The fact that she nourished a babe in her womb had affected Madeline profoundly. She had been twice wed and had not quickened. Her first lord had fathered no children even in his prime, and had been well beyond that when he took Madeline to wife. The few times she'd coupled with her second husband, the poor, overeager fool had spilled most of his seed before he managed to join with her. Hence her compelling desire to have a say in the choice of her next lord!

While the knowledge that she would soon swell with babe added a new urgency to this business of choosing her next lord, in another way it relieved Madeline of much of her concern. Before, she'd hoped to find someone she could laugh with, someone she could experience the full joy of her womanhood with. Now, with this unexpected gift of life within her, she'd come to accept that she could find that joy with her child, if not with her lord. From the first moment she realized that her strange lethargy was not due to the enervating heat, Madeline had felt a wondering sense of joy.

Nor had it taken her long to realize what she must now do. Madeline pulled a silver thread through the unicorn's horn she was fashioning and reviewed her plan of attack.

As soon as Ian arrived home, which should be soon, according to all reports, she would ask to speak to him. Calmly, coolly, she would tell him of her condition. He would be furious, of course, and mayhap beat her.

Nay, he wouldn't beat her. Not Ian.

He would demand to know the father, though, and
Madeline would tell him. She owed him and the child
the chance to establish its birthright, but she had no
expectation that he would believe her. Why should he?
She'd been too proud, too sure of herself, to deny the
rumors that had circulated about her for years. Now
she must bear the burden of that pride.

When he did not acknowledge the child, the only
thing she would ask of him was to sell her wardship
back to the king. From all accounts, John had acquit-
ted himself with great distinction during the recent
battles. 'Twas said the king could not speak enough
praises for his youngest, his best, his most loyal son.
Henry would deny John nothing now, Madeline knew.
She would write him, and be back in the king's ward
within the month. Then she would set about choosing
a lord who would accept her and her child. There'd be
no smiles, this time, no gay games while she toyed with
this knight and that. This time, she had more than just
herself and her own needs to consider.

If the thought that she would lose forever the brief
passion she'd found with Ian gave her pain, she refused to acknowledge it.

On the day prior to Ian's expected arrival, the entire keep hummed with activity. Lady Elizabeth was
everywhere, supervising the cleaning and overseeing
the preparations for the great feast that would welcome the returning warriors. She personally instructed the cook as to what hogs to butcher and what
sides of beef and mutton to dress for the great feast.

Using the keys that dangled from her girdle, she unlocked the storerooms to provide precious herbs and costly spices to flavor the sauces. For the frumenty alone, the frothy dish that would be in itself a main course, one hundred eggs were to be beaten into every eight pints of milk, to which was added chopped dittany, rue, tansy, mint, sage, marjorm, parsley, violet leaves and pounded ginger. The strong smells that wafted from the kitchen sheds pervaded the entire keep.

Added to them was the yeasty scent of fresh-risen dough. Alicia had been given the task of supervising the army of cooks who prepared pies and breads and elaborate pasties in the shape of castles and mythical animals.

Even Lady Elizabeth's young daughter had been put to work, counting the carp pulled from traps in the pond and the strings of trout and pike brought in, fresh caught along the shores of Derwentwater. The stench of the fish heads and innards tossed to the cats in the yards hung on the humid air.

Madeline would have liked to help. She desperately needed something to do to keep her mind from her imminent meeting with Ian. But her stomach seemed to have its own mind in this matter of what was and was not acceptable labor. Madeline had looked but once on the bloody carcass of a pig, and retreated hastily from the dressing shed, her hand over her mouth. Lady Elizabeth's keen eyes had noted her abrupt departure. The wimpled matron had pursed her lips—whether in disgust or disapproval, Madeline knew not and could not, at that moment, care.

She cared greatly, however, when Lady Elizabeth summoned her to her chambers later that evening. Madeline entered the spacious solar, hung with rich tapestries to brighten the blue-gray Lakeland-stone walls, and nodded coolly.

"You wished to see me, lady?"

"Aye, I did." She hesitated, then nodded to a chair. "Sit you down, lady, I would speak with you."

Her years spent with Eleanor stood Madeline in good stead. Folding her skirts about her, she sank gracefully into a lyre-shaped backless chair that faced Lady Elizabeth's and waited for the older woman to say her piece. Madeline had little doubt it had to do with Ian's imminent return, and the fact that Elizabeth would then demand that he make other arrangements for her. The older woman had made no secret of her disdain for Madeline.

Lady Elizabeth plucked at the folds of her blue robe for a few moments, as if distracted by her thoughts. When she lifted her head, her doe-soft brown eyes were troubled.

"It seems I must thank you for what you do with Will."

Of all the words Lady Elizabeth could have said to her, those were the last Madeline expected. She blinked, certain that she'd not heard aright.

"I wasn't sure at first," Lady Elizabeth continued. "But it soon came clear."

"I know not..."

The older woman waved one hand in the air. "There's no need to dissemble. You're much too skilled to keep sending the boy away each day a bit more disillusioned with his ladylove—unless you wished to. Nor would you show yourself to compare so unfavorably with Alicia—unless that was your intent."

Madeline shrugged, still in the role she'd chosen for herself. "'Tis no great loss to me if your son thinks he'll find greater joy in a girl's company than in mine. There are other men about, after all."

"You never meant to attach him, did you?" Lady Elizabeth asked shrewdly, "Even all those weeks ago, at Kenilworth?"

That, at least, Madeline could answer truthfully. "Nay, I never did."

"Did you tell Ian so?"

Madeline's careful poise slipped. "I tried! But he's more than a little dunderheaded, your son-by-marriage."

"I see," Lady Elizabeth murmured, her fair brows rising.

If that was perhaps not the most accurate description of one spoken of by his vassals as a fearless fighter and a man of uncompromising loyalty and uncommon good sense, the older woman didn't say so. She looked down at her own clasped hands for a moment, then at Madeline.

"Mayhap...mayhap I spoke too harshly to you when I first received Ian's message. Is there aught you wish to tell me about you and this dunderheaded son of mine?''

For a moment, a foolish moment, Madeline considered telling her the truth. She acknowledged ruefully that the truth wouldn't endear her to the older woman. The simple fact was that she'd lain with Ian and now carried his child. But she knew the mother would no more believe her than the son.

''Nay, lady, there's naught to tell.''

When she dismissed Madeline sometime later, Lady Elizabeth's brow was crinkled in thought. None of this made any sense. 'Twas obvious to all but a blind woman that Madeline was with child, yet instead of trying to snare Will to husband her, she subtly pushed him toward his betrothed. Instead of blaming Ian, who she'd admitted before had bedded her, she now refused to even speak of him. None of these actions accorded with the woman Madeline de Courcey presented to the world.

Lady Elizabeth rose and summoned her maids to prepare for bed. She was tired, and had much to do yet in the morning before Ian arrived. She had much to think about, as well, after she'd said her nightly prayers and slipped into bed.

Lady Elizabeth was not the only one whose brow was troubled that night. Alicia had heard the malicious whispers about Lady Madeline's inconvenient sickness. There were few secrets in a crowded keep, and none at all among the servants. Her heart aching, Alicia watched a pale, distracted Madeline pass through the women's solar on her way to her own bedchamber. In the past weeks, the girl had progressed from a shy, painful admiration to a deep respect for this woman who presented such a brave front.

She'd been a little shocked at first, when Madeline began to flirt so outrageously with Will, and then with the other men and boys, as well, but she'd soon understood what was about. Each time Will turned from Madeline with a puzzled frown, Alicia had soothed it with the gentle reminder that the lady was special, after all. Each time he'd been excluded from her gay circle, Alicia had made him welcome in hers.

'Twas no hardship for Alicia to take whatever attention Will would spare her. She'd loved him with all her girlish heart for so long as she could remember. He was so tall, so handsome, so overpowering at times.

The first time Will tried to kiss her, when she'd been but a young maid, Alicia had been frightened and overcome by shyness. She'd been so timid then, and he had only kissed her because they were betrothed and 'twas expected of him. Now she ached to feel his lips on hers. Her ripened body longed for more than his kiss. Of late she'd sensed that he had noticed the changes in her, too.

And yet, did she win Will's love, she would do so at the expense of Madeline. And Madeline's need was the greater now. Nibbling nervously on her lower lip, Alicia summoned a maidservant to her side, then sent her with a message for her betrothed. A few moments later, she pulled a light mantle over her chainse and slipped downstairs to meet Will in the walled garden.

"Alicia, what's so urgent that you must needs meet me like this?" Will's golden brows hiked up. "And in your shift!"

"Never mind my shift," she said. "I must speak with you."

The mantle slipped off one shoulder as she took Will's good arm and tugged him to a stone bench. He sat beside her, somewhat disconcerted by the feel of the round, full breast that brushed against him.

"Will, you must speak to Ian as soon as he arrives...about us."

The moonlight bathed her small face in shadows and light, and darkened her violet eyes to a deep, fathomless purple. Will stared down at the delicate features and felt the urge to lift his hand and stroke the smooth skin of her cheek. She was so tiny, so sweet, so gentle to be with. She made him feel much a man, and not a stripling boy.

"Aye," he said slowly, coming to an awareness within himself. "'Tis time."

"He'll understand," she said earnestly.

"Aye." Will couldn't help himself. His good hand lifted to cup the small, smooth cheek so close to his.

Alicia covered his hand with hers and turned to press a kiss into his palm. Her lashes fluttered down, and when she opened them again, tears welled up like liquid silver in her eyes.

"'Twill not be so difficult, will it? Dissolving our betrothal?"

Lost as he was in the magic of her small face, and more than a little mesmerized by the tantalizing glimpse of her curved body revealed by the thin shift, it took a few seconds for Will to grasp her words.

"Dissolve our betrothal? You wish to dissolve our betrothal?" He pulled his hand free, frowning at her. "Oaths were pledged in our name, lady. Sacred oaths."

"I know, I know," Alicia said miserably. "But I will not hold you to them, nor can your brother, not when you tell him about Lady Madeline."

Will jumped up, spurred by guilt that he had once harbored half-formed thoughts of ending his betrothal, just as Alicia suggested, and fury that she would now propose it herself.

"Do you imply that I have violated my vows to you with Lady Madeline? That I have so little honor I would forswear myself with her?"

"Oh, no, Will! No!" Alicia surged to her feet, the mantle slipping off her shoulders completely in her agitation. She placed both hands on his good arm and pleaded with him to understand. "Not you! You're too good to dishonor her or yourself! But—but you love her..."

"Alicia..."

"I understand, truly I do. You can't help but love her! She's so beautiful and kind."

"Alicia..."

"She sparkles so. The rest of us are like wrens next to her, and—ooof!"

With his one arm still bound to his chest, Will's attempt to sweep Alicia up against him and quiet her the only way he knew how met with mixed results. His good arm managed to catch her around the waist and pull her to him. She was so much shorter than he, however, that his kiss bounced off her forehead. She leaned back in his hold, her eyes wide and her mouth open, while Will's confused phrases tumbled out.

"Hellfire and damnation, Alicia! I don't want Lady Madeline. Not the way I thought I did. Well, mayhap I do, a little, but not the way you think. Not to take to wife, in any case."

"She's with child, Will."

The quiet words fell like stones between them. For a long moment, neither moved.

"I know 'tis not your child she carries," Alicia continued softly. "You would not do that to her, nay, nor to me. But if you love her, you will want to..."

Alicia's voice trailed off. She saw that Will was much struck. He stared down at her, but didn't seem to see her. His handsome face was still, his brow furrowed in thought. And then, incredibly, a slow grin etched across his face.

"So *that* explains it. No wonder he was so late coming to the ships!"

"Who?"

He blinked, then refocused on her face. "Never mind, sweetheart," he said, his grin widening. "Worry not about Lady Madeline. I'll see she's taken care of."

"Aye," Alicia said in a small voice. "I knew you would. 'Tis the kind of man you are. You've too much honor to leave her in such distress."

Will's arm tightened around the tiny waist. "Alicia, listen to me. I'm not going to wed with Madeline. My brother is."

"Wh-what?" she stuttered. "Lord Ian? But—"

"And if I didn't have this damned broken arm," he said, interrupting her ruthlessly, "you'd see just how little honor I possess. Don't you have any more sense than to meet a man in a garden wearing nothing but your shift! When we're wed, I'll show you what the sight of your ripe beauty does to me!"

Alicia gaped up at him for a stunned moment, then used both little hands to thrust herself away from Will. Thinking he'd frightened her, he loosed his arm and let her go.

With a singular lack of grace, she scrambled up onto the stone bench and turned to face him. Her hands fumbled with her ties as she peeled the thin linen back to reveal a full, flawless bosom.

"Show me now," she demanded breathlessly.

Anticipation thrummed in Ian's veins as he rode up to Wyndham keep the following afternoon. Horns sounded his approach, dogs barked and cavorted as his troop rode into the bailey, and castle folk tumbled out to greet them. His mother-by-marriage, gorgeously arrayed in a sparkling white wimple, a gossamer veil of purple sarascenet and a gown of the finest brocaded silk, waited for him in the bailey. Will stood tall and sturdy at her side with his betrothed and younger, eager siblings arranged about him.

Ian's gaze scanned the crowd of well-wishers for Madeline's slender figure, but she was not among them. 'Twas as well, he thought with an inner grin. What he had to say to her was best said in private. Schooling himself to patience, he dismounted and went to take his mother's welcome. It was only then that Ian noticed that Lady Elizabeth's smile didn't quite reach her eyes. And that Will regarded him with a determined frown.

"Welcome, Ian," Lady Elizabeth said, giving him the kiss of greeting on either cheek. "I'm glad you took no hurt and are home safe."

"So am I, Lady Mother."

"Come inside and disarm. When you are rested and refreshed, we must talk."

Ian's brow rose at the quiet authority in her voice.

"And I would have a word with you, as well," Will said grimly.

Chapter Fifteen

It was several hours after his return before Ian sent a page for Madeline with word that he desired her presence.

He waited in the small antechamber where he managed the affairs of Wyndham, leaning an arm against the wooden window frame as he stared unseeing at the busy central courtyard. His jaw clenched and unclenched spasmodically while he sought to control his rioting emotions.

In the past few hours, he'd run the gamut from simmering anticipation to astonishment to chagrin and incipient fury. He was not used to being taken to task by either his mother or his younger brother. He'd sustained a heated interview with Will and a scathing one with Lady Elizabeth. Both of them were unstinting in their condemnations, that he would use Madeline so. While he was still reeling from these sessions, old Sir Alymer had petitioned to speak with him. Sir Alymer, who had served with Ian's father in his youth! The man had stuttered and harrumphed and laid out for Ian all the reasons he should be given Lady Madeline to wife. Ian had dismissed his suit with an uncharacteristic terseness.

Jesu! How could one slight female have disrupted his entire household and caused such tumult in so short a space of time? How could she have brought Will from his blind devotion to the realization that she was too much a woman for him, but far more than Ian deserved? How did she make an ally of Lady Elizabeth by flirting outrageously with the male half of the keep—including, it seemed, Sir Alymer?

And how was he to handle the fact that she carried a babe?

Deliberately Ian forced himself to consider the possibility that the child was not of his loins. Just as deliberately, he dismissed it. He shouldn't be surprised that their wild, prolonged and very thorough couplings had born fruit. In any case, the fact that she was with child did not alter greatly his plans for her.

Turning from the window, he crossed to the oaken table that held Wyndham's iron-hasped books. He hooked a finger through the thong of the small leather pouch he'd placed on the table earlier and dangled it thoughtfully. Opening the pouch, he tumbled a small golden band into his palm. The ruby centered on it winked dully.

"You wished to speak with me, my lord?"

Madeline stood in the open doorway, her chin high and her eyes cool. Ian's fist closed over the ring as he surveyed her. She had dressed with special care for this meeting, he saw at once. The chestnut hair that usually managed to curl about her face in soft wisps was smooth and glossy and well tamed within silver fillets. She wore a finely worked chainse decorated with gold and silver embroidery at neck and sleeve, and a bliaut of a deep, vibrant rose. Bright stones glittered among the gold links of the girdle that encircled her still-slender hips.

She looked as different from the tumbled, well-loved creature he'd left asleep at Cragsmore as 'twas possible for her to look. At that moment, Ian wanted nothing so much as to strip away the jewels and silks and discover again the warm ivory skin beneath. Instead, he forced himself to nod and respond in as cool and even a tone as she herself had used.

"Aye, lady. Come in. It appears we have some matters to discuss between us."

She swept into the room. "Aye, sir, we do."

Madeline's heart ached at the way Ian held himself aloof. She hadn't known what to expect, but she had hoped for at least some sign of warmth, of... of remembrance of their hours at Cragsmore.

He stood with his back to the glazed window, bathed in sunshine and shadows. His tawny hair was shorter than she remembered, his face leaner. He'd divested himself of his armor and washed away the dirt of travel, she saw, and donned the rich, golden-hued surcoat that Lady Elizabeth had worked the stitches on most lovingly these last months. He looked magnificent, altogether different from the bristlecheeked, fierce-eyed man who had tumbled her to the bed so many weeks ago.

"Before we begin," Ian said slowly, "I would discharge a trust that was given me."

Lifting one hand, he uncurled his fingers.

Madeline felt cold seep through her as she stared at the ruby ring she'd given Guy Blackhair.

"Did you kill him?"

"Nay. I would have, but he collapsed of wounds taken in battle afore I had the chance. I left him with a churgeon and a promise that we will meet again."

Madeline took the ring he held out to her with a rush of relief. She would not have had Guy killed for his part in her foolish attempt to hold Ian to ransom.

"Although he yet lives, you will not take Guy Blackhair to husband," Ian told her softly.

"Nay," she responded, able to smile now that her initial spurt of fear had passed. "He didn't really want me, in any case. He was quick enough to abandon his plans to kidnap me when I offered him the alternative of taking you."

"Kidnap you?" Ian's sun-lightened brows snapped together. "What are you speaking of?"

Madeline glanced up at him in surprise. "Why, of his plot to take me from Cragsmore. What are you speaking of?"

A rueful gleam danced in Ian's eyes. "The rogue! The damned rogue! He neglected to mention any plot to take you when we spoke."

"You spoke of me?" Madeline's heart tripped. There was no telling what Guy might have said to fan Ian's rage.

"Aye. You should know, lady, that Guy Blackhair won considerable honors for himself in the recent battles. King Henry offered him the fief of Ballieu. In turn, Guy pledged it to me as your bride price, would I give you to him."

"And . . . and what did you say?"

"I told him I would see him in hell first."

"What!"

Madeline stared up at him, her eyes wide with indignation. She had no desire to wed with Guy, but neither did she care for the way Ian dismissed her options so arbitrarily.

"I said the same to Sir Alymer not half an hour ago," Ian informed her.

"Sir Alymer! Did he . . ." Her voice trailed off at Ian's nod.

"He did." Ian paused, then added in a casually menacing tone, "As did Will."

Blank astonishment wiped all other emotions from Madeline's face. "Will? Your brother Will?"

"Aye." Ian rested one hip against the wooden table and folded both hands across his chest, never taking his eyes from her face. "It seems that he and his betrothed between them decided he should speak to me."

Madeline's head whirled in utter confusion. This interview was not going at all as she planned. She shook her head, trying to make sense of Ian's words.

"Lady Alicia much admires you, lady. She told Will he should take you to wife."

"To wife?" she squeaked.

"Aye. Alicia would see you wed to one who would honor you and keep you in your... difficulties."

Madeline drew in a swift breath. Angling up her chin, she met his steady gaze. "I see. And did Will tell you the nature of these difficulties?"

"Nay, but my lady mother did."

"Your lady mother! Holy Virgin, does everyone have a hand in my affairs!"

"So it appears," he drawled. "I'm surprised I haven't yet been accosted by your maid."

"I doubt not she lies in wait for you!" Madeline snapped, whirling to pace the small room.

This was beyond believing! She had planned to discuss her future with him so calmly, so coolly. She'd wanted to be the one to tell him of the babe, yet it appeared Will had already spoken of it. And Lady Elizabeth. And everyone else in the keep, she thought furiously.

Ah, well, it mattered not how he knew of it. She tucked away the little hurt that he would stand there, arms folded and eyes steady on her face, when she needed so desperately some sign, some touch. Whirling she faced him.

Ian's fingers dug into his arms at the sight of the woman who stood before him. Her face was flushed, her eyes wide and glinting with emotions he could only guess at. His every muscle strained to take her in his arms and kiss away the doubt and uncertainty that hovered between them. But he knew that she had yet to say all she wanted to. He waited with a mounting sense of interest to see what she would say next.

She didn't disappoint him. Planting both hands on her hips, she flashed him a look that was all Madeline. There was no shame, no fear, in the green eyes that blazed into his. Only pride, and a strength he would never again underestimate.

"As half the keep seems to have informed you, I am with child. The babe is yours, my lord, although I know you won't believe me."

Ian uncurled his arms and straightened.

"There's no need for insults," she rushed on before he could speak, "nor blame. What's done is done. I ask naught of you but that you give me back into the king's ward, that I may find a husband who will honor me and the child."

"No."

The response was hard and fast and flat. Ian stepped toward her, fighting to control the rage that surged through him at the thought of any other man claiming this woman and the child she carried.

"You'll lie with no other man but me, Madeline. That much I decided before I even left Cragsmore."

She whitened, but refused to back away from him. "I won't be your mistress, Ian. If you had taken time to wake me before you left Cragsmore, I would have told you so."

"Wake you! Jesu, woman, all the king's trumpeters couldn't have awakened you!"

"Hah!" She tossed her head, undaunted. "I'll be no man's leman, nor—"

Ian's hands curled around the soft flesh of her upper arms. "I want no leman. We'll wed afore the week is out."

Ian held his breath, waiting for some sign that she acknowledged his claim. She was so close, only a breath away. He could see the dark flecks in her green eyes, his own reflection in her widened pupils. A pulse beat frantically in the tiny blue vein at the side of her temple as she searched his face.

"I'll not wed with one who thinks me a whore," she said slowly, painfully.

In the space of a heartbeat, she found herself against him, her hands splayed against his chest, her hips cradled by his thighs. She angled her head back and caught her breath at the flames leaping in his midnight blue eyes.

"I don't think you the whore, Madeline. And you'll wed with me, if I must truss you up like a chicken on its way to market and carry you over my shoulder."

"Ian..."

"Nay, no more words. There have been too many words between us already."

He bent his head, but she jerked back. "Do...do you believe this babe is yours?"

"If you tell me 'tis so," he growled, then covered her lips with his.

His kiss was all that Madeline had remembered, and more. Searing, taking, giving. She held back, until her own senses screamed at her to return the pressure of his lips, to slide her arms about his neck and fit her body to his. She ached for him, for the feel of his hands on her skin, for the heat of his skin on hers.

It took all her strength of will, but Madeline managed to battle down her own desires and push herself out of his arms.

"I will think on this, my lord, and let you know my answer."

"There's naught to think about, lady. We'll wed within the week."

'Twas the longest week of Ian's life. Madeline kept to her chambers, refusing speech with him. Twice he sent Lady Elizabeth to reason with her. Twice the older woman emerged shrugging her shoulders. Ian was tempted to kick in the door himself, but he told himself it wasn't necessary. Not yet, at any rate. Did she not emerge from her seclusion by the time the vassals he'd summoned as witnesses arrived, the stout wooden door would lie in splinters. He'd much prefer a willing bride, but he'd have her however he must.

Ian would've been surprised to know that Madeline's stubborn withdrawal was due as much to her uncertain stomach and the heat as to any inability to come to terms with her fate. She was no child, to rail uselessly at circumstance. She knew Ian didn't need her consent to take her to wife. He held her in ward, and 'twas his right to marry her where he would. Nor was she so stupid as to deny her child its birthright. Whether Ian believed the babe his or not, the marriage would grant it all the rights and entitlements provided by the laws of God and man.

But for those long, hot, miserable days and nights, she let him stew, deciding that he could suffer as much as she. At last, knowing she had no choice if she was to keep her dignity, she met with Ian and the priest to record the marriage agreements.

As north-country weddings and beddings went, theirs was not unusual. In a land where many brides were stolen and many more swelled with child before being brought to the altar, no one thought it unusual that Ian should send the woman at his side a fierce scowl when she hesitated before giving the priest her response. And none considered it the least surprising that she had little to say during the long feast that followed, when toast followed ribald toast and strolling minstrels sang songs of marriage that made most of the women present blush and the men burst into laughter.

As he sat beside Madeline at high table, Ian felt himself relax for the first time in a week. He slanted a sideways look at his still, unsmiling bride. Bright August sunlight, as clear and sharp as only the lake country could produce, filtered in through the high mullioned windows of Wyndham's great hall. She'd dressed with care for the ceremony, he saw with some pleasure. Her own pride would not let her shame herself before his vassals and hers. As usual, she disdained the wimple older women donned, preferring instead a thin, shimmering silk veil over pearl-encrusted cauls. Ian's bride gift, a heavy circlet of gold with a huge square-cut emerald set in its center, anchored the veil to her shining mane. Her robe was of the finest damascene, of a color that changed from blue to green to blue again whenever she made the slightest movement. Which wasn't often.

Ian stifled a sigh and leaned forward to cut a slice of the stuffed swan that floated in winged majesty on a bed of leeks and truffles.

"Come, Madeline, when you came to me with your decision, you said that we would each have to make the best of this marriage."

"Aye, my lord."

He refused to let her stiff, wooden voice deter him. Twisting his eating knife in the succulent meat, he held it up.

"Here, lady, you must take sustenance. With what is to come yet this night, and the babe to consider, you must eat."

She swung sideways to face him. To Ian's relief, a hint of the Madeline he knew surfaced in a rueful smile.

"'Tis because of the babe that I cannot eat. Do you put that knife down, my lord, ere I... Oh, sweet Mother!"

Her eyes took on a distant, glazed look, and she swallowed once, twice.

Ian sat up straight in his chair, alarmed by her sudden pallor. He knew little of breeding women, and he had no idea whether she suffered from some serious complaint or a simple ill humor of the nerves.

"Lady," he said quietly, "are you all right?"

"Nay, my lord," she gasped "I'm about as far from all right as I may be at this moment. I...I think I must leave the hall. At once!"

Ian sent his chair crashing over. With one quick movement, he swooped down and lifted Madeline in his arms. The golden circlet tumbled from her forehead as she yanked her veil off and stuffed a good portion of it into her mouth.

Lady Elizabeth's eyes rounded to huge brown circles. Will looked up, startled, and Alicia gasped in dismay. The singers halted in midsong, while all about them the hum of conversation filling the great hall stumbled and died.

As Ian headed for the stairs to the upper story, Madeline choked and pulled at the cloth in her mouth. "Not there! I need air! Quickly, my lord, quickly!"

Two hundred astonished guests, a chorus of singers, an army of squires, pages and serving wenches and a number of assorted dogs and doves perched in the rafters watched Ian stride out of the keep. Kicking at the door before a wide-eyed page could leap to open it, he looked around the crowded courtyard for a private corner. Seeing none, he set his mouth in a grim line and headed through the gatehouse toward the stables, a moaning Madeline in his arms.

As soon as the dim coolness of the stables closed around them, she pushed herself out of his hold and stumbled toward an empty stall. Muttering a thankful prayer, she sank on her knees in the clean straw.

With a jerk of his head, Ian sent the openmouthed stable hands outside. For long moments, the only sounds that disturbed the stillness were the clump of horses' hooves on the dirt as they shifted in their stalls, the smack of the mounts lipping hay, and Madeline's wretched heaving.

When at last she was done, Ian picked up her discarded veil and dunked it in a pail of standing water. To one who'd spent much of his life on the battlefield, there was nothing in a woman's illness to disgust him. He lifted her in his arms, kicked a thick layer of straw over her leavings and carried her to a spot just inside the open door. Hooking one foot around a farrier's stool, he slid it forward and sat down, his wife in his lap.

She took the wet veil with a moan of thanks and rubbed it across her face. To his amusement, some of the sooty darkness of her brows traced across her forehead, but he was wise enough not to mention it at the moment. Not when she scrubbed at her cheeks and glowered up at him as though this were all his fault.

"Does this happen often?" he inquired casually. "Not that I mind, you understand. But this is the first meal you've deigned to take with me since I returned, and I would know what to expect when we share a table in the future."

She gave her face a final rub and slumped against his chest. "It happens often enough."

Ian rested his chin on her head, which had lost its pearl-encrusted caul somewhere between banquet table and horse shed.

"Your lady mother says it takes all women differently," Madeline continued glumly. "It may go on for months yet, or stop at any time."

Ian registered with some interest the fact that his wife took her knowledge of her condition from Lady Elizabeth. For a widow twice over, Madeline seemed to have little knowledge of herself as a woman. For an instant his mind was filled with the image of her as he'd left her at Cragsmore, sprawled in exhausted abandon across the sheets. She'd been wondrously, joyously surprised then, too, by her body's responses. Ian felt a slow curl of desire, low in his belly, as he remembered her shriek of astonishment at her climax. His legs shifted to ease the sudden tight pressure in his groin.

"Ah, well," Madeline said with a sigh, "at least it doesn't last long." She shifted on his lap, seeking a more comfortable spot.

Ian sucked in a quick breath. "Are you better, then?"

"Aye, much."

For all her bedraggled state, Madeline was feeling the slow resurgence of energy that usually came after she had finally rid herself of the nausea. Her leaden listlessness dissipated, leaving behind a gathering sensory awareness. She felt the hot August sun on her skin, heard the steady thump of Ian's heart under her cheek, saw through half-closed lids the iridescent flicker of the flies that buzzed around the horses. In the stall beside them, a dappled rump rippled, and then a coarse tail lashed out and up at the bothersome insects. Madeline rolled back on Ian's lap to avoid the tail's whip, laughing in surprise. He caught her with a strong arm under her back, and his thigh muscles corded under her weight. One muscle in particular poked at her through the thickness of his tunic and her robe. Startled, she looked up to see his blue eyes gleaming wickedly.

"May-mayhap we'd best get back," she stammered, pushing herself off his lap.

"If 'tis your wish."

"'Tis hardly my wish," she said, grimacing down at the soaked, stained veil he held, "but I suppose I have no choice."

Ian cocked a brow. "What, is this the same Lady Madeline who charmed the king's court with her merry laugh and bright eyes? Surely you'd not let a soiled veil dismay you."

"Were it only a soiled veil! I fear to think what the rest of me must look like, including these bright eyes." She wiped a forefinger under her lower lid and held it up to display the remains of her careful paint.

Ian curled a knuckle under her chin and tilted her face up to his. "You look passing beautiful, wife."

To her surprise, Madeline felt heat steal up her neck and stain her cheeks. The woman who exchanged quips with ease and took compliments with a practiced smile was suddenly as flushed and tongue-tied as a stuttering country maid.

His knuckle slid along the tender flesh under her chin and down the line of her throat.

"Do you really wish to go back inside?" he asked, his gaze holding hers.

Madeline's eyes widened, then she pulled her head away with a jerk. There was no mistaking his meaning, nor the sudden heat in his eyes.

"I realize I'm no virgin to be bedded before witnesses to prove my purity," she said coldly, "but neither am I some drab to tumble in the hay."

She would have sailed out of the stable in offended dignity had Ian not swung her once more into his arms, laughing.

"If only you knew, lady, how close you've come to being tumbled in the hay. That day at Cragsmore, when you came back from your wild ride all covered with mud, 'twas all I could do not to drag you into the stable, throw up your skirts and have my way with you."

"Ian!" Shocked, she stared at him as he strode out of the stable into the blinding sunlight. Instead of crossing the bailey toward the keep, however, he stopped in front of a line of tethered mounts.

"Whose horse is that?" he asked, jerking his chin toward a brilliantly caparisoned bay.

"Sir—Sir Eustache's, my lord," the stable lad stuttered.

"My compliments to Sir Eustache. I would borrow his mount."

"My lord?"

"We'll return it afore the feasting is done," Ian said cheerfully, lifting an astonished Madeline into the saddle. She scrambled for a seat, barely righting herself before he tugged the reins free and backed the huge stallion out of the line. With a lithe, easy swing, he was behind her. He settled her across the cushion of his thighs, bracketing her with the solid strength of his arms, and urged the mount toward the open portcullis.

Chapter Sixteen

Ever afterward, Madeline would believe the hours that followed were among the finest she would know in life.

'Twas the first time she and Ian had been alone without strife or conflict between them. There was no Will, no Guy Blackhair, nay, nor even Sir Alymer or the king's son, to divide their thoughts. There was only her, and Ian, and the clean, clear air of the Cumbrian wilds.

As the walls of Wyndham were left behind, Madeline's halfhearted protests dwindled and she leaned back against Ian. She drew in greedily the clean scent of pine and flowering wood myrtle.

They rode for some miles along Derwentwater's shore, which was lined with bare blue rock, grassy banks and forested glens. Their borrowed mount picked its way easily across the tumbling springs that fed the great mere. As they passed the small, wooded islands that dotted the lake, Ian pointed them out to Madeline and solemnly intoned their unlikely names.

Duck Hole and Little Witch's Hat. Castle Rock and
Sturgill Cove. Squinting, she followed the line of his
outstretched arm to peer at the ruins of Saint He-
bert's retreat on a tiny, timbered isle that rose from the
sparkling water.

At length Ian turned the mount inland, away from
the shore. The dappled stillness of the forest enclosed
them. If Ian followed a path, 'twas not one Madeline
could discern. Branches tugged at her skirts, and the
call of curlews in the trees around them shut out all but
the crunch of underbrush beneath the horse's hooves.
Sunlight filtered in shifting patterns through the tall
pines and shorter white-barked beech and ash. Gradually a distant sound made itself heard, a soft, insis-
tent rushing. Steadily it grew louder, and closer.

To Madeline's surprised delight, Ian soon drew rein
at the edge of a pool fed by a tumbling waterfall. The
frothy water cascaded down a series of rocky ledges,
then fell in a misty ribbon of silver into the deep,
sparkling basin. Vegetation grew lush and green all
around the secluded spot.

"Oh, Ian," Madeline breathed. "'Tis beautiful."

"'Tis more than beautiful," he agreed with a smile.
"Many folk hereabout claim this pool was sacred to
the ancient ones who believed their gods inhabited
rivers and glens."

Madeline glanced about the clearing, suppressing
the urge to cross herself. It wasn't difficult to imagine
this spot a place of pagan worship. Its beauty went

soul deep, and pulled at something elemental, something primal, within her.

Ian's cheerful voice shattered the spell. "This is where I taught Will and my other brothers to swim. My sisters, too, whenever they could escape Lady Elizabeth's close watch. If there are any spirits or water sprites slumbering here, they had little chance to rest with us about."

To one brought up in the close, crowded confines of the royal ward, the idea of children cavorting unwatched and unrestrained in this sun-dappled pool was tantalizing.

"The closest I ever came to swimming," Madeline admitted on a laugh, "was the time I tumbled headlong into the fish pond at Poitiers. It took three men-at-arms to haul me out, choking and half-drowned and most indignant. The queen was not best pleased."

Actually, Queen Eleanor's ire had been directed more at her son, Lord John, who'd pushed Madeline into the pond. But for some reason Madeline was loath to bring her friend's name into play between her and Ian right now.

His deep voice rumbled in his chest behind her. "Well, 'tis a matter easily corrected, this half-finished education of yours."

With Madeline held high in both arms, Ian swung a leg over the pommel and slid easily to the ground. Setting her on her feet, he threw the reins over a low-hanging tree branch and loosened the saddle girth. While he attended to the horse, Madeline looked about the glen, entranced. She glanced up at him when he rejoined her, expecting him to stand beside her and share the beauty of the scene. To her surprise, he took her arm, turned her sideways, and matter-of-factly began to unlace the ties that held her bliaut at the side.

She slapped at his hands and edged away. "What are you about?"

Undeterred, he pulled her back to him and worked the ties loose. "I'm undressing you, lady wife."

The spell wrought by the slow ride and the magical scene evaporated instantly, to be replaced by a mixture of indignation and sudden, breathless anticipation.

"'Tis . . .'tis broad daylight!"

"Aye, so it is."

"Ian, you cannot do this."

One golden brow cocked. "And what is it you think I do?"

While she sought for a dignified reply, he lifted the now less-than-pristine blue-green gown over her head and tossed it carelessly to the ground. Ignoring Madeline's sputtering protests, he gathered her shift and tugged it up and off, as well. Feeling ridiculous and unaccountably embarrassed in only her leather slippers, stockings and short undershift, she tried to back away. His big hands tangled in her hair and held her in place.

"Ouch!"

"Hold still," he ordered unsympathetically, untying her braids.

"You could take lessons from Gerda," she muttered as he raked his fingers through the rippling mass. "Ian, you do realize that your guests will think you mad, or most discourteous, should we not return soon?"

"Aye."

"We cannot do this," she repeated stubbornly.

"Aye, lady wife," he replied with a crooked grin, "we can."

With the unselfconscious grace of a great, untamed cat, he stripped himself of the trappings of civilization. His surcoat followed Madeline's robes to the grassy bank, then his finely woven linen shirt. He shucked his braies and chausses and boots and stood before her, magnificent in his nakedness. He belonged to this glen, Madeline thought, swallowing. And to this wild, rugged country. Like the land around him, his body was hard and unyielding, yet beautiful in its sculptured planes and shadowed hollows. The sunlight picked out golden lights in the hair that furred his chest and arrowed down toward a flat, hard belly and lean flanks. She felt a liquid heat gather between her legs at the sight of his manhood, half-roused and nestled against the gilded pelt of his groin.

Madeline knew not whether he owed his coloring to the ancient pagan ones he'd spoken of earlier, or to the Norsemen who'd once sailed up the friths and rivers and plundered these valleys. But when he knelt before her to remove her slippers, she couldn't resist the urge to bury her fingers in the tawny thatch of hair so close at hand.

He straightened, sliding his palms up her calves, and then over the swell of her hips. Through the thin linen, Madeline could feel the roughness of his skin, made hard by years of wielding sword and lance. Of a sudden, she remembered how he had won her in the tourney, and carried her away from all that she knew. Her unthinking pleasure in the moment dimmed, and uncertainty shaded her eyes.

"Nay, no doubts, now, wife," he told her. "You must trust me in this."

She bit her lip, unsure not only of him, but of herself, as well.

His eyes gleamed as he bent and lifted her once more. "Put your arms about me," he instructed gently.

Madeline released a slow breath. Feeling much like one entering an unfamiliar home after a long journey, she raised her arms and wrapped them around the strong column of his neck. Her breasts, swollen and tender almost beyond bearing, ached as they pressed against the hardness of his chest.

"Now, lady wife, we will see about teaching you to swim."

In two long strides, he had cleared the grassy bank and plunged into the pool.

"Ian! Aieee! 'Tis cold!"

Madeline's shriek rose above the noisy tumble of the waterfall. She clambered higher in his arms, trying to lift her rump out of the cold, clear water. He laughed and fell backward, taking her down with him.

When he broke surface, she clutched frantically at his neck, clinging to him like a limpet.

"You wretch! You idiot! You're like to drown me!"

"I misdoubt you'll drown in this shallow pool. And not with all this buoyancy you've acquired of late," he added, grinning wickedly as he flexed his chest against her swollen breasts.

She groaned and buried her face in his neck. "I know, I know! I've become a veritable cow!"

"Well, mayhap, but a most delightful one." He laughed at her muffled snort. "Come, even cows with full udders can swim."

Afterward, when she'd floated and sunk and sputtered and shrieked and, at last, paddled to his satisfaction, they lay on the grassy bank side by side, their faces to the sun. Madeline's short shift clung to her body like a second skin. Her hair fanned out on the grass above her head, a wild, curling blanket of sable against the verdant green.

She kept her eyes closed against the sunlight's glare, thinking that this was not at all the way she'd expected to spend her first hours as Ian's wife. She couldn't quite believe they lay in this glade, so far from the crowded keep and boisterous banquet. The raucous, lewd toasts and suggestive minstrel songs seemed of a different world.

A rustle at her side told her Ian stirred. Opening one eye, she saw him propped up on his hand, a smile tugging at his lips as he surveyed her sprawled length.

"You look like one of the water sprites who were thought to inhabit this glen, all wet and glistening and beautiful."

"I'm not beautiful," she said, closing her eye again. "I'm fat."

"Fat and beautiful."

"Just fat." She pursed her lips. "I've lost my waist."

"So I see. You need it not."

She felt his hand trace her more generous curves. His palm rested on her hip, warm through the coolness of her wet shift.

"I am grown clumsy," she said on a sigh. "As awkward as my maid."

His small laugh gusted against her cheek. "Nay, never could you grow that awkward."

"I have a bulge," she mourned.

His hand curved over her small, rounded stomach. Madeline kept her eyes closed, her every nerve atingle.

"Aye, and so you do."

The bright sunlight danced against her lids. It seemed to Madeline that although she could not see, her every other sense leapt into awareness. When he rolled over and settled his hips between her knees, she heard the smooth slide of his flesh on the thick grass. His scent rose to mingle in her nostrils, sharp and clean and male. And when he kissed the slight bulge of her stomach, she gasped and ran her tongue along her bottom lip, tasting desire.

"Ah, Madeline, you're most beauteous," he said softly, peeling up her shift. "Like a ripe, succulent sacrifice the ancient ones made to the gods who lived in these wilds."

"I thought such sacrifices were supposed to be virgin," she managed on a half laugh, half gasp. "I hardly think you can include me in that rank."

His mouth moved down her stomach, leaving a trail of pleasure where it touched. Heat spread through her loins and traced along her veins. He eased her thighs apart, opening her to the sun and his warm, whispered words.

"To me, this honeyed sweetness is virgin," he murmured against her core.

That particular honeyed sweetness was virgin to Madeline, too. A flush of embarrassment stained her cheeks as his tongue delved into her depths. Flustered, she tried to scuttle back. He allowed no separation, however, no space between them. His hands slid under her buttocks, lifting her to fit his mouth.

"Lie still, wife, and let me taste of you."

With a helpless sigh, Madeline flung her arms over her head and gave herself up to the sensations Ian wrought within her. His breath washed hot and moist against her slick flesh. His tongue rasped against her inner folds. Squeezing her eyes shut, she concentrated fiercely on the slow, spiraling pleasure that

built, receded, and then built again. Time seemed to
lose itself, then rush forward apace. She moaned
softly, and again, not so softly. Of their own accord,
her hips left the earth and thrust upward to meet his
hungry mouth.

Through the ache of his own need, Ian could sense
that she neared her peak. He turned his head and nipped the tender inside of one thigh, then rolled onto his
back, bringing her atop him. In a swirl of silken limbs
and shining hair, she sat astride his hips. Her swollen
breasts teased him with their fullness, but when he
took them in his hands she gave a little gasp of discomfort. Ian contented himself with palming the line
of her ribs, the smooth curve of her waist and hips. He
bent one knee to support her back, near groaning with
the effort to restrain himself until she found a rhythm
that would suit her.

Their joining had been blessed by the church not
three hours ago, but Madeline felt a pagan wildness
stir her blood. 'Twas this glen, she thought, while she
could still think at all. 'Twas the sunlight streaming
through the leaves and the scent of grass crushed under Ian's shoulders. And the sight of his jaw, tight
with the power of his need. She rose, feeling every
ridged inch of his shaft, then lowered herself, sheath-
ing him. She rose again, and then again.

When it burst upon them, their shattering release
brought a cry as old and as primitive as the earth on
which they joined.

Afterward, she lay with her head cradled on his shoulder and her face to the sun. Thick grass cushioned her back and hips. The muted rush of the waterfall drowned out all but the sound of their own breathing, coming slowly back to normal.

"Ian?"

"Mmm?"

"Of all my weddings and beddings, this is the strangest one so far."

Lazy laughter rumbled in the chest next to her ear. "Good. I would not wish you to confuse me in your mind with your other lords."

"As if I could!" she muttered under her breath.

They lay silent for a few moments, and Madeline pondered the strange course of events that had brought them to this moment, this glen. A sudden flutter in her stomach cut into her confused thoughts. She gave a little start, then lifted a hand to trace slow circles over the small bulge.

Ian eased his arm from under her head and propped himself up on one elbow. Frowning, he watched the movement of her fingers. Madeline caught his look, and her hand stilled.

"Did we harm the babe?" he asked, his voice worried.

"Nay," she replied. "We just disturbed his slumber."

His expression thoughtful, he reached out and brushed her hand aside. To Madeline's surprise, his fingers took up the circular pattern, warm and rough-tipped and sure on her stomach.

A slow ache pierced her heart, so strong she had to bite her lips against the pain. At that moment, Madeline would have given all she possessed to gift this man with the knowledge that the child she carried was his. This golden, blue-eyed warrior who had enraged her, tormented her, tumbled her into his arms and given her pleasure such as she had never known. She covered his hand with hers, pressing it against her belly.

"Ian..."

"Aye?"

"I would have you know that...that this child..."

"That this babe is of my loins," he finished, when she could not.

She swallowed painfully. "Aye, although I know there's no way to give you proof of it."

"I don't need proof, Madeline, if you tell me 'tis so."

"How can you believe it?" Her eyes searched his face. "How can I know that you believe it?"

Ian rested his palm on the taut mound of flesh. There were a hundred things he could have told her. He could have said that he'd gained a greater insight into the woman who was his wife during the long hours he'd spent with Guy Blackhair in the churgeon's tent, while the knight hovered between life and death from the sword wound to his side. He could have told her of Lady Elizabeth's surprising defense of a woman she had once despised. He could have shared with her

Will's blunt demand that his brother honor the lady who carried his babe.

But Ian knew that this matter was between them alone, only them, and none other. It depended not on other people's words, whether whispered or ground out with the hoarseness of pain.

"You took my pledge that I would not harm you if you loosed the shackles to tend my wrists," he said slowly. "You trusted in me then, Madeline. You must trust in me now. As I trust in you."

She bit her lower lip, uncertainty clouding her eyes.

Ian bent and brushed her mouth with his. "Trust in me, wife, as I will in you."

The sun was slipping behind Skiddaw peak when at last they returned to Wyndham. The feast had lasted most of the summer afternoon, then spilled into the games that had been organized for entertainment. Shouts and whistles of encouragement filled the twilight air as archers loosed their shafts in the open fields outside the walls to sing toward straw targets. Young squires titled at shields set on spinning poles. Coracle races were taking place on the lake, with much laughter and boisterous advice to the contestants attempting to maneuver the round-bottomed boats around a course marked by floating buoys. As they rode by, Madeline caught sight of Lady Alicia clapping and shouting encouragement to Will, who poled furiously through the churning waters.

If only this day could last forever, she thought with a small sigh. If only the golden sunshine would not fade, nor the shadows creep across the land.

As much as she wished to, however, Madeline could not hold back the march of time. With the close of August, Ian laid plans to move his household from Wyndham. As was both custom and necessity, the great landholding barons changed their residence with the season, leaving one keep when its stores were drained and moving to the next. Such measures ensured the lord kept close to his lands and the vassals knew their lord.

Lady Elizabeth decided to take up residence for the winter in one of her dower manors near Coventry, far enough south to give her ease from the rough winds but close enough to attend Madeline when her time came. She journeyed with Ian and Madeline as far as Bolton, where Will took Alicia to wife amid much revelry and feasting.

It was while they were loading the baggage wains at Bolton that the king's courier caught up with them. The courier brought two messages. One for Ian, summoning him to the king's presence to explain why he married in such haste, without the formality of royal consent. The second message was for Madeline from Lord John. The king's son desired the friend of his childhood to return to his father's court so that he could assure himself she was not ill-used in this joining. Having distinguished himself in the recent battles, John now basked in his father's favor and would use all royal influence to have this marriage set aside, should Madeline wish it.

She drew in a swift breath as the message was read to her. Her gaze flew to Ian, standing across the small window embrasure where they'd sought privacy. With a curt nod and a silver penny pulled from the leather pouch at his waist, Ian dismissed the courier. When he turned to face his wife, his eyes were glittering points of dark blue flame.

"This marriage will not be set aside," he told her flatly. "There are no grounds, and I will allow neither prince nor priest to fabricate them."

Madeline couldn't answer, too stunned by the contents of the message to form a coherent thought.

He closed the distance between them and lifted her chin with a firm hand. "Heed me, wife. If I have to lock you in that damned cell at Cragsmore and fight off the king's entire army, you'll not be free of me."

"Ian—"

"You gave yourself to me, and I will hold you."

"Ian, I don't—"

"I swear it, Madeline."

She yanked her chin out of his hold. "Holy Virgin! I don't wish to have our marriage set aside, and so I will tell the king, and John, and *you,* if you would but listen to me!"

"Why not?"

"What?"

"Why do you not wish the marriage dissolved? You were reluctant enough to enter into it."

"Yes, well, that was before."

"Before what?"

"Oh, for pity's sake!" She turned, exasperated, to stare out the window.

Ian's hand snaked out and brought her back around. He backed her against the stone pillar between the window openings.

"Before what?"

She waved a hand helplessly. "Before...before you took me to the glen. Before I came to share your table and your bed."

And to share your trust, she wanted to add. This trust that was slowly building into love. 'Twas too soon to speak of it, she feared. The tenuous bond was yet too fragile to expose. But it grew within her each day, overlaying the passion that flared whenever Ian took her to bed. It expanded a bit more whenever he smiled that lazy smile of his or even, as he was wont to do, rubbed her back of a night. 'Twas something new to her, something unexpected and a little frightening.

"I'm not ill-used in this marriage, my lord," she said softly, "and so I will tell the king's son."

They took the journey south in easy stages. In deference to her mounding belly, Madeline rode in the four-wheeled litter Ian had procured, accompanied by a chattering Gerda. Madeline kept the curtains pulled well back and often found herself enlivened by the colorful throng of travelers who shared the road. She'd expected the rocking motion of the great cart to be torture, but the sickness that had plagued her for so long eased, then gradually disappeared.

The court lay at Westminster Hall, originally the palace of the Saxon king Edward the Confessor, but much enlarged and fortified by the Norman conquerors. Not far from London, the palace was yet distant enough to leave behind the stench of the overcrowded city streets. It was set among spacious gardens filled with heavy-limbed fruit trees and surrounded by lush pastures. Close by, for the pleasure of the king's hunt, was a royal forest thick with timbered copses and well populated by deer and boar and bulls.

With the peace negotiations between Henry and Philip as yet unconcluded, the court was not as crowded and chaotic as usual. Many of the barons remained on the Continent, making sure they kept possession of the castles they had reclaimed or stolen. Ian had only to slip a handful of coins to the king's seneschal to secure a comfortable set of rooms for him and Madeline, just a short walk from the vast, aisled hall where the king met with his councillors during the day and presided at the banquets each night.

Ian took little note of the palace's fine oaken walls and arched nave when he went to answer the king's summons the day after their arrival. A muscle ticked in one side of his jaw as he waited in the anteroom, marshaling his arguments in support of his joining with Madeline. Only one mattered, however. She was his, and he would have her.

Henry was not alone when Ian was ushered into his presence. Three scribes were perched at tall desks set close to the windows to catch the light, scribbling furiously while the king dictated. William, lord marshal of England, nodded a friendly greeting. But it was the third, richly robed figure who snared Ian's attention. Lord John stood stiff and silent, his dark eyes unsmiling.

A man of immense energy, Henry wasted little time on preliminaries. After a curt greeting, he clasped his hands behind his back and paced the chamber. "Well, de Burgh, what have you to say of this hasty marriage of yours?"

Knowing his king well, Ian minced no words. "I came to desire the Lady Madeline, and have wed with her. 'Twas not done against her will, although I would have taken her so, were it necessary."

Ignoring John's swift hiss of breath, he continued. "The union was blessed by the church. And my lady wife now swells with child."

A sudden silence descended, broken after a moment by Henry's bellow of laughter. "That was fast work, even for you, Ian. Well, well, Lady Madeline always was one to stir a man's blood. You'll have your hands full with her, I doubt not."

"I'll manage, sir."

"And she?" John asked, his eyes angry. "How does she fare in this hurried union?"

Ian turned to face him. "You may ask her yourself," he answered in a slow north-country drawl, "when I bring her to table this night."

The inference was not lost on anyone present. The king's son could speak with Ian's wife—in his presence.

"I'll ask her now." John started toward the door, only to be waved back by his father.

"We'll summon the lady, that we may all hear her answer."

He sent an attendant scurrying with a request for Madeline's presence. Ian kept his face impassive, listening with half an ear as the king filled the wait with talk of the stalled peace initiatives. Philip was impossible, Henry groused, demanding among other things either the immediate marriage of his sister, Lady Alice, to Richard *Coeur de Lion,* or the return of her person and her dower lands. Since the lady had been betrothed to Richard for some twenty years, and had been mistress to Henry for half that time, Ian knew there was little likelihood of the lady or her lands being returned to France. 'Twas, however, only one of the points of contention between Henry and his son that Philip played most skillfully.

Henry was in the midst of an angry discourse against his archenemy when Lady Madeline was announced. She slanted Ian a quick, searching glance as she went past, as though trying to gauge his thoughts. He felt the tendons in his neck tightening, one by one, when she knelt before the king.

Henry raised her up with a strong hand. "Here, here, no need for that, not when you carry a babe." His eyes skimmed down her front, which was considerably more curvaceous than the last time she'd been at court. His red-gold brows rose. "'Twould appear you've carried it far longer than we thought."

Madeline smiled, not at all disconcerted by his frank appraisal. "I cannot dispute the king's greater knowledge in these matters."

Henry, who had fathered eight living children on his queen, snorted. "Nay, I would think not."

Ian watched the byplay between his wife and the most powerful king in Christendom. Despite his tension, he was fascinated by Madeline's poise.

He knew her well enough now, however, to recognize the subtle signs that she, too, felt the strain of this moment. Although she smiled on the king, her movements lacked their usual grace and her back was stiff. It became even stiffer when Henry brought them back to the business at hand in his brusque way.

"Tell me straight, Lady Madeline, is this marriage to your liking? Do you feel ill-used by it?"

John stepped forward to hover at his father's shoulder, his dark eyes intent on Madeline's face.

"I am not ill-used, my lord." Her reply was soft but sure.

Ian saw the swift play of emotions that passed across John's face. Anger, and denial, and a swift, bitter hurt.

The king shrugged. "'Tis settled, then. I'll levy a healthy fine on your lord for being so presumptuous as to wed you without my permission and to make sure he values you as he should. Go and take your ease while I finish this business."

John stepped forward. "I'll escort Lady Madeline to her chambers."

With a naturalness born of long years, Madeline lifted her hand to place it on his sleeve. Only when it hovered just a few inches above his outstretched arm did she hesitate and think to look to her husband. Her eyes met Ian's, a question in their depths that only he could answer.

"I'll see you when I return, lady wife," he told her with a small smile.

Her lips curved in response, and she slanted him a look that was private, personal, and most provocative. "Aye, my lord."

Ian watched them leave, then turned to find Henry eyeing him shrewdly.

"'Twas one of the reasons I summoned you to my presence," the king said bluntly, "this friendship between my son and your lady wife. I want to know whether it will cause bad blood between us."

"It will not, on my part." As he said the words, Ian knew them to be true. In his heart, he'd accepted Madeline's avowal that there was naught between her and the king's son.

"Good," the king stated, "because I have need of you. I would ask a service of you."

'Twas typical of Henry, Ian thought wryly. He'd levy a fine on his barons in one breath and demand a service of them in the next.

"I leave immediately for Giscors," the king explained, pacing again. "Philip wants another meeting at the Tree of Peace to discuss conditions. He insists this time we will come to settlement. Christ's bones, I hope so. Even the pope pushes me to peace, so that Richard can go on with his Crusade."

"I'll need a few days to settle my lady wife," Ian replied, his mind was busy with the logistics of which keep would hold Madeline most safe and secure in his absence.

"Nay, nay, I don't ask you to come this time. The marshal here goes with me, but Chester stays. And you. I would have you remain here, with your lady wife. John will remain, as well." Henry paused, then added with a small shrug, "I wish him to have the counsel of my loyal barons while I am gone."

Behind the king's back, Ian shot William Marshal a quick look. The old knight gave a little shake of his head, as if to say they would speak of this later. Privately.

Ian nodded grimly. In the short hours he'd been at Westminster, he'd already heard whispers that even the king's youngest, most beloved son was becoming disaffected with Henry's inability to loose the reins. After distinguishing himself in the recent battles, John had expected, but had not received, tangible reward.

Cold rippled down Ian's back. If John went the way of his brothers and turned against his father, the king's rage would know no bounds. He could only hope that Henry and Philip reached agreement quickly, and that the king found a way to satisfy this never-ending discord among his sons.

Chapter Seventeen

Contrary to Ian's hopes, the peace talks at Giscors broke down almost as soon as they began. A Welsh knight, believing himself insulted by a French lord, promptly put an arrow into the man's skull, thereby violating the sacred Tree of Peace. Even William Marshal's offer of single combat with any French knight put forth failed to assuage Philip's rage. He withdrew, vowing vengeance. Henry and Richard rode off to lay siege to Mantes.

A month later Henry and Philip met once more, this time at Châtillon, and again failed to reach a peace. Before long, however, the shocking news that Richard Lionheart had opened separate peace negotiations with Philip soon made its way to England.

Ian and the other barons not called to knight service watched the developments on the Continent with a gathering sense of unease. Most of them held lands of both Henry and Richard, and wondered if they would again have to choose between them. 'Twould not be the first time the son warred against the father, nor, Ian predicted grimly, the last. Quietly, he sent orders to reinforce his own holding of St. Briac, set high on the rolling, sea-swept cliffs of Normandy, and saw to the strengthening of his younger brothers' holdings, as well.

He also watched with growing unease the vacillations of the Lord John. The young warrior who had distinguished himself in the previous battles now chafed at being left in England, without say in the peace talks and with little responsibility to occupy him.

Madeline was less disturbed by the tension that seemed to grip the court. In the habit of all breeding women, she focused less on the events unfolding around her and more on the changes taking place within her.

In truth, she often felt herself suspended between two worlds during those long weeks. By day she was surrounded by silk-clad ladies engaged in embroidery or music or gossip. Her evenings were filled with the sounds of trumpets announcing the start of great feasts, and the songs of minstrels.

But her nights, her nights belonged to Ian. Unlike most of those at the court, she made no complaint as autumn passed and the days grew shorter, the drafts colder. She would sit beside Ian at the boards and listen to the talk, knowing that her fecund state gave her the excuse to retire early. And retire she often did, with her husband at her side.

As Madeline ripened, the sensuous, erotic explorations that had characterized the first months of their

marriage gave way to tamer pleasures, and then, finally, to a simple shared warmth. Like a nesting dove,
however, it was a warmth she much craved.

She saw little of John during the passing weeks,
which both concerned and relieved her. Ian hadn't
forbidden her to speak with him, but neither did it
please him when she did. She made it a point to do so
only in the presence of others, but her heart ached at
the disquiet she saw increasingly in her friend's dark
eyes. She wished she could go to him and listen while
he poured out his anger and frustration, then tease
him to laughter. But he was a part of her old world
that she could not seem to fit into her new.

These two worlds collided, then narrowed abruptly
to a small, dark point of pain on a blustery November day.

Madeline sat with a group of courtiers in Winches-
ter's music room, a cozy bower strewn with lutes and
beribboned harps where lords and ladies came to
compose *chansons* or practice their skills on the
stringed instruments or simply flirt. She'd spent many
hours at such pleasures in the past, but had little desire to linger at them now. Now she wanted only to return to her chambers, relieve the increasing pressure
on her bladder, put up her feet and await Ian's return
from the hunt. Her advancing pregnancy made comfort a more immediate concern than the pastimes she
was used to enjoy, she thought wryly.

She glanced up as the door to the music chamber
opened and a group of men entered, laughing. She

searched eagerly for a glimpse of her husband's broad shoulders and tawny hair among them. 'Twas not Ian who detached himself from the group and came toward her, however, but John.

"I would rise, my lord," she said with a rueful smile, "if I could."

His gaze swept her rounded figure. "And to think I once thought you flat, Maddy."

"Wretch," she murmured for his ears alone, glad to see that the cold air and sport had restored his humor. "Did you have a successful hunt?"

"Aye, most successful." He flung himself down on a stool beside her, signaling to the singer who'd been entertaining the company to continue.

Madeline caught the sideways glances cast their way as the various lords and ladies resumed their seats. Her simple enjoyment in John's company faded. 'Twas an awkward thing, this business of trying to hold true to both husband and friend, she thought, sighing. When the song ended, she asked for John's aid to get her to her feet.

"I must go," she said lightly. "If you are returned, my lord will be, also."

He drew her up, but his hand tightened around hers, and a flash of annoyance crossed his features. "I never thought to see you on so short a leash, Madeline. You, of all people."

"Nay, nor I," she replied with a laugh, refusing to apologize or deny that it was a leash she little minded.

He stared down at her for a long moment, then abruptly released her hand and turned away.

Mayhap it was her bulk that made her clumsy, or the discomfort of her bladder, or her sorrow that she could not find her old ease with John. Whatever it was, she didn't see the discarded lute that tripped her and made her foot slide out from under her. She hit the hard tiles with a breathless, frightened cry.

John rushed to kneel beside her. "Maddy! Jesu, Maddy, are you all right?"

The others crowded around as she sat up slowly, her face ashen. "I... I think so."

"Don't jostle her," someone called.

"Get her to bed," another urged.

Madeline sat unmoving on the floor until the black spots stopped dancing in front of her, then raised wide, stricken eyes to the man beside her. "Help me up, John. I'd best go to my chambers."

Ignoring the hand she held out to him, he bent and gathered her in his arms. With a quick order for the king's physician to report at once to Lord Ian's chambers, he swept out of the music room.

The first spasm hit her while they strode through the corridors. Madeline arched in John's arms, gasping, as the muscles of her womb contracted violently.

John cursed and tightened his hold.

The second caught her as they approached the stairs to the upper story.

"No!" she sobbed, convulsing in its throes. "No! 'Tis too early!"

At John's furious order, a footman raced along the corridor to pound on the door of Madeline's chambers. Ian's squire flung open the timbered panel, sent a startled look down the hall and shouted for his master.

Half-undressed and still soiled with the dirt of the hunt, Ian reached instinctively for his sword. The blade was fully out of the scabbard when John swept in.

"Ian," Madeline sobbed, holding out her arms. "'Tis the babe! I fell, and 'tis the babe!"

The sword clattered to the floor. Grim-faced, Ian strode forward and gathered her to his chest. She curled against him, sobbing. Without a backward glance, he turned and carried her to the bed.

"Hush, sweeting, hush..." he murmured into her hair, his voice low and reassuring.

In her distress, Madeline didn't catch the tremor that shook his shoulders when he lowered her to the bed.

John, however, saw it. He stood for a moment, his arms hanging empty at his sides, his eyes filled with a dark pain. Then the portly physician puffed in, his robes flapping, followed shortly by the lady's maid. Soon the room was crowded with attendants, all unnoticed by the couple on the bed. Madeline arched in pain and clung to Ian's hand with both of hers.

The king's son turned and left.

Ian had never known a fear such as had leapt into his heart when he saw Madeline carried into the room.

But the hours that followed magnified his initial fear a thousandfold and flung it back in his face.

She labored long into the night, and all through the next day. The physician poked and probed and shook his head, saying there was naught he could do. The babe came too soon, in his opinion, to survive. It looked doubtful for the mother, as well.

Gerda hovered at her mistress's bedside, trampling on the hems of the ladies who came to give what comfort they could, until one snapped at her to mind her feet. Ian banished all visitors after that, allowing only Gerda and the senior midwife and her attendants to remain. He himself was anchored to the bed by Madeline's frantic grasp.

When she was delivered of a tiny, fragile girl child in the dark hours just before the second dawn, Ian thought her agony at last was ended. The babe gave a weak cry, followed by a louder one when the midwife cleared its mouth. Madeline sobbed in relief, then used the last reserves of her strength to expel the afterbirth. Having assured herself that the babe was whole, she slipped into a sleep that was closer to unconsciousness than to slumber.

Ian said a fervent prayer of thanks for their deliverance and left his wife's side to wash and change. He soon found, however, that another ordeal awaited him.

Gerda came to stand beside him while he splashed cold water over his face and shoulders, her plump face pasty and white. "The babe's too weak to take suck, m'lord. The wet nurse cannot get her to take the nipple."

Ian straightened slowly, a rough towel held to his face, and turned to watch the sturdy kitchen maid who'd been hustled upstairs. The woman sat on a low stool, her swollen breast bared, the distended nipple teasing the swaddled babe's mouth. The infant lay unmoving, without the strength to suckle.

The midwife shrugged and said 'twas God's will. With a shake of her head, she packed her baskets, shooed her assistants out of the room and said she would send a priest. A robed bishop came and went, his words of comfort falling on deaf ears.

Ian was now locked in a struggle more fierce than any battle he'd ever fought. With Gerda's determined assistance, he laid the tiny being on a table and began the slow process of feeding, drop by drop, the milk the wet nurse squeezed out into a cup. The babe's tongue pushed out more than Ian's finger put in, but he didn't give up. Nor did it occur to him to delegate the task to one of the many serving women available at his call. The sense of responsibility that had governed his care of his family since he was scarcely ten years old would not have allowed him to abandon the babe, even had he wanted to. With each passing hour, his determination to save the child grew, as did its hold on his heart.

Madeline came slowly awake. Her lower body ached with a wrenching, grinding hurt that filled her mind for the first moments of consciousness. Her lashes lifted only with great effort, as though they were weighted down. When at last she could focus, she saw that it was dusk. Candles flickered in their holders, and a fire snapped in the great hearth. She moved her head on the pillow, seeking, searching.

At last she saw them, Ian and Gerda and a tiny, swaddled bundle. Gerda held a silver cup. Ian dipped his finger in, then pressed it to the babe's mouth. His brow was furrowed in intense concentration, his muscled body coiled over the child.

"Drink." The low, muted command held an emotion she'd never before heard in his voice. "Drink."

Her throat closed with a piercing ache. She'd longed to be able to give Ian proof the child was his. She saw now that he needed none.

"Bring her here," she called softly.

In the quiet, desperate hours that followed, Madeline's milk replaced that of the wet nurse in the silver cup. She and Ian took turns feeding the child, nudging her awake again and again when she drifted off, dribbling as much of the life-giving sustenance down her throat as she would take.

It was two days before the babe's lips tightened around Ian's finger in a reflexive sucking movement. His eyes rested briefly on her red, wrinkled face, and then he withdrew his finger and brushed a knuckle down a still-mottled cheek.

"Madeline," he called softly to his sleeping wife. "Wake, sweeting."

His lips curved into a grin. When his wife slept, she slept. He shook her shoulder gently, and she jerked awake, her frightened gaze flying to the babe cradled beside her. She gave a small cry of joy when she saw the tiny lips pursed and smacking.

Stiff in every joint, Ian straightened slowly. He felt as though he'd been racked, and yet as he stood beside his wife's bed and watched her put their babe to her breast, an exultation filled him, wilder than any he'd ever known.

While winter closed down outside, bringing cold drizzle and the first brush of snow, Madeline and Gerda kept the fires burning bright in their rooms. The babe, baptized Elizabeth in honor of the woman who braved the roads to come south and help tend her, clung tenaciously to life. Ian was relegated to an outer chamber, his role diminished by his mother's presence. Leaving the women to their work, he went back to the business of men.

Gradually the babe's limbs gained strength, and within a few weeks her cry was as lusty as any of the hovering women could have wished. Unwilling to expose Bess to the risks of travel, Ian kept his family in residence at Westminster.

While they stayed wrapped in a cocoon of warmth and comfort, the world without rushed forward to a bitter winter. Only gradually did Madeline regain an awareness of the desperate situation that now faced the king.

In November, the Angevin's united front had been shattered when Richard, determined to get on with the Crusade he'd pledged himself to, threw in with Philip.

Richard rode up to the colloquy at Bonoulins beside Philip and laid his demands before his father: He would wed the woman he'd been betrothed to for some twenty years, he wanted full rule of Anjou and Maine, and Henry must publicly proclaim him heir of England and Normandy.

Henry refused, fighting resumed, and Ian left for France. The weather worsened, however, and a half-hearted peace was agreed to until the following Eastertide. Nursing his anger, Henry retired to Saumur to spend Christmas with John. Afterward, the king remained in Normandy, while John returned to take up residence at Colchester keep.

Ian himself returned in February. He'd spent the extra weeks investing his holdings around St. Briac with additional men. He'd been prepared to take arms against Richard, should he be called to it.

Still chilled from the miserable winter crossing, he took a few moments to admire the sleeping Bess, then quickly stripped and let his squire take his mail for cleaning. With a groan of pleasure, he sank gratefully into a tub of steaming water. After assuring herself he'd taken no hurt, Lady Elizabeth retired, leaving him in Madeline's care. His wife scrubbed his back and washed his hair and generally ignored his invitations to join him in the tub. When she'd dried him, however, and clothed him in a warm robe, she allowed herself to be taken onto his lap as they sat by the fire in the outer chamber.

Gradually, the sounds of Gerda readying herself for bed died away, to be replaced sometime later by her snores. The maid slept on a pallet beside the babe's cradle, being somewhat lighter at her rest than her mistress, or so she'd informed Madeline.

In the quiet night, Ian gave his wife what details he knew of Richard's break with the king. She pursed her lips over the man's perfidy, but was too used to the chaotic relationship between Henry and his older son to be surprised. Ian's next words, however, caused her considerably more consternation.

"'Tis said that Philip, having won the older son, now courts the younger."

"John will not betray his father," she said flatly.

"Think you not?" Ian asked, resting his chin on her head as he stared into the fire. "I've heard rumors that couriers arrive with increasing regularity at Colchester, bearing secret messages and promises from Philip, and from Richard."

Madeline shifted in his arms to stare up at his face. "Ian, he would not side with Philip. He could not. John believes Henry will yet devolve the lands on him he would wish."

She bit her lip, realizing that she was trying to convince herself as well as him.

Her husband's blue eyes were troubled as they rested on her face. "The king has tried afore to take lands from Richard to give to John, and failed. Nor is he as strong now as he once was. The trip to Saumur tired him unexpectedly."

"What, do you mean he rode only fifty miles a day, instead of the hundred he's been known to? Did you not have to grab a few hours' rest under a hedgerow, then scramble to follow him, as usual?"

Laughter rumbled in Ian's chest. "Nay, I slept in a ditch, as I usually do when with the king."

Madeline snuggled back into his warmth. "There, you see? Henry's invincible, or as near to it as makes no difference. He'll settle this matter with Richard, as he has before, and John must wait for an inheritance."

"I hope you're right. In any case, I'm glad the king's son is now at Colchester and not here." Ian's quiet voice provided a low counterpoint to the hiss and spit of the fire. "I'd as soon you not be again in his company afore you take Bess north."

Madeline frowned into his furred robe.

His breath stirred her hair. "Keep a safe distance from him, at least until the king returns."

Lifting her head, she searched his face. "I have no plans to go to Colchester, Ian."

He nodded, then added, "Nor will you see John if he comes here."

Placing her hands against his chest, she pushed herself off his lap. She stood before him, frowning, her chin lifted in a manner Ian had not seen in many months.

"What is this 'will' and 'will not'? I thought you'd come to trust me, husband."

"I do," he drawled, surveying her tumbled hair and flushed face. "'Tis John I don't trust, nor have I ever. I don't wish you involved in his schemes, wife, if schemes they be."

Her eyes narrowed, but before she could speak, Ian reached out and caught the front of her robe. Spreading his legs, he tugged her forward until she stood at the juncture of his thighs.

"You'd best beware how you glare at me, lady. Such ill humors may turn your milk."

"Or your head, when I clout it! Ian, we must speak of this. I cannot—"

"Nay, no more, wife. No more of the king, or the king's son, or any of the Angevin devils." Lazily he parted the folds of her robe, revealing the sheer shift underneath. "Let's speak instead of how we may work off these excess humors of yours."

Madeline snatched at her gown, unwilling to admit that she was, indeed, suddenly filled with an excess of bodily spirits. They curled in her belly and flooded her veins with a liquid heat.

"We must discuss this sudden desire of yours to order my movements." She jerked her chin toward the bulge in his braies. "And do not think to turn my head with that!"

"Ah, wife, 'tis not your head I wish to turn." Grinning, he slid his hands inside her robe and took her by the waist. With one smooth lift, she was astride his thighs, her center pressed intimately to his. "And I plan most definitely to order your movements."

"Ian, the babe!" Madeline cast a helpless glance over his shoulder at the cradle in the other room. Bess slept quietly, Gerda less quietly beside her.

"Our daughter had best learn now to close her ears," he murmured, sliding her robe off her shoulders. "Or you to still your cries."

"I do not cry," she protested.

"Aye, you do, sweeting. You make the most delicious noises. Sometimes 'tis a little grunt. Occasionally 'tis a shriek."

Ignoring her indignant sputter, he tugged her shift up and over her head.

"And often a mewling sort of whimper, one that I have not heard in far too many weeks."

Madeline saw his gaze drop to the cloth that bound her breasts, wet in spots where she had leaked. His hands gentle, he unbound her.

As he reached up to shape her fullness, she felt a sudden glory in her womanliness. And a stirring of the love that had taken seed when he held her in keeping against her will, had been nurtured during the uncertain weeks after their hasty wedding, and had come to full bloom in the desperate hours while they battled for their daughter's life.

Madeline took his face in both her hands, her eyes willing him to stop his play and listen. "I have not done so before, my lord, but I would thank you."

"For what, my lady?" he answered gravely, his gaze locked with hers.

"For refusing to pay your ransom," she murmured wickedly, leaning forward to slant her lips to his, "and for escaping your chains that night."

With the coming of March, Bess gained in weight. Lady Elizabeth returned to her own holdings and Madeline began to emerge more from her rooms. Knowing they would leave for the north as soon as the ice crusted on the roads melted, she began once more to enjoy the company kept close within Westminster. Her ready laughter soon drifted across the solars, and her merry smile once more dazzled.

Ian propped a shoulder against a pillar and watched his wife, surrounded by her usual court of admirers. He smiled, wondering what it was about her that entranced men so. It wasn't her figure, although she still retained a fullness from Bess's birthing that he found most pleasing. Nor her features, not with that short nose and determined chin. It was more the sparkle in her jewellike eyes, he decided, and the warmth in her ready smile. That warmth kept him enthralled, even as it did the young knight on one knee beside her.

"Please, my lady," the youth importuned, "'tis a song of my own composing. I would play it for you, do you come with me to the music chamber."

"Nay, sir," Madeline replied with a laugh. "I'm too fatigued to walk so far. 'Tis ever the way with aging mothers, you know. Better that you take Lady Sybilla." She nodded toward a shy young maiden seated on a chair in front of an embroidery frame. "She has not my advanced years, and her ear is keener."

The young knight looked crestfallen, but took his marching orders with good-mannered grace. He clambered to his feet and offered the young girl his hand.

"I see she hasn't lost her touch. She can still send men to the lists with just a smile."

Ian turned at the sound of a masculine voice. Guy Blackhair grinned at him, considerably improved since the last time the two men had met. Then he'd been stretched out on a pallet, not fully recovered from his injuries, but strong enough to offer Ian the fief he'd just received in exchange for Madeline's hand. Now his black mustache was neatly trimmed, as was his hair, and he wore a fine black surcoat lined with sable over polished mail. Ian noted with interest the silver swan embroidered above the black bar on his plain white shield.

"Well, well," Ian drawled in greeting, "I see the devil decided not to take you after all."

"Not this time, but if he's patient, I'm sure he'll get his chance."

Ian answered Guy's grin with his own. "What do you here?"

"I've come in escort to my overlord, Gervais d'Evereaux. He brings messages for Lord John from his brother, Richard. When I heard you were here, I left d'Evereaux at Colchester and came to give you that chance to dent my skull, if you think you've the skill for it.''

Ian kept his smile in place, but his mind whirled with the knowledge that a baron known for his disaffection with Henry acted as courier between Richard and John. Before he could probe further, Madeline swept into view.

"Sir Guy! Is that indeed you? I scarce recognized you in such finery.''

The dark-haired knight's grin widened, and he made Madeline a graceful bow. "You see before you the results of diligent knavery, my lady. I finally found an heiress to carry off. She's a bit of a shrew, and somewhat less than pleased with her newly married state, but her estates added greatly to mine.''

Madeline bit her lip, trying to feel sorry for the abducted bride. Somehow she suspected Guy would reconcile her to her fate ere long.

"So how is it that you leave your lady wife so soon?''

"I've come with my overlord, count d'Evereaux, who bears messages from Duke Richard to Lord John.''

Ian covered Madeline's startled gasp. "He came, as well, to give me a chance at denting his noggin. I still owe him a goodly blow, as I recall.''

"What's this?'' Madeline asked, taking her cue from her husband's warning glance. "I thought you two settled things in the heat of battle.''

"Nay," Guy responded easily enough, although his eyes skimmed her face thoughtfully. "Sir Ian wished to, of course, but I foiled him by taking a sword in the side from a rascally mercenary."

"How...how disobliging of you," Madeline sputtered.

"Aye, your lord was most displeased. He was forced to cauterize the wound himself, then carry me to the churgeon when the fever came. Cursing all the way, I might add, and making dire threats of what he would do if I was so inconsiderate as to cock up my toes afore he could take a whack at me."

She tilted her head, surveying her husband. "You did that? You never told me, my lord."

His lazy grin set her heart thumping. "The occasion never arose, wife."

"Wife?" Guy's eyes gleamed as he surveyed the two before him. "'Twould appear there's something he hasn't told me, either. Come, let me take you to table, Lady Madeline, and you can explain how you lowered yourself to wed this ragtag knight."

It was several hours before Madeline and Ian retired and she could probe his reaction to Guy's presence. She nursed Bess, then drew the curtains to their bed, having learned to overcome her dislike of confined spaces in the need for privacy to couple with her lord. Curling on Ian's chest, she whispered to him in the darkness.

"Didn't d'Evereaux side with the Lusignans in their revolt against Henry last year?"

"Aye," Ian murmured, his hands tucked under his head as he stared unseeing at curtains overhead.

"He's allied himself with Richard now, 'twould appear."

"Aye."

"Ian, doesn't it bode ill with you that he would be at Colchester, with messages from Richard to John?"

"Aye. Ouch!" His hand swooped down to cover hers. "Damnation, Madeline, why do you pull my pelt?"

She loosed the tuff of chest hairs she'd yanked. "I want no more of these 'ayes,' " she hissed. "Tell me what you think this means, and what we should do about it."

In a move so swift she could only give a muffled gasp, he rolled over and pinned her to the mattress. "I think it means that John is about to take a step he'll much regret, and 'we' will do nothing about it."

"Ian—"

His hands tunneled in her hair, holding her head steady. "*I* will send a message to John. *You* will do nothing."

"Ian, he must know that we only wish to aid him!"

"I don't wish to aid him," her lord snarled. "I only wish to keep him from destroying his kingdom. 'Tis a fine line we tread here, Madeline, between treason to a king and betrayal of his son. Do not meddle in this. Do not!"

She stared up at him, seeing only the faint outline of his head in the darkness and the glitter of his eyes.

"What—what will you say to him?" she asked, breathless with the weight of his body on hers.

"That I know of his meeting with d'Evereaux. That I know he schemes with Richard. That the king will know of it, too, unless John has the courage to confess it first. Henry will forgive his most beloved son anything if he comes to him and begs his pardon. But if the king must face him on a field of battle, he'll kill him. His rage will know no bounds, and he'll kill him."

"Ian, if I spoke with John, if I told him this, he might— Oh!" She broke off on a gasp of pain as her lord's fists clenched, near tugging her hair out by the roots. He loosed his hold at once, but his voice lashed at her with a sting almost as painful.

"If I thought that you would go to him, I would chain you in far heavier shackles than you used on me, woman. But I need not. I'll take your pledge instead, and trust you to hold to it."

Ian left the next morning to consult with the archbishop of York, currently in residence in London pending a meeting with a papal legate. Bastard son to Henry and much favored by the king, the archbishop was some twenty years older than his half brother John. He'd been given guardianship of the king's youngest son when he was but a boy, and was the only man in England Ian trusted to carry his message.

Two days later, Madeline received a message from Lord John. If she would see her husband again, she would come to Colchester immediately. Without escort, except that which John himself provided.

Chapter Eighteen

"Let me be sure I understand this."

Madeline set aside the wine John had insisted she take and pushed back her chair. She rose slowly, fury vibrating through every bone in her body, and pressed her fingers against the table's edge to still their trembling. The untouched platters of food he'd tried to tempt her with were strewn along the long-linen-covered length between them.

"You don't hold Ian? You lured me here falsely?"

John leaned back in his chair, regarding her with narrowed eyes. "I would have taken him if I could, but he rides too heavily armed and escorted."

"So you will hold me instead? To ensure his silence?"

"Aye." His dark eyes urged her to understand. "You'll be my ransom, Maddy, as you were before."

"Oh, John, you fool! Ian doesn't pay ransoms. He only takes them. I learned that the hard way."

Her scorn sent a surge of red into John's cheeks, a prelude to the famous Angevin rage. "He'll pay this one, if he wants you back. He'll come when he learns I have you, and will buy your release with his silence."

She shook her head at the irony, the monstrous irony, of it all. "He'll not come, John. He'll think I rode to you of my own free will. He'll think I chose you over him, and his honor won't allow him to come for me."

"Aye, he will."

"He won't, I tell you. And to think I've left my babe to be tended by a wet nurse. For this? Oh, John how could you do this? To me?"

A muscle twitched on one side of his jaw. "I needed time. You know my father's rage as well as any, Madeline. I couldn't face him until I sorted this out. Nor could I allow de Burgh to force my hand."

"You've sealed your own doom," she shouted, beside herself. "Ian gave you the chance to go to your father of your own will. Now that onerous task will fall on my lord, and we'll all suffer for it."

"Your husband won't go to my father," John said with a sneer, rising. "He'll come for you. I've watched him with you these past weeks. He's besotted with you. You've bewitched him, like all the rest."

"You don't understand! He made it a matter of trust between us, and I have violated that trust. Or so he'll think. Oh—oh, you ass." She whirled away, unwilling to admit the construction Ian would put on her presence at Colchester.

Her fury fueled John's. He kicked aside his chair and strode around the table to face her, his rage mounting with every step.

"Save that pap for the brat he spawned on you! He'll come. I've seen how he lusts for you. I told you once, long ago, that did you but smile sweetly on him, you'd have him at your feet. 'Twould appear you've done more than smile, madame."

Jealousy, hot and dark, flooded his eyes. Shocked at the depth of it, Madeline tried to step back, away from him, but the table pressed against her legs, blocking any movement.

"Why did you give him what you would not give me?" John demanded, his voice low and dangerous.

"He's my lord! My husband!"

He leaned toward her, breathing hard. "You've had husbands afore, Maddy. After each of them, you came back to me. Always you came back to me."

"John, don't do this! Don't ruin what is between us."

"What *is* between us?" Deliberately he crowded her back against the table. "What *is* this damnable bond that won't be broken?"

"You are my friend," she whispered. "My only friend, ere Ian."

He curled both hands around her upper arms, pressing her hips with his. "It's more than friendship, damn you, and well you know it."

"Nay."

"And yet 'tis not love, is it, Maddy? If you loved me, you would have given yourself to me long afore now." He dug his fingers into the soft flesh of her arms. "Mayhap it's time I take what you will not give."

The sharp tines of an eating fork cut into Madeline's palm as she strained backward, away from him. Her other hand sought purchase among the heavy platters that filled the table.

"John! For pity's sake, don't be so ridiculous. After all our years together, would you take me against my will? Here, on the eating table, among the stewed chickens and boiled carp?"

For a moment, she thought that she had reached him. For one heart-stopping moment, she thought the Jackanapes of her youth would respond to the raillery that had always been their special gift to each other.

Then his lips twisted in a smile that stabbed at her heart. "If I must. 'Tis likely the only way I'll have you, Maddy."

He thrust a knee between hers, forcing her legs apart. One of his hands loosed its hold on her upper arm and slid down to ruck up her skirts.

"John, if you love me, do not do this!"

His hand stilled for just an instant. Black eyes held hers. Madeline thought she saw pain in them, the same pain she felt tearing at her soul.

In that moment, she knew that she could not allow him to destroy himself and her. Her fingers closed around the edge of a platter. Twisting, she swung it around and up with every ounce of strength in her body. Sauce spewed in all directions, splattering her and John both before the heavy plate slammed against his forehead. His eyes widened in stunned surprise, then rolled back in his head as he slumped to the floor.

Sweet Virgin, had she killed him?

Madeline's heart knocked against her ribs so hard and fast she could scarcely breathe. She scrambled off the table edge and knelt beside the sprawled figure. To her relief, she felt his chest rising and falling under her trembling hand.

With a shaky sob, she rose and snatched her furred mantle from the chair where she'd flung it. Throwing it around her shoulders to hide the greasy stains spreading down her robe, she sped toward the chamber door.

She stopped, one hand on the iron latch, and forced herself to breathe deeply, once, twice. Her only hope to escape from Colchester was to ride out boldly, as she had ridden in.

Tilting her chin to a determined angle, Madeline opened the door and stepped into the hall. The wood panel shut firmly behind her as the elderly knight who served as John's chamber steward jumped to his feet.

"My lady! I thought... Lord John said..."

He glanced uncertainly from Madeline to the closed door and back again.

"You thought that I would stay to take supper with the king's son?" Madeline said lightly, moving toward the outer hallway. "Nay, I will not. I must to home. My lord husband awaits me."

He stepped in front of her, his thick brows making a white slash across his forehead. "Lord John said your husband would come for you, and that when he did, we were to hold him."

"Yes, I know." Madeline gave a shaky laugh. "John is ever determined to have his way, is he not? He usually does . . . with all but me."

Her message was not lost on the elderly knight. Having served the king's son for some years, he knew well the rumors that floated about his master and Lady Madeline. In his position as master of the bed-chamber, however, he also knew the rumors were not true.

"I'll not deny he's most displeased with me right now," she admitted frankly. "He sent me away, and charged me tell you that he would not be disturbed until he calls for—"

The sound of booted feet running through the hall cut her off in midsentence. The old knight whirled, his hand going to the sword he wore as guardian of his lord's chambers. He straightened, relaxing his instinctive crouch, when Guy Blackhair came to an abrupt halt a few feet away. Having come with count d'Evereaux, Sir Guy was well-known to the chamberlain.

The dark-haired knight's eyes narrowed when he spotted Madeline. Before he could say anything, she tilted her chin and hailed him in an imperious voice.

"Are you come to escort me to my horse, Sir Guy?"

His brown eyes flicked to the closed door, then back to Madeline. "Do you leave now, lady?"

"Aye. My business here is done."

"Then I am honored to escort you."

"Come," she said brusquely, brushing past the older knight. "I would make haste. My lord husband awaits me. He does not like to be kept waiting at table. He gets a bilious stomach, you know, if he eats too late of an evening."

She swept past him, for all the world like a woman whose most pressing concern was to see to her lord's supper.

"A bilious stomach?" Guy hissed, following at her heels as they rounded a corner. Madeline didn't bother to reply. She picked up her skirts and began to run.

There was no time to explain, no time to waste. Without any question, without hesitation, Guy slapped his hand against his sword to keep it from banging against his leg and raced along beside her. At any moment, Madeline expected to hear an outraged shout and the sound of guards pursuing them. With each step, each slam of her heart against her ribs, she was sure it would be her last.

The months she'd spent in Colchester as a child served her well. With only one false turn, Madeline was able to lead the way through tortuous, winding halls, lighted at distant intervals by flickering torches. At last the halls gave onto a landing above the south entrance. Wide stone steps led down to iron-hasped doors. These stood open, protected as they were by rambling curtain walls and concentric rings of fortifications, but the exit was nevertheless well guarded by men-at-arms.

Madeline stopped at the top of the stairs, dragging air into her starved lungs. As dangerous as it was to delay, they could not rush past the guards, panting and heaving, without alerting them. Guy hovered at her side, his breath harsh in her ear.

"A bilious stomach?" he muttered.

"'Twas the best I could think of!" she gasped. "How did you know I was with John?"

"I saw your palfrey in the stables. There's no mistaking that mare, or her barding. Did you kill him?"

"John?" she panted. "Nay."

"What, could you not get the knife in right?"

Shocked, Madeline twisted around. "Nay, I but knocked him in the head with a platter. Do you think I would stick a knife in one who is my friend?"

His mustache lifted in a wicked grin. "Forgive me, lady. I assumed that a man who brought you to Colchester against your will might no longer be counted among your friends."

"I was not brought here against my will," she admitted with painful honesty, "although John thought to keep me so."

He stared at her. "Good God, Madeline, don't tell me you came of your own accord. Ian will have your head, or whatever portion of your anatomy comes to hand."

"I know." She locked her hands together tightly to still their trembling. "We argued fiercely, Ian and I, about John. I much fear he'll ... not believe my reasons for coming here."

Guy's mustache lifted in a roguish grin. "If he does not, you can just lock him up again until he sees reason."

Madeline gave a sobbing laugh and moved toward the stairs. "If we don't get out of here, and quickly, 'tis we who'll be locked up."

They almost made it.

Guy's brusque authority took them past the guards and out into the courtyard. He sent a man-at-arms scurrying with orders to fetch the lady's palfrey and his own rawboned bay. His hands were steady on Zephyr's bridle as he held her still for Madeline to mount, but hers were shaking so badly she could hardly pull herself up. Swinging into his own saddle, Guy wheeled his horse alongside Madeline's and rode with her toward the yawning gate that guarded the inner bailey.

As they passed through the gate, Madeline threw one last glance behind her at the stark, square keep. The bright Caen stone gleamed white in the winter twilight, a legacy of the first William, who had brought it a century ago from his native Normandy to cover red Roman brick.

They were almost to the bridge that spanned the sluggish moat when the distant rumble of iron-shod hooves reached them.

"Jesu," Guy swore, under his breath. "I hope 'tis Ian. If not, we're caught, lady."

Madeline urged her mount forward, onto the wooden drawbridge. Once across the bridge, they faced only the final barrier of the barbican. She peered through the open portcullis, gauging the distance.

The far rumble swelled to a roll of thunder. A mounted troop appeared topped a rise, riding fast and bearing down on Colchester. In the bright moonlight, she thought she caught a glimpse of blue and white.

Madeline's heart leapt into her throat. He'd come. Holy Virgin, he'd come for her.

Even as she gave a sob of joy, a shout rang out behind her.

"Stop them! Stop that woman!"

The guards atop the barbican raced toward the chains that winched the portcullis.

Madeline kicked Zephyr's flanks.

The horse raised on its hind legs, pawing air, then shot forward. She flew across the bridge and sped through the barbican in a blur of shimmering green and gold. As the mare cleared the second gate, Madeline heard the creak of the iron grill above her.

Leaning low over her mount's neck, Madeline prayed that Guy would make it through. The sound of his horse's hooves was lost in the scream of chains being loosed and the whistle of the great spiked portcul-

lis slicing through the air. It thudded into the earth
with a force that shook the ground. Glancing back
frantically, she saw Guy, only a few yards behind her.

"Ride, woman! Ride like you've never ridden before!"

As if she needed urging!

She tore down the straight, cobbled road, a legacy
of the long-dead Romans. As she neared the oncom-
ing troops, Madeline saw the armored knight at their
head lift his visor and rise up in his stirrups. She waved
wildly and shouted to Ian to follow, then sent Zephyr
plunging off the road so that she could ride around the
mass of the mounted warriors.

She heard shouted oaths, a startled neigh, then the
jingle of bridles yanked hard and thud of hooves
slowing. Within moments, the troop had turned and
followed behind her.

Bred to bear the weight of heavily armed men, the
war-horses had not the fleetness nor the stamina to
gallop too long or too far. The troop was soon strung
out, the differing capabilities of their mounts dictat-
ing their speed. Guy fell slowly back, making Madeline realize that she must rein in or risk losing them all.
She drew in when she topped the high, sloping rise.
Panting, she twisted back to stare over her shoulder.
Colchester huddled in the distance, bathed in the
moon's light. The same bright shine illuminated the
screen of dust their own troop had raised, but showed
no sign of pursuit.

She had done it! She'd sprung the jaws of John's trap, Madeline thought, her heart in her throat. But at what price? Her friend was lost to her now, and Ian— She swallowed as his plunging, snorting stallion drew up behind her.

Throwing himself out of the saddle, Ian stalked forward. He pulled off his great helm and flung it down, taking no heed as it rolled and clanged along the cobbled road.

"Ian . . ."

"Get down," he ordered furiously. "Get you down. Now!"

Madeline decided it was not wise to yield whatever advantage her added height gave her just yet. At her light tug on the rein, Zephyr sidestepped daintily.

"Ian, let me explain why I was at Colchester."

"You'll do more than explain, wife!"

Grabbing the decorated bridle, Ian halted the mare's dance with a ruthless grip. Madeline barely had time to kick her feet free of the stirrups before he transferred his hold to her skirts and yanked her out of the saddle. She tumbled down, landing heavily against him. Her elbow slammed against his metal shoulder guard, sending needles of fire shooting up her arm.

Madeline yelped, rubbing the afflicted spot, and blinked back tears of pain.

"Save your tears," he snarled, jerking her around to face him, "for when I'm through with you! Then you'll have reason aplenty to cry."

Madeline lost her caul and her dignity in the rough shake he gave her. Ignoring the fire that radiated from her elbow, she shoved her hair out of her eyes and pleaded with him.

"Ian, please! Please listen to me! I only went to John because I thought he held you!"

"I knew it had to be something like that, you little fool." He dragged her up almost off her toes in his fury. "Why could you not trust me to see him, and you, through this?"

"Wh-what did you say?"

"Why could you not trust me?" he shouted. "I would have . . ."

"No, no, before that. What did you say before?"

"Before what?"

"Did you not think I'd chosen John over you?"

"No!" he bellowed. "Jesu, woman, of course I didn't think you'd chosen him!"

Madeline stared up at him, feeling neither his bruising hold nor the fiery waves radiating from her elbow. "Why not?"

"What?"

"Why *didn't* you think that I had gone to him of my own will?"

"Madeline, for the love of—"

"Why?"

"Because I know you," he said savagely, drawing her up on her toes again with the sheer force of his wrath. "Because you're stubborn and foolhardy and far too quick to act before you think. But you're more

Merline Lovelace

339

true to yourself and those you hold dear than anyone I know. You would not betray me for him."

Fresh tears sprang into her eyes. Hot, glorious tears. Her throat worked as she tried to hold them back, but they spilled over, leaving wet silver tracks on her cheeks.

"Aye," she whispered. "I'm true to those I hold dear. And I hold you most dear, my lord."

Her tender admission didn't appear to appease him at all. He gave an exasperated snort and spun her around to lead her back to her palfrey.

"As I do you, lady wife, when I'm not racked by the urge to beat you black and blue. Get you horsed. I can see any rational discussion about this night will have to wait until we're both more calm and safely away."

"Where do you take her?"

Both Madeline and Ian swung around as Guy strolled toward them through the gathering darkness.

Ian groaned. "It would have to be you who saved her. Now my sword may never get to slice your gullet."

Guy's rich laughter rolled out. "You may slice away, my lord, or try to. I didn't save her. The lady saved herself. Knocked the king's son out cold."

"Knocked him out cold?" Ian turned disbelieving eyes on Madeline.

"With a gold plate, no less." Guy waved an impatient hand. "I'll let Lady Madeline tell you about it later. I only came forward to offer Ballieu, if you need a stronghold to retreat to."

"Nay. I've sent our babe ahead with Madeline's maid and wet nurse and the rest of my men to Cragsmore. We'll hold there, until Henry arrives. The archbishop of York had word he's taken ship."

Guy's ready grin flashed. "Well, you'll be safe enough there. No man gets in—or out!—of that keep unless Lady Madeline allows it."

Ignoring Ian's huff of laughter, Guy stepped forward to take Madeline's hand. "God keep you, lady."

"And you," she replied breathlessly.

"Mayhap we'll meet again."

"Not if I have aught to say about it," Ian snorted. "Every time you two get together, someone ends up with a dent in his head."

He slid a hand around his wife's waist and swung her up in his arms. Guy's laughter followed them as they rode off into the dark of night.

Two days later, Cragsmore once more rose out of the mists before them. Madeline took in its stark, uncompromising lines with tired eyes, marveling that a keep that had appeared as bleak as a prison but a year ago now beckoned with the illusive promise of safety. Clucking to an equally tired Zephyr, Madeline rode up the incline and across the wide ditch into a yard that held little trace of the squalor that had greeted her so many months ago.

The miles fell from her when she rode into the inner bailey and found Gerda waiting, a bundled, squawking Bess in her arms. Laughing, sobbing with joy, exclaiming each in turn over the other, the two women embraced, then retired to the keep so that Madeline could unwrap the swaddled babe and count each tiny finger and toe to make sure all were still intact.

Ian watched them with a small smile tugging at his lips. They were nothing alike, mistress and maid. One was slender, the other stout as an ale barrel. One was all grace and musical laughter, the other shrill and clumsy beyond belief. But if he had to seal himself within a keep and hold off the armies of Lord John, there were no other women he would rather have sharpening his weapons. Three, he corrected, thinking that Bess had made the fast journey with Gerda and a wet nurse better by far than many of his men. Aye, he told himself, he was well served in his women.

Leaving them to their tasks, he went to ensure the defenses.

'Twas only later, after darkness had fallen and Ian had left the walls to enter the keep and climb wearily to the lord's chamber, that he realized he was sealed within the keep with many more women than just Madeline, their daughter and her maid.

They were everywhere, it seemed. With the additional troops Ian had brought to fortify Cragsmore, every square foot of space in the great hall and the upper chambers had to be used to bed them down. Gerda had shooed the maids out of their normal chambers to make space for the fighting men. A bevy of giggling women now rolled out pallets in the chapel,

the weaving room, the minstrel's gallery and, at
Madeline's insistence, the lord's chamber. She would
not have anyone sleep outside, she'd declared, not in
the icy drizzle that came with winter at Cragsmore.

There was little privacy in any keep, but Ian had
hoped at least to have his lady wife to himself the first
time they'd shared a bed since their hasty flight from
Colchester. He stared about the crowded lord's
chamber in consternation, knowing he couldn't
sneeze, let alone raise the breathless moans in Madeline that he wished to, without a dozen women listening avidly. He didn't mind, but he suspected that his
lady wife might.

Leaning a shoulder against the doorframe, he
watched as she prepared for bed. With Gerda pro-
moted to nursery mistress, Madeline had chosen from
among the crowd of women a young maid to tend her
wardrobe and dress her hair. His wife now sat on a
stool, eyes closed, head back and nary a wince crossing her face, while the girl ran a brush of boar's bristles through the heavy, rippling mane.

Apparently more than content with the arrangement, Gerda sat on a stool nearby, the babe on one
knee, and cooed in time to each stroke.

Ian watched the chestnut strands lift and crackle, as
though they had life of their own. His hands curled
slowly into fists, imagining the feel of that curtain of
living silk.

Unaware that she was watched, Madeline heaved a
sigh of sheer sensual pleasure and shifted on the stool.

Her nipples pushed at the sheer fabric of her shift, causing Ian's loins to tighten painfully.

A plump maid kneeling on a pallet nudged her neighbor with an elbow and jerked her head toward him. They both broke into giggles.

Ian had no doubt what had caught their notice. He was as hard as a rock. Shaking his head wryly, he stepped over a makeshift pallet and crossed to his wife. Grasping her wrist, he pulled her off her stool.

"My lord!"

Madeline's gasp startled a hiccup out of the babe, causing Gerda to cluck in disapproval.

Holding his wife by one wrist, Ian marched into the private solar. Madeline stumbled after him, negotiating her way around scattered blankets.

"Ian, where do you go? There's no more room in here than in the other chamber."

Disdaining to answer, he maneuvered his way across the solar. Just before he reached the winding tower stairs, he snatched up a rough blanket.

"Ian, what in the world—?"

He tugged her down the stairs and shouldered open the door to the small, disused storeroom. It hadn't been disturbed since last he was here, Ian saw in the dim light. It was still small and dank and bare. And blessedly empty.

With a grunt of satisfaction, he slammed the door shut, wrapping them both in a cocoon of darkness.

Chapter Nineteen

When the banners were first spotted in the distance, Ian was inspecting the shelters built on logs thrust into special holes in the outer wall. Should any attacker make it across the ditch lined with sharpened spikes, men protected by these shelters would pour boiling water on them, then drop the huge boulders stacked on the walls behind.

"My lord!"

Ian jerked upright at the sound of Ralf's shout.

The man-at-arms raced along the wall, his sleeves flapping. He was still scarecrow-thin, although the punishment Ian imposed on him for his part in the ransom attempt had been adding flesh to his bones. Ralf had been sentenced to a lifetime with an indignant Gerda, who wanted to know how it was she was given to a man who hadn't even asked for her dower of a silver coin. Ralf would no doubt soon be as round as the maid, Madeline had assured Ian when she arranged the match.

"My lord," he panted, "a troop's been sighted coming along the valley road."

Ian strode to the west wall and peered over the sheer precipice at fields still bare from winter. "Are all the villagers within the walls?"

"Aye, lord. And as many swine as we could round up. The herders have taken the sheep and cattle high up into the hills."

"Alert the men. I'll go advise Lady Madeline."

He found her in the great hall. Bess lay in a basket on the table, gurgling, while her lady mother directed the small army of women and children who sorted blankets and stored hastily gathered possessions. Ian stood beside one of the huge timbers that supported the overhead arches, thinking how he'd once questioned her ability to order this keep. There was no doubting her authority now, nor her competence.

In the midst of assigning a family of nine to a sleeping space in one of the alcoves, Madeline looked up and caught sight of her husband. He looked so different from the man she'd first met in the vast hall at Kenilworth, she thought. The smooth, handsome earl whose blue eyes had captured hers across a crowded hall bore only passing resemblance to this knight in mail and gambeson.

But, had she the choice, Madeline would not have traded this keep for Kenilworth, nor this warrior for the lord who'd taken her arm and led her away from Will so long ago. She walked to his side, reading the expression in his eyes.

"So they come?"

"They come."

"Is it Henry? Or one of John's men?"

"We'll know soon enough."

"Whatever happens, my lord, I would you know that...that..." She broke off, glancing around the ring of interested spectators. She turned back, lowering her voice. "That I love you well, my lord."

His lips curved. "And I you, Madeline de Courcey."

It arced between them, the need to hold each other, to have some last moments with their bodies touching and their breaths mingled.

Ian contented himself with a hand curled under her chin. He lifted her face, studying her eyes in the thin sunlight filtering through the high, narrow windows. They met his gaze, wide and thick lashed and fearless.

"You're much a woman, Madeline de Courcey."

She stood on the ramparts beside him later, wrapped in a thick cloak against the March winds. Her heart pounding, she watched the troop as it climbed the winding path from the valley floor. A golden lion on a field of red fluttered from the pennon held by the mounted herald. Henry's device.

Ian's hand was steady as he took hers to lead her down to the outer bailey. There would be no attack, not by the king's men. But when Henry heard what Ian had to tell him, any disaster might follow.

Madeline stood beside her lord, her hand gripping his. She shifted her shoulders to settle her crimson cloak more evenly, then lifted her chin.

It dropped, leaving her openmouthed with astonishment, when the king rode through the gates, his son but a half length behind him.

Ian's fingers tightened warningly over hers, and then he led her forward. She swept the king a graceful bow, then offered greeting as lady of Cragsmore.

"I welcome you, my lord. And . . . and your son, Lord John."

"Well, Madeline," Henry observed as he dismounted, "you're looking less cumbersome than when I last saw you." He placed his hands at the small of his back and bent backward to loose muscles corded from riding, looking around as he did so. "Jesu, what a dismal place."

"But strong," Ian supplied, stepping forward to greet him.

Henry straightened, eyeing him. Behind the king, John swung out of the saddle. The three men stood for a moment, unspeaking, unsmiling.

'Twas Madeline who breached the silence, slipping into the role she'd been trained to since childhood. With a practiced smile, she gestured toward the stairs to the keep.

"Will you come inside, my lord? 'Tis almost as dismal within as without, but at least 'tis warm."

She buried her shaking hands in the folds of her robe as she followed the king into the great hall. Her

nerves stretched tighter and tighter with tension, but
she dared not look at Ian. Or at John. It seemed to
take eons before the men were served flagons of
mulled wine and one end of the hall was cleared to allow them privacy. They gathered in a walled alcove,
none of the others close enough to hear. Madeline
swallowed, wondering what it was she would hear.

To her sharpened senses, the king seemed slower, his
movements less frenetic than they usually were. But
when he downed the last of his wine, some of his energy returned and he began to pace the alcove.

"I cannot stay but an hour. I must make Chester yet
this night, and be at Carlisle by next week to meet with
William of Scotland. I hope to gain his assurances that
he won't attack when my truce with Philip expires at
Eastertide."

Behind his back, Madeline's eyes met Ian's. He gave
his head a little shake, warning her not to say anything yet. To let the king take this conversation where
he would.

"There will be war between Philip and me," Henry
said heavily. "Between Richard and me. When the
treaty expires at Eastertide, there will be war. I want
to see for myself the state of the border keeps."

"Wyndham will hold for you, my lord," Ian put in
quietly. "And all of Margill."

Henry threw him a quick look. "Aye, you'll hold
the north, you and Northumberland and York. And
John will hold the south."

"Will he?" Ian asked.

The king waved an impatient hand. "Aye, he will, though his brother thinks to subvert him to his cause. John met me when I landed and told me how Richard, damn his soul, sent d'Evereaux to meet with him. He told me how his brother tempted him with the promise of greater lands than I would give him."

Ian's eyes locked with John's. Madeline held her breath as she watched these two men she had never thought to see face-to-face again.

"Ha!" the king snorted, unaware of the drama going on behind his back. "John knew better than to believe Richard's promises. That devil I spawned would never loose his grip on one acre of his soil, nor share one half measure of his power."

Madeline thought that Henry surely must hear the echo of himself in the son he castigated. He ranted for a few moments more, then suddenly stopped in midstride, cursing.

"You will show me to the garderobe, Lady Madeline. I must have eaten spoiled meat, so much do my innards rack themselves."

She hesitated, loath to leave the two men, but having no choice. Turning, she led Henry to a privy chamber. As soon as he had closeted himself, she whirled on one heel and sped back to the great hall. She ran breathlessly down its length, little caring that she lost her veil and her dignity in her mad race.

Her heart thudded painfully against her ribs as she stopped in the opening to the alcove. The two men eyed each other, grim-faced and tense.

John spoke slowly, as though every word were pulled from him by red hot pincers. "I would have told him of my own accord."

"Would you?"

"Aye, but I was...was not prepared to have my hand forced."

Madeline, more than anyone, knew what it cost the king's son to acknowledge his own failing. Lifting her chin, she sailed toward them.

"'Tis done. 'Tis done and behind us. And, by the holy Virgin, if the husband I love and the friend of my heart don't settle matters between them here and now, I swear I'll knock you both to the rushes."

She looked so fierce and fearsome, with both hands clenched at her sides, hair flying wildly about her head and eyes shooting green sparks, that Ian could only stare at her. Wondering how it was that one slight female had come to order his universe, he drew in a slow breath, then turned to the man beside him.

"I think she means it, my lord."

The white lines that bracketed either side of John's mouth eased. "Aye, I believe she does."

* * * * *

Author Note

Have you ever turned off a main highway and wandered into a place so unexpected and magical that you never wanted to leave? That's what happened when my husband and I first discovered England's Lake District one chilly spring a few years ago. Its sharp, rocky peaks, thousands of clear mountain lakes and tumbling waterfalls enchanted us as much as they have many of England's greatest poets, including William Wordsworth and Samuel Taylor Coleridge. The harsh climate also breeds tough, self-reliant men—just the kind of hero I wanted for *His Lady's Ransom*.

It might interest you to know that the last of King Henry's sons did, indeed, turn against him. In June of 1189, Philip and Richard marched against Le Mans, which Henry and John held. Henry, in failing health, sent John to safety and withdrew. With his father's strength declining, John decided to place his fate in his brother's hands. In July, the two brothers stood beside the French king at the colloquy at Colombier. Henry agreed to their conditions, and died a few weeks later—some say of a broken heart.

Harlequin® Historical

What do A.E. Maxwell, Miranda Jarrett, Merline Lovelace and Cassandra Austin have in common?

They are all part of Harlequin Historical's efforts to bring you longer books by some of your favorite authors. Pick up one of these upcoming titles today and see what a difference an historical from Harlequin can make!

REDWOOD EMPIRE—A.E. Maxwell Don't miss the reissue of this exciting saga from award-winning authors Ann and Evan Maxwell, coming in May 1995.

SPARHAWK'S LADY—Miranda Jarrett From this popular author comes another sweeping Sparhawk adventure full of passion and emotion in June 1995.

HIS LADY'S RANSOM—Merline Lovelace A gripping Medieval tale from the talented author of the *Destiny's Women* series that is sure to delight, coming in July 1995.

TRUSTING SARAH—Cassandra Austin And in August 1995, the long-awaited new Western by the author whose *Wait for the Sunrise* touched readers' hearts.

Watch for them this spring and summer wherever Harlequin Historicals are sold.

Take 4 bestselling love stories FREE

Plus get a FREE surprise gift!

Harlequin® Historical

WOMEN OF THE WEST

Exciting stories of the old West and the women whose dreams
and passions shaped a new land!

Join Harlequin Historicals every month as we bring you
these unforgettable tales.

May 1995 #270—JUSTIN'S BRIDE
Susan Macias w/a Susan Mallery

June 1995 #273—SADDLE THE WIND
Pat Tracy

July 1995 #277—ADDIE'S LAMENT
DeLoras Scott

August 1995 #279—TRUSTING SARAH
Cassandra Austin

September 1995 #286—CECILIA AND THE STRANGER
Liz Ireland

October 1995 #288—SAINT OR SINNER
Cheryl St.John

November 1995 #294—LYDIA
Elizabeth Lane

Don't miss any of our Women of the West!

RUGGED. SEXY. HEROIC.

OUTLAWS and HEROES

Stony Carlton—A lone wolf determined never to be tied down.

Gabriel Taylor—Accused and found guilty by small-town gossip.

Clay Barker—At Revenge Unlimited, he *is* the law.

JOAN JOHNSTON, DALLAS SCHULZE and MALLORY RUSH, three of romance fiction's biggest names, have created three unforgettable men—modern heroes who have the courage to fight for what is right....

OUTLAWS AND HEROES—available in September wherever Harlequin books are sold.

HARLEQUIN ®

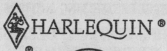

HARLEQUIN ®

Coming in August!
Award-winning author
Jasmine Cresswell's

Rakes and Rascals

Harlequin Regency Romance presents
The Abducted Heiress and *The Blackwood Bride*—
together in one exciting volume!

The Abducted Heiress is Georgiana Thayne, who has
for years disguised her wit and beauty in order to avoid
marriage to her odious cousin. But life takes a turn for the
adventurous when Viscount Benham comes to Town....

The Blackwood Bride is a supposedly dying woman from a
London workhouse. But Viscount Blackwood's bride is
made of sturdier stuff than he imagines, and what had
been intended as a very brief marriage of convenience
soon becomes inconvenient in the extreme!

Rakes and Rascals. Available in bookstores in August.

THREE BESTSELLING AUTHORS

HEATHER GRAHAM POZZESSERE
THERESA MICHAELS
MERLINE LOVELACE

bring you

THREE HEROES THAT DREAMS ARE MADE OF!

The Highwayman—He knew the honorable thing was to send his captive home, but how could he let the beautiful Lady Kate return to the arms of another man?

The Warrior—Raised to protect his tribe, the fierce Apache warrior had little room in his heart until the gentle Angie showed him the power and strength of love.

The Knight—His years as a mercenary had taught him many skills, but would winning the hand of a spirited young widow prove to be his greatest challenge?

Don't miss these **UNFORGETTABLE RENEGADES!**

Available in August wherever Harlequin books are sold.

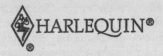

HARLEQUIN®

As a Privileged Woman, you'll be entitled to all these Free Benefits. And Free Gifts, too.

To thank you for buying our books, we've designed an exclusive FREE program called *PAGES & PRIVILEGES*™. You can enroll with just one Proof of Purchase, and get the kind of luxuries that, until now, you could only read about.

Big HOTEL DISCOUNTS

A privileged woman stays in the finest hotels. And so can you—at up to 60% off! Imagine standing in a hotel check-in line and watching as the guest in front of you pays $150 for the same room that's only costing you $60. Your *Pages & Privileges* discounts are good at Sheraton, Marriott, Best Western, Hyatt and thousands of other fine hotels all over the U.S., Canada and Europe.

Free DISCOUNT TRAVEL SERVICE

A privileged woman is always jetting to romantic places. When you fly, just make one phone call for the lowest published airfare at time of booking—or double the difference back! PLUS— you'll get a $25 voucher to use the first time you book a flight AND 5% cash back on every ticket you buy thereafter through the travel service!

HH-PP3A

FREE GIFTS!

A privileged woman is always getting wonderful gifts.
Luxuriate in rich fragrances that will stir your senses (and his). This gift-boxed assortment of fine perfumes includes three popular scents, each in a beautiful designer bottle. <u>Truly Lace</u>...This luxurious fragrance unveils your sensuous side. <u>L'Effleur</u>...discover the romance of the Victorian era with this soft floral. <u>Muguet des bois</u>...a single note floral of singular beauty.

YOURS FREE!

$50 VALUE

FREE INSIDER TIPS LETTER

A privileged woman is always informed. And you'll be, too, with our free letter full of fascinating information and sneak previews of upcoming books.

MORE GREAT GIFTS & BENEFITS TO COME

A privileged woman always has a lot to look forward to. And so will you. You get all these wonderful FREE gifts and benefits now with only one purchase...and there are no additional purchases required. However, each additional retail purchase of Harlequin and Silhouette books brings you a step closer to even more great FREE benefits like half-price movie tickets... and even more FREE gifts.

L'Effleur...This basketful of romance lets you discover L'Effleur from head to toe, heart to home.

Truly Lace... A basket spun with the sensuous luxuries of Truly Lace, including Dusting Powder in a reusable satin and lace covered box.

Complete the Enrollment Form in the front of this book and mail it with this Proof of Purchase.

PROOF OF PURCHASE
Offer expires October 31, 1996

HH-PP3